CHRISTMAS
ON THE ISLAND

A Novel

Jenny Colgan

WILLIAM MORROW
An Imprint of HarperCollins*Publishers*

CHRISTMAS ON THE ISLAND. Copyright © 2018 by Jenny Colgan. Map copyright © 2017 by The Flying Fish Studios. All rights reserved. Printed in the United States of America. No part of this book may be used or reproduced in any manner whatsoever without written permission except in the case of brief quotations embodied in critical articles and reviews. For information, address HarperCollins Publishers, 195 Broadway, New York, NY 10007.

HarperCollins books may be purchased for educational, business, or sales promotional use. For information, please email the Special Markets Department at SPsales@harpercollins.com.

Originally published in the United Kingdom under the title *An Island Christmas* by Little, Brown Book Group in 2018.

Library of Congress Cataloging-in-Publication Data has been applied for.

ISBN 978-0-06-285007-2
ISBN 978-0-06-286920-3 (hardcover library edition)

18 19 20 21 22   TS   10 9 8 7 6 5 4 3

Praise for
JENNY COLGAN

'This is the perfect book to curl up with . . . the mouthwatering descriptions of baked goods will make it hard to stave off the Christmas pounds'
—*Express*

'A good-hearted and humorous slice of Cornish life'
—*Sunday Mirror*

'If you like your Yuletide tales with real characters and plenty of fun, this is the one for you'
—*Heat*

'A cracker . . . the one must-read this festive season'
—*Sun*

'Fast-paced, funny, poignant and well observed'
—*Daily Mail*

'Sweeter than a bag of jelly beans . . . had us eating up every page'
—*Cosmopolitan*

'As fresh and invigorating as a breath of sea air'
—*S Magazine*

'A perfect beach read'
—*Good Housekeeping*

'A quirky tale of love, work and the meaning of life'
—*Company*

'A smart, witty love story'
—*Observer*

'Full of laugh-out-loud observations . . .
utterly unputdownable'
—*Woman*

'A chick-lit writer with a difference . . . never scared
to try something different, Colgan always pulls it off'
—*Image*

'A Colgan novel is like listening to your best
pal, souped up on vino, spilling the latest gossip –
entertaining, dramatic and frequently hilarious'
—*Daily Record*

'An entertaining read'
—*Sunday Express*

'Part-chick lit, part-food porn . . . this
is full on fun for foodies'
—*Bella*

Dedicated to the memory of Kate Breame,
(1979-2018), with love from all
of your FFF family.

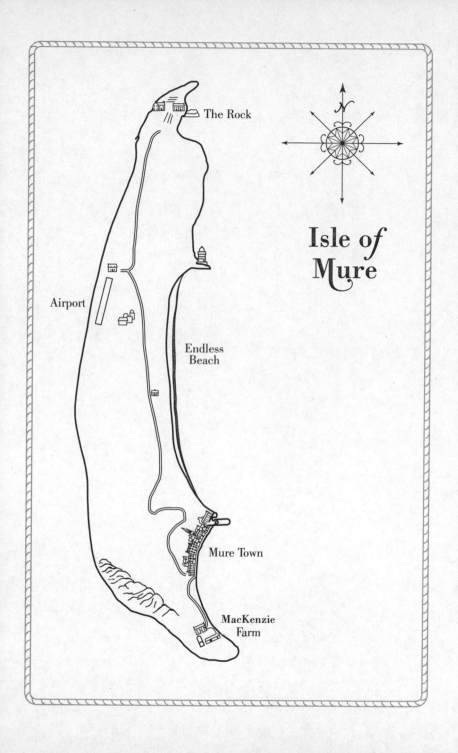

'Beware the snow dancers. They are beautiful, and pale, and oh they can dance; and you will think they are going to carry you away. They arrive with the tinkling of bells, and swirl and swish and you will run out to dance with them, and they will surround you, and beckon, 'Come with us, child—you can dance for ever more.'

And many is the lost child who chased and ran, as the flakes swirled and laughed and moved on, leaving them frozen by the shore, craving their distant bells forever, as they heard stories of ice mountains and deep ice kings.

And sometimes the child is entirely engulfed; is taken and lost by the snow dancing and never seen again. And perhaps they are happy dancing in the frozen ballroom of the Deep King. But perhaps they are not. So. Best not to risk it, la.'

Chapter One

In winter, the mornings are very dark on Mure, the tiny island high up off the coast of the north of Scotland, halfway to Iceland (or, it occasionally feels like, to the North Pole when the west winds blow in).

Beautiful; cosy, stark and astonishingly clear when the clouds lift – but the nights last a long, long time.

Dogs of course don't really care that much about whether it's dark or not. They just roughly know when it's time to get up and start working on their very heavy schedule of 'snuffling', 'hoping for a morsel' and 'mmm, stink!'

I wouldn't tell you that it's absolutely obligatory to have a dog if you live on Mure, but I can't see any good reason why you wouldn't, and nor would any of the island dwellers. It's safe, there are few cars – and those there are don't travel very quickly along the pitted farm tracks.

There are exciting moors to run across and coves and beaches to swim in, and lots and lots of sticks, and seals to wuff at, and sheep poo to roll in, and lots of other dogs to play with, and cosy fires to flop in front of when you have finished gambolling, and barely anyone uses a lead and you're allowed in the pub. Mure is paradise for dogs.

Many people agree with the dogs' assessment of things.

The farm dogs sleep in the barn, with the gentle heat of the cows blowing over their flanks, and warm hay beneath them. On the MacKenzies' farm – which is up a small hill off the southernmost tip of the island, just along from the high street, with its pink and yellow and red shops, brightly painted to counteract the low winter skies and bring cheer in the darker months – they snooze there, contented, sheep dancing in dreams that make their paws twitch.

All except Bramble, oldest and most beloved of the sheepdogs. He's been retired for years, but nobody begrudges him his spot: as close to the wood-burning stove in the old farmhouse kitchen as a dog can technically be without actually being on fire. He snuffles and snores a great deal and tends to like to be up and about early, which Flora, who lives there, thinks is ridiculous: seeing as he is an old dog and sleeps twenty hours a day, then surely some of those hours should be between five and seven in the morning?

Although, to be fair, Flora is up early too as she needs to get to work, down in the Seaside Kitchen on the main street. It's an extremely short commute.

Along the high street, the gift shops are yellow and

peppermint green, the chemist is a faded blue, the beauty salon a brand-new fuchsia nobody likes and the fishmonger is a pale orange. Then there is the old, peeling, black-and-white Harbour's Rest, the hotel which acts as a bar and rites-of-passage point: weddings, funerals, birthday parties, anniversaries. It is somewhat carelessly presided over by Inge-Britt, an Icelandic girl, who doesn't have a dog as she likes a lie-in in the morning, even as her pint glasses are growing sticky on the unwiped tables.

And two doors down from there, in palest pink, is the Seaside Kitchen. Flora came back to the island a year or so ago, to work on a lawyering job. She had been raised on Mure and left for the bright lights of London, many years before. She had thought she would never return. She'd dreaded doing so.

But in the way that life will often throw things at you that you will never expect, the job didn't entirely pan out and instead, she fell back in love with the land of her forebears, as well as the lawyer who had brought her back there, Joel Binder.

Joel. Well. He's a difficult one. Flora loves him regardless (and possibly a tiny bit because) of this. Flora is, let us say, very much up for a challenge.

So she pushes herself out of bed, because she knows if she doesn't get up first, her father will, and she can't bear the thought of his old, arthritic feet crossing the freezing flagstones of the kitchen before she has a chance to fuel up the stove and put the kettle on to boil. He can get up when he hears the whistle.

She pulls the tangle of hair out of her face. She is unusual to look at, Flora, although not for the islands: generations of intermingling blood between Celts and the Vikings means that she has the palest skin imaginable, white as the foam on the waves; hair that is not blonde, not brown, but almost colourless; pale eyes that change with the weather from blue to green to grey.

In London she faded into the background. Here she is a part of the wild foaming sea; the pale cliffs; the white seabirds and seals. She looks like part of the landscape.

Sleepy old Bramble is all bounce at this time of day, huge tail knocking off anything left on low chairs, as Flora embraces his warm hairy tummy, gets the kitchen started and hauls herself off to the shower. Joel isn't here right now: he's in New York, coming back for Christmas, and for certain reasons, Flora is not displeased about this, in the dark, quiet early hours of this morning.

They bounce down the street together, Flora and Bramble, Flora full of what she needs Isla and Iona, the two pretty young island girls who work in the café with her, to do that day: cakes, pies, pasties – and hand out fruitcake as fast as they can. She started making whole fruitcakes back at the beginning of November, as a good Christmas cake needs time to mature, then selling them by the slice. And she took the risk of making one every day, unsure – particularly as the ingredients were expensive and hard to source on the island – as to whether this would pay off, or if they'd be left with dozens of unwanted fruitcakes in January.

Anyway, since the beginning of December (which was only the week before now) they had absolutely gone like the clappers. Some people were having a piece every day, and Flora was thinking of putting a quota system in place, just for the sake of their arteries. Even with the cost of the ingredients – all of which were absolutely top class – and the famous Seaside Kitchen discount card (a necessity so she could raise prices for tourists and summer visitors – the only thing that could keep them running through the winter without penalising the much lower-paid workers who lived there all year round) – it was still a very good money-spinner, and she would keep making a new one every day which would still give them three weeks' marinating time.

Bramble would get as far as the door of the Seaside Kitchen and no further, even though he tried his damnedest. He knew the score. Flora led a very tight ship as far as cleanliness was concerned. Inge-Britt would have let him in at Harbour's Rest to snuffle around the tables for old peanuts, but she wasn't awake yet.

So Bramble trotted patiently, every day, off on his rounds.

Mrs MacPherson was clucking up the high street with Brandy, her highland terrier, as she always did, first thing. She'd told Flora after seventy you never slept and Flora had tried to smile sympathetically while wondering exactly how much Mrs MacPherson would sleep if given half a chance. On Mondays, when the café was shut, Flora didn't get out of bed until lunchtime, and if Joel was there, she'd try and get him to take the day off too and, well, that tended to lead to other things . . .

. . . but she wasn't going to think about that now.

Bramble said good morning to Brandy by politely sniffing the other dog's bottom, then carried on his way to the newsagent, where Iain, who ran it, would hand him the previous day's papers. That day's papers didn't arrive until the first morning ferry at 8 a.m., which didn't bother Flora's father at all. He took a paper every day but maintained they were all rubbish, so it hardly mattered when the news arrived.

Iain's dog, Rickson, lay down in the back of the shop. He growled lazily. He'd spent too many years going on paper rounds with other dogs who barked at him and protecting Iain from wee lads who wanted to shoplift penny sweets and so he was, frankly, just a bit grumpy. As was Iain, to be fair. They made a good couple.

Bramble gave Rickson his customary wide berth, as Iain patted him on the head and handed over the *Highland Times*. Then he trotted confidently back up the high street, passing Pickle, Mrs McCrorie's horribly over-spoiled Jack Russell, who only ate roast chicken, Mrs McCrorie liked to announce to everyone, much to the horror of the village. Dogs on Mure were working dogs on the whole; they existed as part of the farms and homesteads. It was still in living memory for many islanders when chicken was a rare luxury for the locals: you were far more likely to eat seal (as many still did), and fish was the staple diet day to day.

Bramble didn't stop past the harbour, where Grey, the pale-eyed northern huge bugger of indeterminate origin – a stray who had somehow wound up on Mure from a Russian fishing boat (legend suggested he was a shaved wolf) and had hung around the docks until the fishermen had adopted him and now gave him the scraps even the birds didn't want – looked up from his ceaseless scanning of the horizon; he huffed back down again as he saw it was only Bramble, nails clacking on the ancient cobbles, his head held high with the newspaper in it, proud of his daily duties.

Nor did Bramble head up towards the Endless Beach, which started on the northern end of the high street, just in front of the old manse currently inhabited by Saif Hassan, one of the island's two doctors (the other being more or less useless), a refugee from Syria, and his two little boys, Ash and Ibrahim.

Saif was aware that Christmas was incoming – one could hardly avoid it, between the television adverts and the incomprehensible non-stop onslaught of missives from the school regarding tea towels and calendars and something called a pantomime which even repeated googling had given him absolutely no insight into.

But the boys were in a state of excited frenzy about it all, and given they had had a two-year separation, he wanted to give them a wonderful Christmas, just as soon as he had figured out what that was meant to consist of exactly.

Further up the beach, if Bramble had not been quite so lazy, he may also have encountered Milou, with his owner, Lorna MacLeod, out for a blow before school, even as there was only the merest hint of pink on the horizon this late in the year. Lorna stayed well away from the old-manse end. Her year-long crush on Saif was useless because he was still in love with his wife, even though he had no idea where she was – trapped somewhere on the winds of war, or dead, or worse. Nobody knew.

She looked back on that year with huge nostalgia now. Once upon a time, before the boys had returned even, he would meet her here on the beach, where he was usually to be found before the working day, waiting for the ferry to come in; waiting for news of his family.

And she would be walking Milou, and they had fallen in to talking, and become friends – real friends – and both had looked forward to those early mornings, sometimes windy or sharp with cold, sometimes so beautiful you could see a million miles across the world and the sky was a vast canopy above them that went on for ever; days so pure and glorious that it was impossible to believe, in the splashing of the tide and the peeling of the gulls, that anything bad could ever happen out there, beyond the wide island horizon.

Anyway. Before, when they were friends, she had made the ghastly error of revealing her hand – and that had not gone well. Not at all.

So Lorna stayed away from Saif's end of the beach now. And anyway, he was busy, raising the two boys who came to her school and who were slowly, very gradually begin-ning to fit in with their fellow playmates, shedding their tentative accents and nervous dispositions – Ash at least.

The half-starved little souls who had arrived, petrified, without a word of English in the cold springtime were now transformed. Good, decent Mure food, much of it from the MacKenzie farm, had filled them out; Ib had grown two inches and looked more like his father every day. So. That was good, she supposed. That was how she had to think about it. Good things were happening. Just not, she thought a little gloomily, to her.

The water was too cold even for Milou this morning, which was very rare, and Lorna turned up the hood of her parka and turned back to the harbour. There was no busier time at the school than Christmas. She had a *lot* to get organised.

Bramble padded across the adjoining road that led to the Rock, Colton Roger's grand project, which at the moment was in a state of some neglect, certainly not helped by Bramble cocking a leg and taking a long pee all over the cornerstone.

Colton was a brash American who had arrived on Mure determined to coat it in wind farms and turn it into a profitable proposition, but had ended up rather falling for the place just as it was, and building his life there.

Colton's dogs were ludicrous: purebred huskies, made for show rather than bounding across snowy wastes, which meant they were inbred, blue-eyed and quite alarmingly stupid, not that it really mattered as they weren't called upon to do anything more strenuous than stand outside his gravelled drive gates like large white statues, and to be more or less in the vicinity when Colton needed to tell people how much he'd paid for them.

That had been before Colton had got sick. He had a nasty cancer, and was being nursed by his husband, Flora's brother Fintan.

The house staff paid attention to the dogs; Fintan had no thoughts for anyone other than Colton. So far, Colton's unofficial prescription of palliative care consisted of as much morphine as he could source – which as a billion-aire was quite a lot – and as much fine whisky as he could drink – again, quite a lot – which meant he was pretty sleepy a lot of the time. Fintan had more or less given up work to care for him, but actually there wasn't much to do; there were nurses for the tricky stuff so Fintan just had be there when Colton stirred, to try not to be more than a hand's grasp away.

It was the hardest thing he'd ever had to do in his life.

Bramble marched steadily onwards, back up the hill towards the farmhouse, loftily ignoring Bran and Lowith, two of the younger sheepdogs who were allowed to joy-ously bounce around on the hillsides all day but absolutely did not have in-front-of-the-fire privilege. When little Agot, Flora's niece, had been very small, she'd never had to be warned to stay back from the fire: Bramble would simply nudge her out of the way without preamble. As a result, tiny Agot had learned to cuddle in under Bramble's warm fur, like a huge slightly smelly blanket. Although she was four now, she hadn't ever got over the habit, and Bramble hadn't ever minded.

Bramble loped up the muddy track, the winter frost crackling across the fields, the puddles solid and the air so shockingly clean it caught in your throat, and nudged open the old farmhouse door and padded across the old worn flagstones, paper still in mouth. Eck, Flora's dad, was at the kettle and turned round slowly – cold mornings these days meant he felt like an old engine; it seemed to take him for ever to get moving. Bramble lifted his head up obligingly so Eck could take the paper from his jaws, and the toaster popped up at exactly the right moment with some of Mrs Laird's wonderful bread, just in time to be spread with the glorious butter Fintan made on the farm and a quick sit-down with tea by the fireplace – one slice for Eck; one slice for Bramble, who chomped it up efficiently as they sat in peaceful early morning contemplation together, and another day on Mure began.

Chapter Two

Even though only the first early birds were coming through the door looking for good coffee and a slice of mincemeat tart, Flora found herself to be exhausted. The tiredness she'd started to feel was completely unlike anything she'd ever experienced before: every night she fell asleep in seconds.

Oh God. How was she going to tell Joel?

It wasn't that she thought he didn't love her. Even though he found it hard to say the words, she knew he did. And that – even when he was working on Colton's projects overseas – all he wanted to do was come home to her.

But the last year had been hard. She'd finally found out about Joel's very difficult childhood in and out of foster care, and understood more about why he needed extremely careful handling. He had never known a home, there had been domestic violence and he'd been fostered around a number of placements until he'd won a scholarship to boarding school aged twelve.

Clever, handsome and ruthless, he had done extremely well in corporate law and all the perks that came with it – the girls, the watches, the hotels. The idea of settling down on a small island with a pale local girl would never have occurred to him in a million years. Flora was still surprised that he had. She couldn't see what Joel could see, because she'd been born and raised there. But for Joel, the longer he'd spent on Mure, the more he'd warmed to it. He'd come to see the value in a world that followed seasons, not a stock market ticker; the patterns of the farming calendar rather than CNN. He had found something there, and in Flora, that he'd never had before in his life: peace of mind. Domestic trappings – and there was little more domestic than Flora's old farmhouse kitchen, her troupe of brothers marching in and out at all hours, her father dozing by the fire, dogs everywhere – had started to appeal to him, even as he kept his cottage at the Rock.

Joel found it fascinating: Flora didn't even realise for a second what she had – what he'd never ever had – in a loving home. At first it had scared him beyond all sense. All his life he had run so fast, trying to leave his childhood behind him, thinking that if he was on a private jet or wearing an expensive suit, he would be safe.

The island made him feel safe; Flora made him feel safe. It had taken a nervous breakdown trying to handle Colton's affairs in the middle of Manhattan that had finally made him realise it. But he was dreadful about articulating it to Flora.

So Flora had been patient. Very patient. She couldn't help it; she had adored him since she'd interviewed at the firm six years ago.

Except. Now something had happened which, on balance, she should have predicted. Birth control bought over the internet (when you grow up somewhere with a population of about a thousand, secret internet shopping came as a boon on a par with electricity) plus as healthy a sex life as you can imagine when the nights are long, the fires at the Rock are very cosy and the person you're with has been someone you've adored for years who suddenly appears to want to have lots and lots of sex with you ...

You can see how it happened. But jings, the timing, Flora knew, absolutely could not be worse. Could not be a bigger spanner in the works.

Of course she'd dreamed of having his baby – one day! And 'one day' was absolutely ages away! Years and years and years.

After they'd bought a house and decorated it and chosen things together ... Okay, she couldn't imagine a universe in which Joel would actually look at wallpaper patterns, so scrap that. Right. Well. Maybe they'd just buy a lovely house together – there weren't a lot of houses for sale on Mure, for sure. There weren't a lot of houses full stop. But they'd find something lovely; she had dreams of one of those gorgeous contemporary eco homes they did on *Grand Designs*, all glass and wooden beams, even though, if she was honest with herself, she was more of a lots-of-tatty-cushions-and-old-worn-blankets-and-lots-of-books-and-mugs-of-tea person than a minimalist.

Anyway. Those were the dreams she'd had. That's as far as they'd got. Cushions and south-facing windows. And if she was that far ahead, Joel was probably miles behind her. Miles. She sighed. He was barely recovered from the summer. It was an awful thing to land on him, a dreadful thing to do, and she truly hadn't meant it, not at all. It was his fault if anything, grabbing her every time he walked through the door . . .

So at least working in the shop and him being away gave her a bit of breathing space as she worked up how best to tell him.

This trip he was on was the first piece of proper work he'd taken for ages – he was selling off companies for Colton, who was attempting to divest his money and spread it among various charities without alerting anyone – and she was incredibly worried about him.

Fortunately, instead of checking into a hotel, he was staying at his therapist's apartment. His therapist, Mark, had known him as a boy – had been his child psychiatrist – and they maintained an active friendship with a lot of counselling thrown in. Mark, who was childless, had confessed to Flora before that the greatest regret of his life was not taking the clever, terrified boy into his home and adopting him when he was little, and so he had spent his life trying to make it up to him. He and his wife, Marsha, were the kindest people Flora had ever known, and if

15

anyone could keep an eye on her boy while she wasn't there, they could.

It occurred to her that she might talk to them before she talked to Joel. They could definitely help.

On the other hand, it felt wrong to ask them for professional advice, and there was a limit to how much Mark could discuss. Plus it felt really wrong to tell other people before she told the father of the baby.

A baby! Even with all the worry, she couldn't quite get her head round the entire thing. I mean, it was incredibly inconvenient. And she was terrified of telling Joel. And she couldn't afford it, and she didn't have enough time and the farmhouse could hardly handle a baby which would crawl over Bramble and straight into the fire . . .

She stroked her stomach thoughtfully. Even so. A baby!

Chapter Three

It was bitter outside, and Flora smiled at her customers' faces as the door banged open in the wind, letting in gusts of frosty air, their expressions shocked by the harshness of the wind outside.

'There's snow on it,' warned the old ladies, who always warned about snow even though they very rarely got any for long. There would be snow on the air, but the wind seldom let up for long enough for it to actually stay on the ground. Snow on Mure was a living, dancing thing; a whirlwind that ran through on its way to the mountains and deep-filled glens of the highlands.

When she was a very little girl, Flora remembered, her mother had found her dancing out there one night and had told her the story about the spirits in snow that stole children away, and she'd remarked that she was half snow child already – quite blue – and that children of the sea shouldn't mix with children of the snow, and so had taken her back indoors and warmed her up with creamy hot chocolate, and then Fintan had woken up and complained vociferously about who was getting hot chocolate, so he had had some too before they were sent back to bed each with a hot water bottle, a whacking great kiss and a cuddle from their mother, who smelled of chocolate and flour and everything safe.

The snow coming, Flora knew, was not the reason she was thinking about her mother that morning, even as she used her strong pale arms to stir the thick fruitcake mixture, Isla and Iona making a tidy production line of scones and sandwiches for the morning crowd. She glanced around. There was Mrs Johanssen, obviously on her way to bother Saif. She liked to have a weekly appointment, more or less just to discuss herself and her ailments, which were, for a woman of seventy-eight, quite extraordinarily minor. She was in fact a medical miracle and as strong as an ox, having done heavy manual labour while eating lots of fish and turnips for the previous seventy-seven years.

It was entirely to Saif's credit that, despite his heavy workload, he treated her as seriously as he treated anyone else. At the Seaside Kitchen, Mrs Johanssen would ask for a plain scone, and check four times with them that it didn't have raisins in it as that played havoc with her digestion.

The knitting group was also in. They didn't spend

much money and were mostly using her fuel to keep warm rather than their own, but Flora couldn't begrudge them: they helped with the overspill from original Fair Isle knitters from the south so the beautiful, intricate garments could still be labelled as locally made, and they shared a pot of tea and a couple of scones and sat next to the radiator to help warm up their arthritic hands, bent into twisted twigs by years of contorting needles. The rhythm of the clicking was a nice accompaniment to the work, along with the ever-present hum of BBC Radio nan Gàidheal, which played all day.

A few spots of snow tossed and played outside, and Arthur, who made the beautiful earthenware cups and plates for the café, as well as being a loyal customer, stood outside looking mournful. He lifted his head.

'No,' said Flora.

'I'm just saying ... '

'I read your petition,' said Flora. 'If I start letting dogs in the café, where will it end? Lions? Buffalo?'

'There's just not that many buffalo on Mure.'

'What about all the people who are allergic to dogs? What if they get hair in my scones?'

'I'm just ... ' Arthur narrowed his eyes. 'You're in a cranky mood this morning.'

'I am not. I'm just slightly weary having to explain the dogs ban nine hundred and forty-nine times a day.'

'Just because you don't like dogs.'

'Arthur! What kind of bugger doesn't like dogs? I *have* a dog. I just don't like pawprints in the flour!'

From outside, Ruffalo, a vast oversized beagle/terrier cross who had absolutely no idea how big he was, crooned a low howl.

'If you didn't pamper him, he wouldn't be upset by a bit of sleet,' said Flora.

'It's hard to look at an upset puppy,' said Arthur thoughtfully.

'He weighs more than a small car!' said Flora. 'I don't force you to come in.'

'When you make those cheese scones you do,' said Arthur, and Flora nodded her head complacently.

The door opened again, letting in a huge draught. Flora smiled; it was Charlie and Jan, who ran the Outward Adventures courses on the island, sometimes for corporations to make money, and sometimes for disadvantaged youngsters – Joel helped out with the latter from time to time.

'Teàrlach!' she called; most people used the Gaelic form of Charlie's name.

'You are not taking your mites out on a day like this.' She started pouring Charlie's tea the way he liked it. He stamped his feet and blew on his fingers, then wiggled them, revelling in the warmth. Jan didn't, looking around at the Seaside Kitchen as she always did, as if she considered heating a terrible wanton extravagance and Flora's life one of unparalleled ease and leisure.

'Och no,' said Charlie, accepting the tea gratefully. Jan watched the interaction beadily. She didn't trust

Flora, who had kissed Charlie for about ten seconds once while she (Jan) and Charlie weren't even dating. The fact that they had subsequently gone on and got married hadn't dissipated the tension quite as much as Flora had hoped.

'Um, would you like a tea, Jan?' offered Flora meekly.

'I'm working,' said Jan, as if Flora had offered her a double vodka Bru.

Charlie handed over his cash and Jan looked at that too, as if scandalised Flora would actually take money just because she ran a business.

'No,' Charlie went on, happily oblivious to the undercurrents as always. He was a blissfully uncomplicated man. 'No, it's corporate this week. A firm of accountants from Swindon.'

Flora peered outside. Despite it being 10 a.m., it was still pretty murky out there. She saw a group of unhappy-looking men and women in unflatteringly large waterproofs, blown sideways by the wind, and couldn't help but smile. They were doing worse than Ruffalo.

'Tell me they're paying thousands of pounds for the privilege,' she said.

'They are indeed,' said Charlie gravely. 'And they have Loch Errin to kayak across before lunch.'

Flora beamed. 'Oh *God*, they're going to hate it. Have they even kayaked before?'

'Nope.'

'It must be a force four. Are you taking tea out to them?'

'Nope.'

'Oh Teàrlach, it's not like you to be cruel.'

'I'm not being cruel. Look at them.'

In a huddle, the Swindon accountants were chatting ferociously to one another.

'See? They're debating whether to mutiny, whether to just leave and how much they hate us. They really, *really* hate us.'

Flora nodded. 'I'm not surprised.'

'Well, that's how it works,' said Jan. 'Team-building. They're bonded in their hatred for us.'

Flora blinked.

'I never knew how that worked before. It makes a lot of sense now you say it like that. But the boys get sausage rolls!'

Charlie shrugged.

'The boys get anything we can give them ... But yes, order me up fifteen of your plainest sandwiches for later. Use yesterday's bread if you like.'

'I will not!' said Flora, scandalised.

'... and charge top dollar please.'

'Well, that's not strictly necessary,' said Jan.

'No, do it, *yarta*,' said Charlie. And the localised term of endearment – 'my darling' – fell out of his mouth before he could stop it, and Jan glared at him and Flora squirmed a little as she took back his tea mug (he had his own, hanging up on a rack at the back) and waved them on their way.

* ❋

By lunchtime it wasn't looking much better outside, and it was obviously going to be a slow day inside, at least until 3 p.m., which was the precise moment everyone working up and down the high street in Mure decided that they needed a piece of Christmas cake. Flora feared withdrawal symptoms come January. Plus the fishing fleet came in at 4 p.m. and they needed mountains of tea and toast and to be shepherded into the furthest corner so they wouldn't stink up everybody else.

Flora decided to slip out and take lunch to Fintan, who would be on vigil up at Colton's place. In the summer, they'd spent a lot of time down on the beach, and everyone had managed to pop in.

Now, as Colton weakened, fewer people were able to casually drop by, even as Colton was withdrawing into himself. It was a time for family now. Just for them.

She packed some Cumbrae pinwheel and bacon roll with a cranberry jelly she'd been experimenting with, and headed out to her father's mucky old Land Rover.

As soon as she pushed the door, she understood why everyone had come in that day looking so shell-shocked: the weather had deteriorated since the morning and now the wind caught you by the throat the moment you opened the door. It blew right through you, and Flora shivered inside the down jacket that was a necessity of life on Mure, pulling her scarf up over her nose and mouth. Tiny bits of snow mixed with rain threw themselves against the side of her head and she jammed down her pompom hat, but her hands were still freezing by the time she got to the car ten metres away, parking not really being a problem this time of year.

It took for ever for the rusty old heating to start up, though it barely mattered as the wind whistled through the tarpaulin at the back, and Flora set off.

Chapter Four

Colton's mansion was quite something. It had been an old rectory at one stage, remodelled and extended to turn it into – well, a home fit for a billionaire, Flora supposed, as she went up the immaculate gravel drive, past the grumpy peacocks – who must be *freezing*, surely – the security gates opening to an unseen voice when she gave her name.

The snow in the air was thicker here as they were on higher ground; the house perched on the edge of a cliff which looked down over water to the north – seemingly endless, all the way to the pole – save for one field of wildly spinning windfarms, zipping around today like futuristic whirligigs. All of the waves were cresting white. It would be a long and miserable slog for the fishermen today, even the ones born to the sea.

The heat when the door was opened to her (round the back; nobody on Mure ever used their front door and few people locked either) was as shocking as the cold had been.

Colton kept his house – and had done, even before he got sick – at tropical temperatures so he could pad about in his bare feet if he felt like it on the underfloor-heated stone flagstones imported from Italy.

Flora couldn't get her top four layers of clothing off quickly enough. She glanced around. Fintan was coming down the hall. Normally such a sprite, he looked older these days, warier. Flora glanced around.

'It's gorgeous,' she said.

And indeed it was. The entire house had already been decorated for Christmas, even though it was barely December. Huge swathes of ivy looped around the old banister in the great hall, holly covered every fireplace, and fires roared in the downstairs library and sitting room, even though there was nobody in them.

Flora found it heartbreakingly sad. It was such a beautiful house, immaculately, beautifully restored, exactly like the Rock, the hotel Colton had bought just to the east of where they were that was meant to provide every possible comfort to visitors and tourists. Only it hadn't quite worked out like that now he was ill. She looked in the kitchen; every type of herb and spice was arranged in futuristic bottles on perfectly dusted floating shelves. The whole place should have been buzzing with parties and children and families and joy because such an amazing thing had happened: Colton and Fintan had both found the loves of their lives in each other, and they were newlyweds.

Instead it felt like a mausoleum, and she could tell Fintan could see it in her eyes.

'It's all right,' he said right away, shrugging. 'Bit over the top.'

'I brought lunch,' said Flora. She didn't want to give him a cuddle as it would feel patronising, weirdly. Also, until their mother had died, they hadn't really been a family that did that. Instead she waved the Tupperware box.

'Oh, actually there's already a chef here,' said Fintan distractedly. 'So . . . '

'Fine,' said Flora. 'I'll eat it. I'm starving—'

She stopped herself. She was always starving these days.

'Anyway.' She changed the subject. 'Is he awake?'

Fintan nodded.

'He's not bad today. Want to come and say hello?'

Moving up the stairs was rather spooky; Flora knew there were other people in the house, but she couldn't hear anyone. The thick, soft carpet muffled their foot-steps too. The house smelled of expensive perfumed candles in various variations of fig and orange peel and mulled wine, but underneath it, they couldn't entirely dissipate a very slight but distinctive disinfectant smell.

Even though Flora saw Colton as often as she could, it was still a shock every time. She recalled the strong, tall, wiry American she had first met striding into a boardroom in the heart of London two years ago; brilliant, mercurial, utterly confident. Insufferably so. She smiled sadly to think of it, and followed Fintan as he pushed aside the heavy wooden door leading to the master suite.

The heavy curtains that covered the vast bay window had been opened, leaving a clear view of the tempest outside. It was an astonishing, bewitching vista at any time; more dramatic now with the waves dancing and snow all around. Flora steeled herself, turned to the diminished figure on the vast hand-carved four-poster bed.

Only the four-poster had gone – of course it had – replaced by a hospital bed; inevitable of course. Colton had to be protected now. And Flora remembered from when her mother died, years earlier, once you brought that bed home . . . She didn't want to think about that. Instead she pasted on a smile.

'Hey!'

It hurt so much to see him like that. He'd always been thin, but lithe; healthy in that way of Californian tech billionaires.

Now he was cadaverous. He looked far, far older than his forty-seven years: his face was sunken, his lips beginning to turn in, his eyes milky and unfocused. He had always been so vital, so full of bounce and ideas – some good, some utterly ridiculous. Such a vigorous man. And now this thing was punching the life out of him, blow after blow, day after day.

Flora sat down on the bed and gave him the gentlest cuddle she could manage. He smiled weakly and she saw with relief that he recognised her. He didn't always. There were good days and bad, but she didn't see so much of the bad. She just cooked for a traumatised Fintan when he popped into the farmhouse for five minutes, when he just wanted to sit down and have a vast cup of tea and some shepherd's pie that wasn't cooked by specially flown-in vegan anti-cancer diet chefs, and hug Bramble, and hide his tears in the big dog's fur, and if Innes's daughter Agot was there, let her rattle on to him about developments in PAW Patrol and someone called Shellington who was a doctor and also a sea otter, and to whom she was apparently quite attached, then sing 'The Stick Song' for nine hours.

Flora could sense that Colton wasn't ready to talk at this point, and anyway, what was there to say? Colton had made it perfectly clear that his wishes were to be respected – in a legally binding document he'd had Joel draw up for him in the summertime after his first diagnosis.

No experimental cures. No life-prolonging – and misery-prolonging – chemotherapy. As far as Colton was concerned, he had made his plans and said his goodbyes and was now letting the tide go out, ever so slightly; the waves came less far up the beach; the sea got further and further from view, bit by bit.

Fintan, of course, did not agree. He hadn't even come out to his family until he'd met Colton and had fallen completely and utterly in love for the first time in his life. And now it was being taken away and he simply couldn't bear it. Flora wanted to tell him that he'd meet other people, that he'd fall in love again. But she'd seen them together, seen how crazy they were about each other. And she didn't know if she'd be speaking the truth. She knew the way she felt about Joel could never ever be replicated, which was why she was currently so terrified.

So. They just all tried to be there: for Colton here, and Fintan back in the familiar farmhouse kitchen, where the old clock ticked away on the mantelpiece above the roaring fire alongside the old pewter bowl, a wedding gift that had belonged to Eck's mother and now contained keys and assorted odds and ends, not that the house was ever locked. The drift of post on the sideboard that piled up until Innes sighed and started doing the accounts. The kettle that must have boiled a hundred thousand times. The old huffing Aga. Just the little familiarities of home, where you didn't have to pretend not to be sad. You didn't have to pretend that everything was going to be all right, that it was going to be a great day. You could simply come home and be as grumpy or silent as you liked; Eck wasn't much of a one for talking anyway.

'Could you nip home and see Dad?' asked Flora, knowing Fintan sometimes needed an excuse to get out of the huge house. He nodded eagerly. 'I'll be back soon.' And he kissed Colton very gently on the cheek and, with a guilty look on his face, escaped.

Flora patted Colton's shoulder. 'How is your awesome morphine today?' she said.

'Good,' Colton croaked. 'Also I'm going to ask the doc to up the whisky scrip.'

'Brilliant idea!' said Flora in a stupidly cheery voice she didn't recognise. She blinked.

'When is the doctor coming anyway?'

Colton stared vacantly into space.

'I don't ... I don't really know when it is now,' he whispered.

'Do you want some water?' said Flora, and Colton nodded, and she lifted his neck up and helped him sip a few drops. Even that was a massive effort for him. His skin felt like paper under the incredibly expensive flannel pyjamas he was wearing. There was nothing to him.

'Everyone gets like this in the winter,' she went on. 'Four hours of twilight then you have absolutely no idea where or when you are.'

Colton blinked.

'Has Fintan been reading you the stock market reports?' she continued.

There was an untouched *Financial Times* sitting by the bed, along with the *Economist* and *Time*.

Colton's mouth wavered a little.

'I don't ... He reads, but I don't ... I don't really. It's too complicated for me to follow ... '

He waved a translucent hand. Flora frowned.

'I've got a magazine in my bag,' she said, taking out a weekly she'd nicked off Jeannie, the doctor's receptionist, who bought them all for the waiting room then read them later in the Seaside Kitchen and left them behind, whereupon the girls would wait till nobody was looking and pounce on them.

'I could read you my favourite section,' said Flora. 'It's called "Celebrities Doing Fake Paparazzi Posing on the Beach".'

Amazingly, Colton's eyebrows perked up and his gaze briefly focused.

'Okay good!' said Flora, making herself comfy. 'Now. Here's Gina. She was in the jungle and vomited four hundred grubs over everyone and she's famous now ...'

Which is how Saif found them half an hour later, comfortably side by side as he dealt with the extraordinary change in temperature from the outside to the inside by hurling off as many layers of clothing as he could.

This was Saif's second winter on Mure, but somehow he'd managed to forget the first one. Maybe you had to forget it, he'd thought, scraping ice off his car that morning, or you'd never make it to another one. Like childbirth.

'Hey,' he said, and Flora had smiled to see his handsome, serious face – he had long dark hair that always seemed in need of a cut, and a short beard and the slightly panicked look around his huge dark eyes that you could see in most working parents. 'I thought that was Fintan's place.'

'It is normally,' said Flora. She glanced at Colton, who appeared to be drifting off to sleep.

'He just needs ... a bit of time away ...'

Saif nodded.

'I understand.'

'How is . . . ?'

Saif looked at her, his face as grave as ever.

'I'm sorry, I can only talk to . . . '

'Oh yes, of course, I know. Sorry.'

She stood up.

Saif softened.

'I would say . . . as expected,' he said.

It didn't matter, Flora mused, how often they were given the terrible news. It still seemed almost impossible to believe that Colton would one day not be here. So she chose not to believe it, which meant it felt like she was constantly being retold.

Saif came over to the bed – a nurse materialised from nowhere to help him, one of a battalion Colton had on call, very quiet and discreet. Saif roused Colton long enough to check his vitals and nod his head. Flora knew it was her cue to leave, but she couldn't, not quite yet.

'Okay, well, everything is as expected, yes?' said Saif, glancing at his watch and timing Colton's thready pulse. 'Stable, meds are good, pain is good, yes?'

Colton grunted. 'More whisky.'

'I do not hear that.'

Although Colton didn't notice Saif's slight nod to the nurse.

Saif packed up his bag. 'I'll see you tomorrow.'

* ❄

Flora caught up with him in the hallway.

'Um, do you have a sec?'

Saif looked pained. This was the terrible problem with working in a very small community: anyone who saw you generally had something they wanted to ask you about and if you said yes to one person you'd have to say yes to everyone and he'd spend the rest of his life doing it.

'Flora! Please make an appointment with Jeannie.'

'Jeannie will scream and misbehave and I will lose all hopes of confidentiality and if I even go into your stupid surgery there'll be ninety-five people in there I know and they will all come straight in the café afterwards, you know they always do, so they'll just be asking if I'm contagious and if it's safe to eat the food and word will get about and my business will fail and close down. Is that what you want, Saif? Is it?'

Saif knew he was being played, but he was a very kind man. He folded his arms.

'I'm not examining you.'

'You don't have to.'

Flora swallowed. Now she had to say it out loud, something she had never said before. She realised how nervous and scared she was. It was kind of hilarious, kind of ridiculous: a stupid, stupid sentence and she wasn't sure she was going to get through it. She took a deep breath. She'd been very tearful recently anyway for one reason and another.

'I'm pregnant.'

Chapter Five

Saif's first instinct was to smile and offer his best wishes. Then he remembered that it could go two ways, so he bit it back and put his stoic mask up again. On the other hand, he could only assume that if she didn't want to continue with the pregnancy, she probably wouldn't have cornered him on a staircase.

'So this is ... good news?'

Flora's eyes widened. 'I don't know. I mean, is it? I think so. I mean, it's too early. I mean, we've hardly been together for five minutes. Is that good for a child? I don't know. And Joel is basically still in recovery, and—'

Saif held up his hand.

'Sorry – I am asking: you want to keep baby?'

'Oh! Yes. I ... Yes. Yes, of course! Actually ideally I'd

like to keep it … inside … for about two years, so we at least have the chance to, you know, move in together. Anyway. Sorry. This isn't your problem. I just wanted to ask. Could you mark it on my notes? And send me for scans and stuff? Without me having to come in right away?'

Saif narrowed his eyes.

'Have you told Joel?'

'I am definitely and absolutely in the process of considering getting around to telling Joel,' said Flora.

Saif blinked. There was absolutely no doubt that he owed Flora a lot of favours, not least the number of times he'd been called out to an emergency on Mrs Laird's (who looked after him and the boys) day off and he'd had to deposit Ib and Ash in the café with two orange juices and a scone between them and trusted her to keep half an eye on them until he got back.

'All right,' he said. 'How many weeks – you know?'

'The test said 3+,' said Flora. 'Are those right though?'

'As right as anything we could do in lab. Did you buy test in town?'

'Hahahahaha!' said Flora. 'I don't think those are even real tests they have on the shelf. Can you imagine? Nobody local has bought a pregnancy test on Mure since they arrived. No, I got it sent under plain wrapper from the mainland.'

'You make good spy,' said Saif, starting off down the stairwell.

'I've been a lot of things,' said Flora. 'I like being a café-owner best.'

'Well, I hope you like next job as much,' said Saif, finally allowing himself to smile as he left the enormous building.

Flora didn't like to think about how difficult everything was about to get, but she took a deep breath as she watched him go. Phew. Well. That was the first bit over with. She felt rather shaky. She had said it out loud. instead of just continuing to walk around in a daze as she'd done for the last few days, completely unable to believe it despite the fact that statistically she could more or less see what had happened. He was pretty hard to resist, Joel Binder.

She sighed.

Oh God. No, she wasn't going to think about that right now. But she was going to do something she wanted to do desperately. Tell someone who'd be pleased. She could hear the Land Rover roar into the drive, which meant Fintan must be coming back.

She went back into the bedroom and lay down beside Colton, whose eyes were half-closed again.

'I'm going to tell you a secret,' she said quietly. 'Don't tell anyone, not even Fintan.'

'I forget . . . stuff,' said Colton.

Flora reached for his hand.

'You're going to be an uncle again,' she whispered into his ear, and squeezed his hand very hard.

It took an age, but eventually she felt the gentle pressure of a return squeeze on her hand. She glanced up. There was a tear running down the side of his face but he couldn't lift his hand up to reach it. She gently wiped it away.

'Agot,' he rasped finally, 'is going to *hate* it.'

'I know,' said Flora. 'I know.'

Chapter Six

There was no doubt about it, Lorna was flustered. Christmas was a crazy time in every school, and Mure primary was no exception even if there were only thirty-eight children in the whole place. The school was divided into two classes: the lower school, which Lorna took as well as being headmistress, and the uppers, which the saintly Mrs Cook did, as well as doing her best to help out with the admin. The fact that Lorna had as much government administration to cover – and often more, seeing as the island schools had to constantly prove that they were managing with all the children together – as vast primaries with six classes per year group and an office full of secretaries and administrative staff felt wildly unfair to Lorna, but she got on with it.

Because otherwise she loved the school. It was perched

above the town, up a hill (which the children sledged down in the winter whenever the snow lay) and was in the traditional Scottish school style: a red sandstone building with old traditional carved entrances for boys and girls, no longer used of course, and a flat playground with hopscotch grids painted on. Inside, huge old oil radiators kept them cosy on the wildest of days, even though the windows rattled. When the school had opened, one hundred and forty years before, the locals had been sceptical: it was seen as a foreign intrusion on their way of life. The radiators had changed all that. Hardy island children, used to unheated rooms, draughty cottages and outside plumbing, flocked to the cosy environment of the school room, warmed their chilblains on the heater, were reluctant to return to the fields. The old guard had warned it would make them soft. And perhaps it had, for subsequent generations had started to move off the island. It was only now that people were coming back, lured by the island's promise of peace and beauty and calm, and good Wi-Fi, more or less, depending on the wind.

It didn't stop Lorna worrying though. Canna's school, near Eigg, had closed the previous year after its last four pupils had moved away. You could never be complacent about it.

And now there was the nativity play to get underway. Parts allocation was always a nightmare. Plus the amount of farm children who thought it was totally unreasonable that their favourite coo didn't get a part was an annual challenge.

Lorna frowned at the register. It would make sense to ask Ibrahim, Saif's son, to play Joseph. After all, he and his brother, Ash, were the only Middle Eastern children they had. On the other hand, would it be insensitive to ask him to act out a major part in a Christian story as a non-Christian? On the other hand, why would that matter? On the other hand, would she look tokenistic by putting the only non-white child in the main role? On the other hand, if she didn't cast him would she look ridiculously racist, seeing as he was right there? On the other hand, might Saif not like it? If it was literally any other parent at the school, she would just call them. And there was that history, hers and Saif's.

Therefore, of course nothing could happen even if it was seemly for a teacher to date a parent, which it wasn't. And he barely spoke to her, which was also a fact to consider in the whole mess. So she tried not to consider it at all, just get on with things.

She wrote 'Joseph – Ibrahim Hassan' on the cast list. Then she crossed it out again. She remembered, nostalgically, her teacher training in Glasgow, where there was a healthy mix of children of all sorts of backgrounds and this kind of thing didn't matter. Here, people would notice. She wrote his name in again; it would be good for Ib, a very reserved, slightly sullen boy (for which nobody blamed him, given he'd lived, age eleven, through things most people could never imagine) to be up on stage, applauded, clapped, made to feel important.

On the other hand, would she be accused of patronising

41

and favouring the little refugee boy, handing him the starring role, when his English could still be a little patchy? On the other hand, what could be better for his English than being made to speak up loudly and clearly . . . ?

Lorna slammed her notebook shut. This could wait until tomorrow. She'd ask Mrs Cook; her counsel was worth having. She glanced at her phone. It just said, 'Harbour's Rest?' which was Flora code for 'A crisis is happening!' It was after 5.30. Okay. Joel would be up to some nonsense again, but it might be fun to shut off her own stupid brain for five seconds, enjoy a G&T (the wine in the Harbour's Rest was utterly unspeakable) and maybe Flora could even come up with a solution. She popped into her car and trundled down the hill, windscreen wipers batting furiously through the storm.

Chapter Seven

The Harbour's Rest had its usual little line of old chaps who came in after a hard day out in the fields or on the sea for a whisky and a chat or, just as often, the chance to not chat, to just sit by the fire and read the paper or pat their dogs or simply take a little comfort and cheer out of the storm.

Lorna had grabbed their usual seats at the bar so Inge-Britt could chime in with any useful ideas of her own to their conversations, but Flora indicated the corner booth, the furthest in the room, even though it was right beside the door and every time someone came in, a wind blew right in and down your neck. Lorna frowned. Then Flora went to the bar and came back with a G&T for Lorna and a Diet Coke for herself.

It was very strange. Lorna generally thought of herself

as quite a balanced person. She'd had her ups and downs in life: both her parents had died and her brother worked the rigs so she could often be lonely without her family around her, even as close as the community was. She had been – okay, was – extremely fond of a man who couldn't love her back.

But she loved her job; she loved her cosy little flat on the high street, where you were close to everything and could see the comings and goings; she loved Milou, and knew everyone on the island and could honestly say she didn't have an enemy in the world. She had a little money put away, and also had her health and her friends. Lorna was a cheerful soul on the whole, not inclined to bemoaning her lot.

So she was surprised by how much this caught her in the gullet. How outstandingly and instantly jealous she was. All at once; like she'd been punched, winded with purest envy.

'You're not,' she said, aghast.

Flora looked furious.

'Seriously,' she said. 'You think I'm that much of a piss-head I can't . . . '

But she couldn't keep it up for long.

'Fuck a duck,' she said. 'Yes. I am.'

There was an agonising pause before Lorna remembered what she was meant to be doing at this point: jumping up and flinging her arms around her friend, delighted.

And she was, she told herself ferociously. She was delighted. She was.

'OMG, are you crying?' said Flora. 'Don't start to cry – I mean it. I'll cry too.'

'Don't cry.'

'Why are you crying?' remarked Inge-Britt on the way past to make a very lacklustre attempt at cleaning the loos. 'Is one of you up the duff?'

'Good,' said Lorna. 'Can we move back to the bar now? I'm freezing here.'

Lorna looked at her friend as they moved their stuff. She looked pale, but Flora was always pale, her skin so white it was practically translucent. Her mother had been the same; it's why they'd got their reputations for being selkies, seal spirits that came to land in mortal form. Flora laughed it off, but Lorna always thought there might be something to it. Flora's niece, Agot, was even fairer, her hair an almost pure white. She looked like – and indeed was – a tiny witch.

But yes, she was possibly a little paler than usual, with tiny blooms of pale blue shadow under her eyes. And . . .

'Jings, have you got tits?' asked Lorna. 'You have! You have *never* had tits. Joel is going to be delighted. Even more delighted, I mean.'

Flora grimaced.

'Ah,' she said. 'Ah. Well . . . '

There was a long expectant pause.

Lorna looked up. That was the thing about being very old friends with someone: they didn't have to say anything for you to know exactly what they meant.

She took another sip of her drink and felt awful for her

jealousy. Flora didn't have life easy either. Lorna liked Joel – or she thought she probably did; he was quite hard to get to know. And he didn't half put her friend through it. She knew he was difficult and had had a difficult childhood, but even so she didn't think it always excused how often Joel didn't exactly put Flora first.

Lorna looked for a way to say, 'You haven't told him?' that wouldn't sound sarcastic or oddly triumphant or pitying or anything else that she didn't want to convey, and finally gave up and went back to the old speech they'd heard at their grandparents' knee.

'*Doch dhu naw telt?*' she said as gently as she was able.

Flora sighed and suddenly looked close to tears.

'Don't worry about me,' she said. 'I suddenly appear to do this *all the time*.'

'Do what?'

'Cry. Leak. Literally all the time. I cried the other day when I saw Bramble.'

'What was he doing?'

'Eating the gas bill. Seriously, nothing!'

Lorna nodded and put her hand on Flora's arm.

'Och, sweetie. But he's going to be all right! He'll be thrilled! Surely! I mean, you're a couple and everything...'

Flora blinked and rubbed the tears away from the corner of her eyes.

'For five minutes we've been a couple! I barely know him! Except I know that he comes from somewhere where family is basically a dirty word.'

Lorna tilted her head.

'Well, maybe he's been looking for a family all along. And you're it.'

'Yeah, me plus an extra person? Lorna, where are we going to live?'

Lorna looked up suddenly as if a lightbulb had gone on. 'What?'

'Well, I was just thinking . . . I mean. I've been thinking since last year what to do with the farmhouse. It's getting really neglected and rundown, and I don't have nine hundred brothers to run the place like you do. It needs selling, Flora.'

'If I need a desperately falling down farmhouse I can just stay at home, thanks,' said Flora.

Lorna shook her head.

'No, no, that's not what I mean. I mean, if you guys paid me rent, you could move into the flat. Then I would have enough money to do up the farmhouse and sell it.'

Flora blinked at this. Lorna's flat was her haven. Any entertaining that went on, Flora normally did it at the farmhouse as everyone knew to come there anyway. Otherwise they'd meet in the pub or the Seaside Kitchen. Lorna hadn't had a boyfriend for three years since Gregor, a nice twinkly fisherman from Eigg, whose genial good nature, fisherman's hours and easy-going manner had meant they had all completely failed to notice that he had another girl in Rhum. And probably in Eigg too.

But that was off the point: the flat was really lovely. It was just by the side of the seafront, which meant it had the views but was mostly protected from the very harshest of the weather in that it looked out on the cobbled streets leading back from the harbour, and was completely unobtrusive unless you were looking for it. It was in a curved sandstone building, with little carvings along the outside. Downstairs housed the tiny Museum of Mure, home to ancient artefacts, beautiful, intricate Celtic jewellery and international flotsam washed up from shipping routes over the centuries as well as the tiny library which was so fervently overheated that Lorna barely needed to turn hers on.

There were two high-ceilinged reception rooms. The first was a soft lounge with a large fireplace, where Milou stretched out on the old Persian rug and an oversized sofa took up the entire back wall. Lorna had painted it in dark reds and greens, so that it was like being inside a cosy jewellery box.

The back room, with a gorgeous brand-new kitchen that had cost an utterly terrifying amount of money to get shipped over from the mainland, faced south, and got every single ounce of sun there was to be had, if there was any at all. It had a sliding glass door at the back which led out onto what was technically a fire escape landing, but Lorna had filled it with beautiful plants and had great big waterproof cushions that she scattered out there in fine weather, so in fact it was more like a tiny oasis, and she and Flora had spent many happy evenings sitting out there with a bottle of wine, looking over the little shambling rooftops and setting the world to rights.

Then there were two bedrooms; one vast, and two bathrooms. It was a perfect little TARDIS of an apartment. Flora blinked.

'You mean it?'

'It's up two flights of stairs,' shrugged Lorna.

'Yes, but there's nobody else in the building,' said Flora. 'I could just dump the buggy in the stairwell. Oh God. Oh God. I'm going to have to buy a buggy. Oh God. Oh God.'

'Stop panicking,' said Lorna. 'Or at least panic about one thing at a time.'

Flora nodded.

'Oh God. I'm going to have to go to Aberdeen.'

'Uh . . . ?'

'Buggies. They have buggies in Aberdeen. They've got a John Lewis. I read on the internet you can't have a baby without John Lewis.'

'Seriously, Flora,' said Lorna, almost cross with her. 'This isn't about John Lewis.'

She thought about it.

'On the other hand, there's one good thing about this so far.'

'What's that?' said Flora

'You know for a fact Joel doesn't stalk your internet use.'

Flora gave Lorna a very hard stare.

Lorna ignored it, swigged more of her gin and tonic, then lowered her voice and took her friend's hand.

'Do you want this baby?'

'Yes,' said Flora fervently. Then she looked up.

'But I want Joel to want it. And I don't know if he can.'

Chapter Eight

Oddly enough, Flora was staring at the phone the next day, trying to will herself to pick it up, when it rang anyway. She blinked, but it wasn't Joel.

Instead it was an international number and she assumed it was what it generally was – American tourists coming for a visit who wanted to know if the Seaside Kitchen was gluten-free. She would kindly and patiently explain that no, they weren't, but everything was locally sourced, and for a surprising amount of people this amounted to more or less the same thing and they came anyway.

'Hello? Seaside Kitchen?' she said cheerfully. There was some crackling on the end of the line, as if someone had dropped the phone.

'HELLO?' came a voice. Then another voice behind it.

'Don't be nuts – you don't need to yell like that. It's only Scotland. She's not deaf.'

Flora felt herself relax as she recognised the tone.

'Mark?' she said. 'Marsha? Is that you?'

'See?' said Marsha's voice. 'She can hear you perfectly fine.'

Hearing their voices brought back the memory of the summer when Mark had been utterly instrumental in helping Joel back from the brink of a nervous breakdown and had shown him how to find himself again in the fresh air of the islands – and by walking, helping, looking after himself Joel had had the time to mend and be able to come back to Flora, to gather the strength to carry on. Flora owed Mark an awful lot.

'Hello? Hello? Are you there?'

Flora came back to the present.

'I'm on Mure, Mark, not the moon.'

'Okay. Right. Okay. Well now. Look. Say no if you want to.'

Flora's attention perked up. Usually if people said 'Say no if you want to' they meant 'If you say no, our relationship is over for all time'.

'Uh-huh?'

'Well, I was thinking . . . I found your island just so, so beautiful when I came and, well, Marsha really wants to see it now, and we were thinking that maybe we might come for Christmas?'

Flora blinked.

'Mark. I have to tell you. You were here in July. When it was sunny and warm and light all the time.'

51

'Uh-huh.'

Flora glanced outside at the snow flurries dancing around the harbour lamppost. Although it was nearly nine in the morning, it was as black as pitch outside.

'Okay, it's really not like that now ... '

'What's it like?'

'Well. Pitch-dark all day really. And windy. Very, very, very windy.'

There was silence.

'I mean,' said Flora, 'obviously we'd love you to come.'

'I thought we'd ask you,' said Marsha, 'because we haven't seen Joel since he got here and then it was only for five minutes. And he said call you ... '

'I'm not sure where you'd stay ... '

'Colton invited us to the Rock,' said Mark. 'Of course, that was a while ago. Back in the summer. But he always said it was at our disposal ... '

'Oh no, the Rock would work,' said Flora, perking up. It was lovely there. If Colton had plans in place to keep it open, that would work very well. 'And you could spend Christmas Day with us?'

'Would that be okay?'

Flora thought about it. She'd only met Marsha once, but had found her wise, direct and sympathetic. And discreet. And she knew Joel as well as anyone in the world. Surely she would be the best person to confide in? Mark and Marsha didn't have children. In a funny way that almost helped; Marsha was as direct and non-judgemental a person as Flora had ever met.

'I'd love that,' she said, the warmth in her voice over-spilling down the phone. 'I'd love to see you both. But you're not allowed to complain about the weather.'

'We won't complain about anything,' said Mark. 'It's just . . . '

Marsha took over. They had to be on speakerphone.

'It's just so wonderful to see you two settled,' she said. 'We couldn't be more delighted.'

Ah, thought Flora. But she didn't elaborate.

Chapter Nine

The one good thing, Flora realised, was that being pregnant didn't give you much in the way of sleepless nights. As soon as her head hit the pillow, she was out like a light. A combination of being pregnant and not drinking Inge-Britt's gin and tonics out of dirty glasses, she assumed.

She sighed as she padded through to the kitchen in her thick socks. She thought enviously of Lorna's flat. She had underfloor heating in the kitchen and every time Flora went around there she immediately took off her shoes. It was such a luxury.

She poured out the tea. Joel was coming home the next day. They could talk about it then. One more day. One more day to get through.

Flora turned up at the Seaside Kitchen to find Isla and Iona, giggling and looking quite unlike themselves.

'What's up with you two?' she asked suspiciously. They were boy-mad, the pair of them, and always up to mischief, so it could be almost anything. But probably boy-related.

Iona blushed.

'Nothing. Nothing at all – everything's fine; we had a good take yesterday.'

Flora checked the safe. They had indeed; unusual for the time of year.

'Did Charlie's lawyers have a walkout?' she asked warily. It was not entirely unheard of for a lone soul to peel off from the main group, digging and hacking their way through great storms inland back to the coastal high street to cower with a bowl of hot soup and a toasted sandwich in the corner until their hands had stopped shaking. Flora took pity on them enough to serve them, but not enough not to dob them in when Charlie called looking for them.

Isla shook her head. 'No. Not them. It was—'

'Sssssh!' said Iona.

'Okay,' said Isla. 'Yeah. Okay. Sssh.'

Flora ignored whatever they were up to and looked at the calendar.

'Oh lord,' she said. 'I've got to plan the nativity party. It's incredibly soon.'

Her mother had started a tradition when she'd had four children at school that after the nativity play, everyone went to their house for a party, and it had become one of the fixed points of the December calendar.

'Are you going to be dancing?' said Isla. Flora shook her head. She had a very real sense that her highland dancing days were over.

'God no,' she said. 'You can, though.'

'I've got no choice,' said Isla sadly. 'Mrs Kennedy corralled me already.'

'Did she indeed?' said Flora, noting that her martinet of a dancing teacher hadn't asked her this year. Was she already showing? No, that couldn't be remotely possible. Surely not.

'Anyway, that doesn't matter. What matters to us is that we have a contract to provide three hundred mince pies.'

The girls groaned.

'Everyone loves a homemade mince pie!'

'Yes, but they're . . . '

Flora knew what they meant. The mincemeat was sticky and gloopy by the time they'd left it to marinate properly for a few days; the little bits of suet tended to creep up the side and keeping that much pastry flaky and light in so many tiny packages was not difficult exactly – but it did get very, very repetitive.

'Come on,' said Flora, trying to jolly them on as she inspected the great slabs of cake being pulled out of the oven for the hungry visitors to come, and deeming herself satisfied. 'We'll do a hundred each. Oh God, no. That sounds just as bad. Okay. Production line.'

She looked at the accounts for yesterday for a second. 'Actually, call it time and a half if you stay on one evening and do it.'

This cheered the girls up sufficiently and she went out to turn the sign on the door to OPEN.

* ❄

Around eleven o'clock, the girls started giggling again. Flora was back in the kitchen. God, how could she still be tired? She'd slept about nine hours the previous evening. She grabbed another coffee. Even though she was drinking decaf now, hopefully it would psychologically fool herself into perking up.

She heard the heavy tread of male footsteps – and it sounded like a lot of them – clumping into the café, so she popped her head around the kitchen door.

Standing there was a bunch of slightly awkward-looking young men. They all had razor-short buzz cuts and were wearing heavy great coats. They were all white, and many were tall and handsome, with high cheekbones. Isla and Iona were grinning at the front of the glass display cabinets, and even the Fair Isle group seemed to have put their knitting down for a second.

'Hello?' said Flora cheerily. The lead boy of the group stepped forwards, looking embarrassed. He was holding a hat in his hand.

'We like ... seventeen ...'

He pointed to the Christmas cake. Flora looked up

at him. His accent was strong and suddenly she had an inkling where they were from.

'*Da*, of course,' she said, smiling. The young man looked surprised. 'You're Russian?'

There was some huddled debating of the men among themselves in a language that was quite obviously Russian.

'*Da*,' said the man finally, reluctantly. Isla and Iona giggled their heads off while scooping all their Christmas cake into a large bag. Flora would have some disappointed customers come teatime.

'Fishing?' said Iona.

They were so clearly not fisherman, Flora nearly laughed. They were all wearing military greatcoats for starters.

'*Da. Da.* Fish,' said the man, stuttering and growing uncomfortably pink as the girls giggled away.

Flora nodded cheerfully.

'Fishing it is,' she said. She knew they'd be in serious trouble if anyone started prying into whether or not there were any nuclear submarines in the area. So best just not to ask.

The handsome young man thanked them, paid and turned to go, when Iona, pink as a shellfish, ran up to him and thrust a leaflet for the Mure Christmas party in his hand.

'What?' she said innocently as she returned to Flora's disapproving glance. 'He's gorgeous. They're all gorgeous.'

'They don't speak any English!' said Flora.

58

'She wasn't planning on talking to them,' said Isla.

'Shut up, Isla!'

'Calm down, everyone,' said Flora, as the click of the knitting needles started up again. 'And, Iona, just try not to cause a major international military incident.'

Chapter Ten

Saif, as usual, was running late, trying to chivvy the boys up the hill. It was snowing properly today, with more flakes lying on the ground, so they were forcing their way into a blizzard. Mrs Laird had knitted the boys balaclavas so you could see almost nothing of their faces apart from Ib's long eyelashes poking out, crystalled with snowflakes. He was going to be quite dramatically handsome.

It was in Ash, though, that Saif saw a lot of Amena, his beautiful wife; the boy had the same heart-shaped face and high cheekbones, and that sudden, thrilling smile.

It didn't make getting them out in the morning anything less than a nightmare though. Literally the first full line in English they'd ever learned at home, rather than at school, was Saif hollering at them to put their shoes on.

It was strange, Saif reflected, that they spoke English at home now. Neda, the social worker and counsellor who contacted them frequently to see how they were getting on, had stressed that they ought to speak Arabic at home and English at school, so the boys could keep their home ties.

But somehow, it felt too difficult to Saif. Arabic was the language they'd spoken when they were a family – a full family. It was the language Amena had sung in when she had rocked the babies in the summer courtyard, with its contrasting scents of diesel from passing cars and the scrappy pomegranate bush they tried to keep alive in the corner, as they hung out tiny onesies to dry.

It was the language of the cartoons they had watched together as babies; Ash constantly squirming as Ib sat, concentrating intensely. It was the language of their cousins; the aunties; all the people they did not see now; all the people they might never see again.

No. The only way to deal with this new life was to live in it. Ash's fondness for baked beans; Ib's enjoyment – of all things – of *The Fresh Prince of Bel Air*, a show about which Saif found nearly everything incomprehensible, particularly the fact that it appeared to be about thirty years old.

It kept the past at bay. Neda told them they were losing something. Saif felt bitterly that it was something they had to lose; otherwise, how could they move on? How could they exist, except in the day and space they lived in now? How could he deny them that?

Except at night, when he would twist in his dreams in which Amena would be waiting at the door of their little section of the courtyard, and the boys could not recognise her, nor speak to her in the only tongue she knew, and he would wake up – Ash in his bed as often as not – curled around the sheets, bathed in sweat and wonder how long? How long?

Then he would look at the beautiful form of Ash, and think of his other boy, sleeping peacefully at last in the great, gloomy bedroom next door, the stars bright, the moon distant and far away, watching over them in peace and safety, and think, It is for them you are here. Hold on. Hold on.

* ❋

That morning there was something of a kerfuffle around the school gates. The other parents had at first been wary of Saif – not because they had anything against him personally, but because Ib, after his difficult experiences, had been, not to put too fine a point on it, a monster. He bit. He kicked out. He shouted in a strange tongue. He was invited to nothing.

Things were starting to settle a little: Ib was a talented footballer player and, it turned out, as soon as they put a stick in his hand, a good shinty player too, and there was always a shortage when putting a side together on their small island.

So he'd become a little more accepted, although he

remained reserved and wary. Ash, with his undersized frame and appealing ways (not to mention his beautiful big eyes) had become a firm favourite among the girls, and was petted and indulged wherever he went. Saif wasn't sure this was ideal – boys and girls hadn't mixed much at the schools he'd been to – but things were different here, he supposed. At least he had someone to sit next to at lunchtime.

The other parents went silent as he approached, but Saif didn't really notice that kind of thing. Pinned to the board was a list and he gradually realised it was a cast list for something called a 'Nativity Play'. Against the name 'Joseph' was Ibrahim Hassan, and against something called an 'Innkeeper', which he'd have to google, was Ash.

Everyone was looking at Saif to gauge his reaction. He didn't have the faintest idea what his reaction was supposed to be. He would have to ask Jeannie, the GP's receptionist, but he knew she was a terrible gossip for anything she didn't absolutely have to keep private, like the medical records. He so missed having Lorna as a friend.

He missed her for a lot of reasons; he felt so strongly for her. But it could not be and that was that. It was hard. He was thirty-four; fit, young, healthy. And when the boys had gone to bed at night, he was so lonely, and sometimes, walking to work in the morning, would catch himself dreaming of her glorious red hair, her beautiful freckles, her warm laugh.

But it was impossible. He was married. He had made vows. The fact that he was so attracted to her simply meant he must always stay absolutely away from her. For everyone's sake. He could not give Lorna what she wanted from him.

There was still no news from Syria; Amena's own family had scattered, mostly in Turkey, and communication was difficult and brief. All he could piece together was that she had left one morning to get food for the boys, and never come home.

Saif was a scientist. He was trained in rational thinking. Occam's razor – the scientific concept that the simplest explanation for anything is almost certainly the correct one – applied here.

But there was always a chance. A tiny chance that Amena was still alive. And the tiniest chance of his boys having a mother; of his family being restored. He had to believe it. He had to.

But he missed his friend very much.

Chapter Eleven

There was the normal row of old ladies waiting, some with their reluctant husbands in tow, when Saif got back to the surgery. He eyed them up. Diabetes management, hypertension, mood stabilisers and for Mrs Giffney – with whom he'd made a terrible mistake a month or so back when, being unable to think of anything to cure her mysterious side pains which didn't conform to any pathology of anything vaguely dangerous and probably had more to do with her comfortable padding and habit of carrying her dog on one hip when it rained, which was always – he had suggested a traditional rubbing herb they used back home rather than expensive heat gels. This had apparently worked brilliantly (and coincided with a period of unusually dry weather) and ever since then Mrs Giffney had been convinced he was some kind of traditional shaman and told everyone to ask him for traditional remedies, which a surprising amount did.

Saif believed the time and attention complementary methods could bring you were enormously helpful; the actual ingredients themselves rather less so, otherwise he would happily co-opt them into his medical practice. But there was no convincing Mrs Giffney, nor any of her cronies who had taken to turning up and asking if he didn't have a poultice or any herbs instead of the statins he was suggesting. He'd admitted defeat eventually, bought some dried coriander from the internet and suggested taking a pinch with the actual medicine he'd given them, being emphatic that it would only work if his instructions were carried out to the letter.

'What is "nativity"?' he asked Jeannie as casually as he was able. He knew the story, more or less, but was unclear as to what was going on in the school.

Jeannie smiled broadly.

'Oh yes, they've taken the leads, haven't they! Just swanned in apparently, snapping up all the good roles because of being from the Middle East?'

Jeannie always knew everything.

'Is this bad?'

'I'm only teasing,' said Jeannie. 'It's the highlight of Christmas. The children do a nativity up at the school. Then there's a big party at the MacKenzies' farm.'

She frowned, seeing his worried face.

'Don't you want them to be in the show?'

Saif squared up.

'We are in a new place,' he said, wondering if the authorities would want to know if they'd joined in. 'We will do ... whatever ... is required.'

'It's usually not considered a chore,' said Jeannie. 'It's usually considered great fun. But it's not compulsory.'

Saif sighed. 'No, no, it's fine.'

'Christmas is going to be hard for you,' said Jeannie sympathetically. She meant because he'd be alone. Saif thought she meant because he'd never done it before. They both nodded their heads gravely, and he took up the day's set of notes and headed off to his consulting room.

Chapter Twelve

Joel hated New York. He hated all cities. Even at its twinkliest, snowiest, most beautiful best, the air was still full of exhaust fumes and hot dog smells and people shouting and cars honking, and out-of-towners trying to cross Midtown.

Colton was doing what doctors called 'getting his affairs in order', which in Colton's case was rather a lot, and Joel was there just to make sure everything was watertight. Ready. Colton wanted to be ready. All of his money was earmarked for charities, except for the Mure properties: the house and the Rock hotel would pass to Fintan to look after. It was a simple straightfoward process, and therefore everyone was going absolutely apeshit about it.

But there was another dimension too – it was a testing. Joel had undergone a minor breakdown in the summer – so this was an adjustment, as Mark liked to say, to his new, calmer way of life. It had been tough on all of them. But if he was still to work a little, he needed to test himself. He was there for three days, staying with Mark and Marsha so he wasn't by himself in a hotel room, and they were keeping him away from spending too much time by himself.

The first night he'd arrived, though, he'd been amazed by how calm he'd felt. He'd sat with Mark in their beautiful top-floor pre-war apartment on the Upper East Side, the fire blazing in the little parlour, the windows closed against the city noise outside.

'I like it more with snow blowing,' he'd observed. 'Feels more like home.'

'Yup, that's New York,' Marsha had said, kissing him. 'Always freezing or boiling.'

'It's like this all day every day at home,' said Joel, smiling. 'You get used to it.'

'Did you just use the "h" word?' said Mark, coming in wearing a huge jumper that made him look like a Greek Santa Claus.

Joel smiled more broadly.

'Thanks again for last summer,' he said.

Mark shook his head. 'Oh, it wasn't us,' he said. 'Thank that girl of yours.'

Joel rolled his eyes.

'Well,' he said. The couple looked at him expectantly. 'What?'

'We were just wondering how it's going,' said Marsha. 'Not that it's any of our business of course . . . '

Chapter Thirteen

Flora was baking spice cookies and thinking maybe she should just phone Joel. No. Maybe she could ask Fintan for advice, take his mind off things. No, that wouldn't work either. The more people who knew before Joel, the worse this was going to get, and that was absolutely a fact.

She was hemming and hawing about this, ignoring the girls completely, when the bell rang out front again. At first she thought it was the Russian sailors back to see Iona, but this man wasn't of military bearing at all: he was large, wearing blue jeans with a big belt, his belly spilling over the top. He also had a check shirt on and an odd blouson jacket affair, unzipped, which seemed unwise in this weather. He had heavy eyebrows, a high colour to his skin and looked to be in his fifties – and not ageing particularly well.

Flora pasted a smile on. A tourist, making the completely correct assumption that Christmas in the islands might be an unusual experience and something to tell their friends, but failing to read the small print about the weather.

'Hello,' she called out. 'Can I help you?'

The man narrowed his eyes.

'Hi.'

He was American, as she'd guessed the second he came in.

'Can I help you?' she said again, still smiling politely. He didn't smile back, which wasn't particularly American of him; normally people from the USA were delighted just to be there, and felt the need to explain that their great-grandmother had either come from the island, or somewhere quite nearby, or Ireland which was the same thing, wasn't it, sweetie, well, never mind, but they were on some kind of a package tour deal.

'I'm looking for someone,' he said in a slightly over-dramatic way. Flora imagined a piano player stopping playing the piano in an old-timey Western bar.

'Oh yes?' she said carefully. However much she'd been away, and however far she'd travelled, she was a Mure girl through and through. She knew everyone on this island and they knew her and she didn't know this guy. So she kept smiling politely, but felt a little wary.

The man moved closer. He glanced around the Seaside Kitchen as if he didn't think much of it, which put Flora on edge even more.

He looked up at her; his eyes were a grey-blue, and reminded her of someone, but she couldn't quite work out who.

'I'm looking for Colton Rogers,' he said, and it was almost a growl.

Flora blinked. There was just something about him she ... she couldn't say what it was. Maybe it was heightened senses. Maybe being pregnant made you more careful of people, she thought. Or maybe he just ... didn't look very nice.

'Would you like a tea or a coffee?' she said.

The man glanced disdainfully at the big clanking coffee machine.

'Nah,' he said.

Flora wished the café wasn't quite so quiet this morning. There was a dense freezing fog outside too, which added to the slightly sinister atmosphere.

'So, why are you looking for him?' she asked politely.

The man sighed, and suddenly looked very tired.

'He's my brother,' he said.

Flora realised why his eyes had looked familiar. They were the same steely colour as Colton's. Although Colton's softened when he smiled and had a network of wrinkles around them ... Well, they used to. It was the strangest thing: ever since he'd got sick, his face had slackened – from the medication she supposed. And his wrinkles had gone – it was almost completely smooth. And as he'd lost weight, he looked bizarrely young, like a child.

This man looked different, but you could see it. If

you concentrated. Flora, though, couldn't imagine him throwing his head back and laughing. At anything, really.

She busied herself clearing up.

'Does he know you're coming?' she asked.

The man snorted.

'No. Colton isn't interested' – it came out as 'innerested' – 'in nothing to do with us. After all, we're just his blood family.'

Flora blinked.

'Well, I can't . . . I mean. Have you spoken to Fintan?'

The man's brow creased.

'Who?'

Chapter Fourteen

In the end, Flora smiled as well as she was able, excused herself, then went back into the kitchen and called Fintan immediately.

Fintan's voice was hushed but he got up and moved, saying soothing words to Colton as he went. Flora heard the heavy door shut behind him.

'How is he?' said Flora.

'He's dying,' said Fintan harshly. Then he collected himself. 'Sorry, Flores. We had a really really bad night. I kept imagining he'd stopped breathing.'

'Fuck,' said Flora. She didn't know what else to say.

'He's worse than when you saw him. I'm losing him,' said Fintan, his voice sounding teary. 'He just gets further and further away. And I can't see him any more. Not the person he was.'

'He's in there somewhere,' said Flora.

'I don't think he is,' said Fintan. He stuttered and his voice choked up a little.

'Flora . . . I think he wants to go.'

Flora didn't say anything. She agreed. Colton's world now was full of pain, eating him from the inside out. Of course he wanted to go. There was only one exit route, heartbreaking as it was for all of them.

'He won't . . . he won't stay here for me,' said Fintan, his voice a whisper.

'I know,' said Flora.

She absolutely didn't want to give him what was coming next.

'There's . . . there's someone in the café,' she whispered.

'Huh?' said Fintan, not catching on.

'There's somebody here . . . '

'Are you . . . wait. Are you being held up? Is it a robbery?'

'No! Why would you think that?'

'You're whispering! I wondered if you were being held hostage.'

'Why would I call you?'

'Oh, thanks very much.'

At least he sounded more like himself, thought Flora.

'No! I mean, there's a bloke here. And he claims to be Colton's brother.'

None of Colton's family had attended his wedding. They had mostly disowned him when he came out as gay and so he had absolutely no interest in having them there – he called them a bunch of lardass rednecks.

'Oh, for Christ's sake,' said Fintan. 'He didn't even tell them which island he lives on.'

'Yeah, if only he hadn't invented the internet,' said Flora.

'He didn't *actually* invent the internet . . . he just monetised quite a lot of it . . . '

Fintan sighed.

'What do you want me to do? Tell him Colton doesn't live here? Just flat out lie to him? I don't like him.'

'Ah, you're getting back your island mistrust of outsiders,' said Fintan. 'That's good. Oh Christ, I don't know. What if Colton'd want to know?'

'Would he?'

'He says he doesn't, but, you know. Bravado. I mean, you know. Even if they're as annoying as – for example – you. Your family, in the end . . . '

'Does his mother even know he's dying?' said Flora in a quiet voice.

There was a long pause. Then Fintan said, 'Right. Let me try and talk to him. What's his name?'

Flora shrugged, which was evident even over the phone.

'Oh, you are a crap detective. Right, Colton's going to take a nap . . . I'll pop down. Don't let him leave.'

'How am I going to do that?'

But Fintan had already hung up.

✳ * ✿

Fintan re-entered the room cautiously. The heavy curtains were open, but the thick mist outside made it feel as if they were floating out to sea. Colton was awake, but his eyes were unfocused; he was staring at nothing, and it was hard to tell if he was actually there at all.

'Colt?' said Fintan, padding across to the bed. He got a half-smile in response, which was at least a good sign.

Fintan sat on the end of the bed and reached his hands to Colton's, taking care to avoid the cannula.

'Okay. Well. Apparently your brother's in town.'

The effect on Colton was astonishing. It was as if he'd been given a shot of adrenalin. He tried to sit up and managed to lift his head off the pillow. More importantly, his eyes focused and he looked, for a moment, like his razor-sharp old self.

'Tripp? That sonuvabitch? Seriously? He's got a nerve!'

Fintan stared at him.

'What?' said Colton. 'I don't want him anywhere near me.'

'Um ... '

'I mean it, Fintan. Are you hearing me? I hate that bastard.'

And at that moment, Fintan loved Colton's brother more than anything else in the world for lifting the curtain, for bringing Colton back to him – even furious.

'I am hearing you,' said Fintan, sitting down and grasping Colton's hand harder. 'Right. Tell me what you want done to that bugger.'

Tripp had accepted a full-fat Coke and was sitting drinking it morosely, staring at his phone.

'What's your Wi-Fi password?' he growled.

'I'm afraid we don't have one,' said Flora. More than one person hooking on to their sparse allocation of the island's limited Wi-Fi made it fall over instantly, so she'd simply decided against it. Also, it kept miserable, wet holidaymakers from setting up camp all day for the price of a cup of tea. She sympathised, but she was only scraping a living as it was – the little library had one if anyone was desperate.

'Goddammit,' he said.

'And I still haven't heard from . . . Fintan.'

The man didn't react to this, just sat back as if he were intent on staying until he got a response, which evidently he was.

'Would you like something to eat?' said Flora, trying to be polite.

'Yeah, I could use a burger,' said the man. Flora frowned. 'Um. I'm afraid we don't do burgers. I've got some quiche.'

'Quiche?' said the man as if she'd suggested he eat a bicycle. 'Yeah, no thanks.'

He looked around.

'Got any pancakes?'

They didn't normally do pancakes either, but Flora

desperately wanted to vanish into the kitchen for a bit and had no objection to making something as incredibly simple as a stack of pancakes so she smiled and said, 'Sure thing,' as he requested maple syrup and bacon, both of which she could manage. (She wasn't sure how many he'd want, so she made nine in the end, of which he ate nine and looked slightly regretful there weren't more. During this period, no fewer than four separate groups of people came in, looked at what he was eating and decided they too wanted pancakes, and as they were super-easy to make and cost absolutely nothing, Flora ended up putting them on the menu full time and they turned into an absolutely brilliant little brunch money-spinner. So there was at least one reason why she turned out be grateful that she ever met Colton's brother.)

'So, you're here for long?' she asked.

He took a long pull of his cola.

'Dunno yet,' he said. Then he turned back to his food.

✫[*] ❅

Fintan came charging down as soon as Saif came in to do the daily check-up. He stopped short when he saw the man sitting there, chewing stolidly through the pancakes, then edged his way to Flora, making her go through to the kitchen with his eyes.

'He doesn't look very nice,' he said once they were by the kitchen burners and Flora had turned the radio up.

'I know,' said Flora. 'Want me to tell him just to leave?'

'Well. Here's the thing,' said Fintan.

And he explained about Colton waking up, suddenly becoming so attentive.

'Hang on,' said Flora. 'You're saying that this is a good thing he's here?'

Fintan had great big shadows under his eyes.

'He's back,' he said. 'Flora, he's back. He's animated. He's with me! Actually in the room!'

'He's furious!'

'He's fucking furious,' agreed Fintan. 'But Flora . . . otherwise he's just going to sail away to nothing.'

'You're saying getting Colton annoyed is the way you're going to play this?'

'Oh God,' said Fintan, his face downcast. 'When you put it like that, it sounds awful.'

Flora sighed. Fintan looked at her as though for the first time in a while.

'What's up with you? You look fat.'

'Shut up,' said Flora. 'But also I was just thinking . . . about families, you know.'

'Dysfunctional units one has absolutely no control over however annoying they are?' said Fintan.

'Yes. That too. But . . . even so. I mean, if I had a son or . . . I mean, if one of you guys was on his deathbed.'

'Even Hamish?'

'Even Hamish, yes, shut up . . . I mean,' said Flora, 'it's the only family he's going to see.'

'Well, it's not,' said Fintan. 'Because he's got me.'

'I realise that,' said Flora. 'I'm trying to be helpful here.

80

There's two good reasons you should let this guy see him. One, because it's woken up Colton. Two, because ... I think it might be the right thing to do.'

'What if he's a total arsehole though?'

'You can't choose your family,' said Flora. 'Surely you know that by now.'

They smiled at each other for a second, their old feuds long forgotten.

'You are looking fat though,' said Fintan. 'Ooh, are you making pancakes? Can I have some?'

Chapter Fifteen

Tripp was staying in the Harbour's Rest, Flora noted the next morning as she got to the Seaside Kitchen and noticed a massive, gleamingly shiny SUV parked outside the hotel. Most people didn't bring cars to Mure: they weren't encouraged on the narrow track roads, and anyway, the island was built for walking; for taking in every new view around every bend; avoiding every grouse waddling along in the middle of the road like a self-important toddler; watching the heron take wing; wondering about life on the ancient wandering stone walls; and the bright purple foliage; or the sun changing the shifting colour of the towering hills. You could get around Mure pretty fast in a car. But the rather better question was: why on earth would you want to do that?

So Flora made a deduction that this was where he

was, and she was proven right about half an hour later when he staggered in, rather blearily – she wondered if he'd fallen to the blandishments of Inge-Britt's line of dusty whisky bottles – and made a remark about the coffee at the Harbour's Rest which might be seen incredibly rude (by anyone who'd never tried the coffee at the Harbour's Rest).

How could two brothers not even share a roof for one night? pondered Flora. What had happened? How could families fall apart so fast?

Then she pondered Joel's family, stroked her stomach thoughtfully and tried not to worry.

⋆ * ❄

Tripp was feeling jet-lagged and confused. Why was it so damn freezing round here? He thought of all the instructions he'd been sent with following the hastily convened family meeting back in Delaware.

It was unanimously decided he should be the one to go, seeing as his stupid sister was in the middle of yet another divorce so was making it all about her, and his parents were getting frail. Also, his father was still such a dick by making a big deal about Colton being a fruit. I mean, God, he didn't care for it either, but that wasn't the problem.

Tripp sighed. At the time, coming over here, to Scotchland or wherever the hell he was, seemed easy. He'd walk in and sort Colton out, like he always did when he was little and Colton was such a weed, such a nerd, showing Tripp up, never there to play games or mess about in the yard. Always inside, clamped to that stupid microcomputer, trying to fit it together to light up a circuit or make something buzz, like, big furry deal.

He was easy to push around though. It was all the rage at high school, making Tripp's pathetic little nerd brother's life a misery. Tripp thought it was hilarious. That would teach him not to behave like a proper boy. He was showing the family up, and their father agreed with him. Janey, their sister, she didn't care about either of them. Pa thought Colton should learn to hold his own and stand on his own two feet; learn to fight back. But the snivelling, trembling kid never did, and the names the other kids called him were revolting.

Tripp found Colton pathetic, embarrassing. Didn't he know that all you had to do was hit back? Get into a fight, that's all it took; even if you lost, you still got respect. It wasn't difficult, was it? Okay, so he didn't want to play football, he was lanky enough for basketball. Or just *something*. Not locking himself in the science lab every lunchtime, for Christ's sake; walking the long way home. Tripp had no idea how they'd actually ended up in the same family. Colton even exasperated their mother, with his constantly running nose and mild asthma and hay fever. Anything that came round, Colt caught it. Tripp was perpetually sure he was putting it on just to get a day off school, like a pussy.

Tripp himself had graduated high school and gone on

to work with his dad, selling cars. He was good at it too: a cheeky word for the ladies, a bit of talk with the men about the game, job done. He stayed in the same town and married the hottest girl from his high school – who turned out to be an utter pain in the hole, even as it became increasingly clear that she thought exactly the same thing about him.

Colton had gone at eighteen, off to the furthest college he could get to – Caltech, whatever the hell that was. Tripp had pretty much lost interest after that.

Until his stupid, pathetic little brother started to get in the papers. It was small things at first: little notes in business sections of papers that Tripp didn't read, but that his mother carefully folded away.

Then more and more, he'd moved into the main sections with a lot of noise being made about some information-gathering service Tripp didn't really care to understand, and words had been thrown around, like 'disrupter' and 'wunderkid' and then things he very much did want to read, like 'billionaire'.

He never came home. Never. Not for Thanksgiving. Not for Christmas. He didn't attend either of Tripp's weddings, nor Janey's. He did on each occasion send them a large cheque, enough to buy a house with. Janey had sniffed, cashed it and never mentioned him again. Tripp had tried to call him once or twice but never remotely made it past his secretary.

Colton had paid off his parent's house too, quietly, without ceremony; repaid his college tuition, plus a certain amount of extra money which, had they counted it up, was precisely the average cost, adjusted for inflation, of raising a child from zero to eighteen.

And then nothing, which, rather than making the Rogers family grateful, made them even more annoyed. A few hundred thousand – what was that to a billionaire? And what made it worse: the rest of the town knew he was part of their family. There were whispers everywhere: why weren't they rich? Why were they still living in normal houses, driving normal cars? Why did Colton never come to visit? Mrs Rogers felt socially embarrassed at her card games in a way she normally preferred to make others feel. Their father never mentioned the son who had gotten away; who had humiliated him by paying off his mortgage. Janey couldn't care less. But it burned in Tripp. He made a good living from the car lot, of course he did. But he had to bust his balls there every day – in the freezing cold, in the hot sun, out there dawn to dusk. He didn't know what Colton did all day, but he'd seen pictures. It looked like a lot of private jets and being on the cover of magazines, as far as Tripp was concerned.

Then, suddenly, it had been all over the papers – Rogers divesting from all his investments; pulling out from many of his industries. It had spooked the market – his stupid little brother could actually move the entire stock market, it transpired. It had made headlines. Rogers had gone into hiding. Which was quite natural for an eccentric billionaire apparently. But for the family, it was concerning. What was he doing? What was he trying to hide? And, more importantly, what the hell was he doing with all that money?

Meanwhile, their father had gotten older and frailer and more curmudgeonly than ever, and it was becoming obvious their mother could no longer cope. They needed money to look after him; neither he nor Janey had anything put by after the divorces, and they couldn't throw their mom out of her home.

A profile in Forbes had talked in passing about the increasing amounts of time Colton was spending on a remote Scottish island without having redeveloped his plans for a golf course at all – work hadn't even started. That was enough for the family to get together and find out what was up, and ... Well, Tripp didn't like to see it as begging. Implying, that was all. That the family needed looking after, and he had billions. So. It was only fair.

Flora brought him a coffee anyway. After all he was, in a funny way, her brother-in-law. He looked utterly exhausted.

'Sleep well?'

He looked at her. There were massive bags under his eyes.

'Nah,' he said. 'Not with all those dogs barking.'

Flora frowned. None of the dogs on Mure were notorious barkers, as far as she knew, and she knew them all. I mean, the sheepdogs when they were working, but not at night ... Oh.

'Those aren't dogs,' she said.

He glanced up.

'Eh?'

'You mean the seals.'

'Seals?'

'Yes, you know . . . fat grey things.'

'Well, I'll be. I didn't know they bark.'

It was becoming clearer and clearer to Flora that there were an awful lot of things that Tripp Rogers didn't know, and she was very careful not to let anything slip that wasn't her place to tell him.

'So are you . . . are you going to see Colton today?' she said carefully, worrying about what she was saying even as she spoke the words.

'I hope so. I have to wait to hear from his manager guy.'

Flora frowned.

'You know . . . I can't remember his name. The faggy-looking one.'

There was a pause. Flora was suddenly terribly tempted to pour the coffee jug all over his hand. Just in time, she remembered how famously litigous Americans were. Even so. There were limits.

'I'm sorry,' she said. 'I'm afraid I won't have language like that in here. You'll have to leave.'

'You're shitting me.'

'Nope,' said Flora. 'Up you get.'

Tripp's eyes wandered through to the kitchen where Iona was grilling the first square Lorne sausage slices of the day, their aromatic scent making its way tantalisingly through to the main room. Big fresh puffy loaves of bread, courtesy of the redoubtable Mrs Laird, had just arrived on the counter, warm and fragrant. His saggy face fell.

'But where . . . ?'

'You can eat in the Harbour's Rest,' said Flora, knowing full well that Inge-Britt rarely got around to breakfast for another half an hour, and not caring in the slightest. She was white with anger.

'I mean, a man can't say a thing these days.'

'You can,' said Flora coldly. 'You can say whatever you want. Just not in my establishment.'

'Jeez,' said Tripp, muttering something under his breath that sounded a lot like it began with a 'b' and heaving his large body from the chair. He turned to leave and Flora was momentarily annoyed that she wasn't going to find out what the hell was actually going on. But rather less annoyed at that than she was at anyone who would come in and be rude about her brother. That was her job.

Chapter Sixteen

Tripp was in an even worse mood after a frankly rather indigestible breakfast peeled off Inge-Britt's dirty grill. He went outside, stretched, ignored completely the beautiful pink of the fresh morning: yesterday's fog had cleared and there was a glorious vista in front of his eyes: the harbour to his right; the clear pale water stretching across to the mainland, so far away; the early ferry bringing people and supplies, reversing in carefully through churning water down at the little dock.

All Tripp could think of was how weird it was going to be, seeing his brother for the first time in twenty years. He could still kick his ass though.

He was going to pull a number on him about visiting his parents. They were still at home, but only just. His pa spent the whole day watching Fox and screaming conspiracy theories at anyone who would stay long enough to listen. He needed help; his legs were shot now.

The cute girl in the hotel – it was a dirty hotel, but she was pretty hot – had told him just to follow the upper road to the top of the island. He'd asked if he could get lost and she'd looked at him like she didn't understand the question. So he got up in the cab of the SUV and was halfway out of town before he realised that he was driving on the wrong side of the road and that's why everyone was flashing their lights at him. He was in a thoroughly bad mood by the time he got to Colton's gates at the Manse, and even crosser when he had to get out of his warm truck and into a piercing north wind to lean down at the gate's microphone, announce himself to someone and show his face to the camera. He was his brother, for Chrissakes, not some burglar that had come all the way to this hellhole to rob it.

The gates cleanly and quietly opened ahead of him and he started up the magnificent driveway, getting crosser all the time at the manicured gravel, the pruned bushes leading up the way, a deer that scampered across his path, and was that a peacock?

Finally Tripp approached the beautiful old stone house and saw the lavish updates – the beautiful stained-glass greenhouse extension now housing a gym and pool complex; conifer shrubs lined up in neat rows at the window boxes; behind the house itself a perfect lawn leading right to the beach edge; every front window facing directly over the sea; then, to the side, the town and the harbour and what looked to be a hotel. Probably the one mentioned.

Anyway, by the looks of things, the reason Colton was withdrawing from everything wasn't because he'd lost all his money, which was something. There was a large garage, one door ajar, through which he could see several cars gleaming, including a huge Range Rover. A gardener was carefully working the lawns.

Nervous now, Tripp blew steam out of his mouth and stepped forward to the huge black-painted front door. As he did so, it was opened silently by a woman wearing a black and white dress, who smiled politely and ushered him into the huge kitchen which, in contrast to the perfect period exterior, was a futuristic professional space, with two ovens, a sub-zero fridge, a dining table for twelve and, sitting at a separate breakfast bar, an unsmiling Fintan.

* ❄

Fintan stood up. He was also nervous: Tripp was a big man. Colton had literally never ever mentioned him except to say how he wasn't having his family at his wedding, and that they had never accepted his sexuality.

But since the name had come up, all through the night, Colton had been restless, stirring, wanting to engage with the world. Before, he'd been turning his head to the wall. Now. This was something new.

Fintan hadn't the remotest idea whether he was doing

the right thing; whether it wasn't cruel to agitate Colton like this, just so he, Fintan, could reach into his world one last time; could spend just a few more moments with the person he loved more than anyone in the world.

He made a mental note to talk to Saif about it sometime. The reticent doctor had become a great source of comfort to Fintan in these times: he didn't spout platitudes – perhaps did not even know them – and was never anything but honest and direct. It was a rare gift.

This, though. This he was handling on his own. Flora had texted with just three words – DICKWAD ON APPROACH – when she'd noticed that Tripp's car had disappeared from where it was blocking the light to the Seaside Kitchen, hideously parked on the harbour front in the entirely selfish but unfortunately correct assumption that Mure didn't have someone busy enforcing traffic laws.

In the weak winter sunlight, the pale grey of Tripp's eyes reminded Fintan of his brother, but that was the only point of similarity he could see. He took a deep breath.

'You want to see Colton?'

Tripp shrugged.

'He's my brother.'

'I'm aware of that. Do you know who I am?'

And, after a split second, Tripp did know.

'You're his . . . '

He couldn't say 'boyfriend'. People just didn't talk like that in Coppell, Texas. I mean, the idea of it. There was a gay bar in Austin, but they were all like that up there.

Tripp turned bright red. He'd never said the phrase before but he'd heard it on TV.

'Are you his ... partner?'

It came out like 'pardner', and sounded so cowboy Fintan almost giggled. He couldn't be more different to his brother, not really. This next bit was going to be rather fun.

'No,' he said. 'I'm his husband.'

Indeed, Tripp's face was so comical, Fintan felt ashamed of himself. The man's mouth actually fell open, for goodness' sake.

'Uh, okay,' Tripp muttered. 'Right.'

Inside, Tripp was raging. What did this mean for them then, Colton's blood family? I mean, it couldn't be a real marriage, could it? They couldn't be husband and husband. They weren't going to have kids or anything. Or were they? He looked around for evidence of any kids' stuff around.

'So I take it you haven't seen Colton for a while?' said Fintan. 'It was good of you to come,' he added grudgingly.

'Oh yeah?' said Tripp. He hadn't considered that anyone would think that at all. He just wanted to have it out with Colton, make sure Mom and Pop were looked after ... and, by extension, himself of course. 'Well, we'll sure have to see about that.'

'Well ... you know ... ' said Fintan.

Tripp frowned. 'Know what?'

Fintan blinked. He'd assumed, of course, that Tripp had heard and had come to say goodbye. But it was

becoming increasingly obvious that that wasn't the case.
Well, if he hadn't known Colton was married . . .

Oh Lord.

'Tripp, would you like to sit down? Glass of water?'

'I'd just like to see my brother please.'

'Seriously. Sit down.'

Chapter Seventeen

Fintan laid it out as plainly and dispassionately as he could, which wasn't very. It was never going to get easier, he knew. There was never going to be a morning, however beautiful. However lovely the room he woke up in; however gorgeous the view. He found it hard to get to sleep anyway. If he slept in Colton's room, there was the beeping of medical equipment and a nurse coming in every two hours, and he started awake every time Colton breathed strangely or turned over or made any sort of noise.

But sleeping alone in another part of the huge house was as lonely a place as Fintan had ever been. The bed was too big; the thick carpet too quiet. He got restless, and paced.

Secretly, he would really have loved to have gone

home, slept back in the farmhouse, had Flora and Innes and Hamish close by, his dad, Bramble coiled up snuffling by the stove, lost in dreams of being a pup, and so he snuck down whenever he could.

But otherwise this was his vigil; he would stand watch. Until the end. The beautiful house was his prison, and he was his own guard.

*   *   ❄

He didn't say any of this to the large American man sitting staring around the kitchen in disbelief. Tripp had taken off his basketball cap but didn't seem to know what to do with it, so he kept putting it down and picking it back up again.

'But he can't be ill,' he said, then twisted the cap around his fingers. 'Jeez,' he said. Then he blinked.

'I mean, he never even told Mom . . . '

His voice turned quieter.

'He must have really hated us, huh?'

Fintan shrugged.

'Honestly, he never speaks about you at all.'

Tripp blinked again.

'Ha. That's kinda worse.'

'What happened?' said Fintan. 'What happened in the family?'

'Oh jeez, it was a long time ago,' said Tripp. He squirmed. 'Actually, can I get a cup of coffee?'

Fintan moved over to the machine.

'I mean, you know. There just . . . there weren't a lot of boys like Colton when I was growing up.'

'Maybe you weren't looking hard enough,' said Fintan.

'Sure,' said Tripp. 'But that's a long time ago . . . '

His face was pained.

'I think . . . I think Mom would have liked to have seen him again. You know he never once came home? Never gave anyone a chance to . . . apologise.'

'What was your father like?'

'To me, great. To Colton . . . well. They never did quite see eye to eye.'

Fintan left a silence.

'He wasn't . . . I guess he wasn't quite what Dad had in mind for a son.'

'But you were?'

Tripp frowned.

'I'm sorry, sir, but I don't think I need the third degree off of you.'

'Your brother-in-law.'

Under different circumstances, Tripp's face would have been, once again, pretty funny.

Fintan stood up. 'I'm going to talk to him. Stay here please.'

* ❄

It was different today. Most mornings, Fintan would sit and cuddle and cajole Colton into squeezing his hand, or would talk about local news and gossip as if Colton could understand him, whether he could or not, and Colton would drift in and out.

This morning, Colton was lying on his back, not his side, and his hands were clenched; his entire body, wizened as it was, gave off a tension.

And as soon as Fintan came through the door, the first thing Colton did was mutter, 'Is that son of a bitch here?'

For Colton to speak first was a very rare thing these days. And it gave Fintan so much pleasure to pretend, just for a moment, that his boy was back.

'Yes,' said Fintan, sitting down on the bed and kissing Colton on the head.

'How does he look?'

'Fat.'

'Good.'

'There's nothing wrong with being fat,' chided Fintan just as he would have done. Before. 'He looks a hell of a lot better than you.'

'Does he really?'

'No.'

Colton sniffed. 'Can you help me put a clean shirt on?'

Fintan picked out a faded blue chambray he'd always loved: it matched Colton's eyes perfectly. He was gentle, aware of Colton's paper-thin skin: his fingers sank into it; he could make out the veins beneath it.

'Goddamn,' was the only thing Colton said. The shirt hung off him. 'Can I have cologne too? I smell sick.'

It was true; Colton smelled of disinfectant and

medicine. It wasn't his fault. Fintan went and retrieved the Marc Jacobs scent he'd always loved, now stowed in Colton's bathroom; Fintan, personally, couldn't bear to smell it anywhere near him. Not these days.

'Okay, how do I look?' said Colton after Fintan had raised the hospital bed so he was more or less properly sitting up and, as an afterthought, had found a pair of Colton's beloved white trainers. It had been an extremely long time since Colton had actually worn shoes.

'Death warmed up,' said Fintan, knowing it would make him smile. Saif had been by earlier, and Fintan had made it clear that the more alert Colton could be that day the better. Of course, that also meant more pain, and Colton tried not to wince. Even if he'd had nothing wrong with him, being that thin would make sitting up painful for anyone.

'Do you want some make-up on?' said Fintan.

'Oh God, can you imagine?' said Colton. '"My brother, fairy to the end".'

And the jolt it gave Fintan – the joy of hearing Colt make a joke, make conversation, be with him in the moment – it was bliss; a moment stolen, even as Colton winced in the bed and Fintan had to pretend not to notice it; had to try not to see what this was costing him.

'You ready?'

Colton nodded.

'Also, do you want me to kick him in the fanny at any point?'

'Fanny means "ass", right?'

'No,' said Fintan, and Colton smiled through cracked lips, and Fintan came close and smeared them with Vaseline, then rubbed it off so it didn't look too weird. Then he kissed him and smelled the aftershave and felt a very odd sensation of wanting to cry and have sex all at once; and didn't pull away until Colton winced again.

Chapter Eighteen

Tripp couldn't help but stare. He had never been in such an incredible house in his life. It was just beautiful: the huge open spaces of the kitchen, with massive windows at the back looking out over the immaculate, frosted lawn, as a deer bounded and flickered down the lower path, startling a squirrel in the small stunted tree. And the view: the sky was vast above, a bright, freezing blue; the sea all the colours at once. This was not the kind of thing Tripp normally noticed, day to day. He noticed if it was hot again; he noticed when Denny's changed their menus, and when the Cowboys were playing.

Something like this though – Tripp had been to Cancun and Toronto and had considered himself pretty well travelled. But this was as far away as he'd ever been. The vista outside looked like something from a children's book, but the perfect insulation of the house meant you felt utterly enclosed and cosy, even as you looked out at the cold world beyond. It was ... well. It was different, Tripp allowed.

He suddenly remembered his brother as a child; he must have been eight or so. An uncle whom Tripp's father had not had much time for had given Colt a gift: a circuitry set. You had to connect up all the wires and build lights and small motors. Tripp had gotten one too, but he hadn't had enough patience to work it and had ended up kicking it to bits all over the room they shared. Then Colt had managed to get his working – you could press buttons and have a buzzer and a light turn on – but had managed to do something extra to it as well, which meant it rotated Janey's little ballerina, the one she had on her jewellery box. He'd simply borrowed it and managed to make it turn on the circuitry board. He was showing it to his mother, who was more interested in her magazine, and their father had come in and hollered at him for playing with a doll.

He remembered his jealousy of his younger brother's achievement, and then the harsh, visceral pleasure he'd taken in his father's utter disregard. Colton's face had been utterly crushed. He'd gone back to their room, whereupon Tripp had attempted to figure out how Colt had put it together, had been unable to do so and finally, in a fit of frustration, had kicked the entire thing to bits.

Colt didn't tell their parents. Hadn't even mentioned the circuit box ever again, not even when Uncle Howie had come over and his father was, as usual, ragging on him because he didn't like sports.

He didn't know why he was remembering that right then.

The hallway was carpeted and silent as he trod through it, feeling his caterpillar boots were out of place somehow. Fintan had come to fetch him, and was walking ahead rather than beside him. Tripp felt a sudden burst of fury about the uppity faggot but tried to damp it down. A calm head was needed if he, Tripp Rogers, was going to come out of this on top. And coming out on top was very much what he was used to doing, as both his ex-wives had found out to their cost.

He'd read profiles of Colton in later years – obsessively – even set up a Google alert for him. Some strange form of masochism, or partly pride. Nobody at home ever mentioned him; people in town knew better than to bring up the Rogers boy who'd vanished and made good. Not people who knew what was good for them anyway. And Rogers was a common enough name that people arriving in town for the first time or coming to the lot weren't likely to make the connection.

So it was just Tripp, reading business acquisition news he didn't understand, or profiles about the 'mysterious billionaire', which made him sound like Batman. He read a piece on his plane in an odd sterile rich man's magazine. But he'd never quite managed to square the rangy, heroic-looking figure in the profiles with the irritating kid brother he remembered ... he felt himself getting defensive. It was just what brothers did. Brothers fought. That was how it was. Things were different then. Colt had taken everything too seriously, as he always did. He was over-sensitive. It was all normal.

Nevertheless, he took a deep breath when he got to the stout oak-framed door at the end of the corridor.

'Are you ready?' said Fintan, turning back. His tone was flat.

'Sure,' said Tripp in a tone as far away from how he really felt as he could muster.

But he wasn't at all prepared for what was waiting for him behind that door.

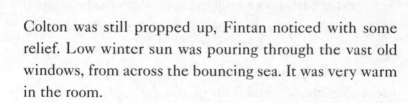

Colton was still propped up, Fintan noticed with some relief. Low winter sun was pouring through the vast old windows, from across the bouncing sea. It was very warm in the room.

'Do you want a window opened?' said Fintan, and Colton shook his head, which he couldn't move without difficulty. Tripp on some level realised this, and walked around the foot of the bed until he was in Colt's eyeline.

There was a long silence while the two brothers looked at one another. Fintan stayed by the window. He would have liked to get some fresh air in the room. He would have liked Tripp not to be there. But. But.

'Hey,' said Colton eventually. His voice wasn't much more than a croak.

'Hey,' said Tripp.

'What, you come to laugh, or what?'

Everyone paused. Fintan had never heard such a bitter tone in Colton's voice – never.

'What? NO,' said Tripp. 'I didn't ... we didn't ... we didn't know you were ill.'

'Right,' said Colton. 'So ... just the money then.'

'Mom was ... Mom and Pop were wondering where you were. And I volunteered to come see you.'

Colton nodded.

'Out of the kindness of your hearts?'

'You're still their son.'

'Yeah, well, lucky me,' said Colton.

'You never came back. Even once.'

'To what? To you kicking me up and down the football field and laughing with your buddies? To Dad screaming at me to be a man in front of the whole neighbourhood? I mean, tell me more of what I'd be missing in that one-horse shithole. Vote for Trump, did ya?'

'Don't upset yourself,' said Fintan, feeling like a fussy old woman.

'So, how much?' said Colton. 'How much do you want to go away, huh? Christ, I never imagined your face being the last thing I see.'

Tripp felt a hot flush steal over that face.

'It's not ... '

'No?'

He irritably tried to move his position, but couldn't. He winced, and Fintan was on the bed instantly, trying to cushion him a little. Colton was breathing heavily as he leaned against his husband's shoulder.

'Well then,' he said. 'What is it?' He turned to Fintan. 'Aw shit, we're going to need Joel for this. Is he back?'

'Today, I think. Flora will know. I'll fetch him.'

* ❄

Tripp had in fact felt, when he walked in, incredible pity for the emaciated figure on the bed. For someone younger than him to be so very ill was horrible to look upon. And this was his only brother, after all.

But then Colton was still being exactly the kind of dismissive snob who had so enraged Tripp all those years ago, always having to be cleverer, always treating Tripp like a subnormal Neanderthal. And now he was being practically dismissed.

'My lawyer will talk you through it,' said Colton. 'I'm warning you, there's not as much in it as I'm sure your grubby hands were hoping for.'

And he fell back in the pillows, effectively dismissing his brother. In fact, it had taken every ounce of Colton's strength to talk for so long, and all he could think about was his next dose of morphine and how quickly the nurse could get in there. But unwittingly he had hardened Tripp's heart without giving it a second thought.

Chapter Nineteen

'YOU FAT, ATTI FLOWA.'

Flora had popped by to grab the Land Rover to go pick up Joel from the airport. She was nervous. This was an understatement.

Agot was there, staring at her curiously.

'Haven't you got some sticks to be singing about?'

'DOAN BE SILLY,' scoffed Agot. She stood up. 'I COME TO AIRPORT FOR UNCLE JOE.'

'He's not your uncle,' said Flora. 'And no, you can't.'

'BECAUSE OF KISSING?'

Hamish looked up from the corner.

'No,' said Flora.

'AWW,' said Agot. 'FLOWA SAD.'

'I'm fine! I'll see you later!'

'Flora sad?' said Hamish worriedly as Flora grabbed the keys and hurried out to the car.

*   *
    ❄

Joel was jet-lagged when he got down from the plane. Flora picked him up from the shed which acted as the airport, which wasn't exactly a hardship, as it was four minutes' drive from the farmhouse, and took him back to the Rock. He was tired and zonked out enough that he didn't notice how oddly she was behaving.

Joel had a room in one of the cottages in the grounds. It was beautiful: the ancient stone exterior, smooth wooden panelling inside, heated floors and a huge claw-foot bathtub in the black and white bathroom. Flora adored it; it was the loveliest hotel imaginable. She wasn't looking forward to the day it filled up with noisy tourists marching about playing golf and complaining about the wind and scaring away the birds. For now, it felt like their own little private universe.

It was only a room, though. Not a home. They needed a home.

Joel was frowning at his phone even as he kissed her. She stiffened, wondering if he'd noticed anything, but he wasn't looking at her.

'Colton wants to see me. Immediately.' He looked up.

'Well, that's good news, isn't it? I haven't been able to talk to him for weeks. I thought it was looking very grave. Saif wasn't saying much, but . . . '

Flora explained about Tripp.

Joel's face closed up.

'So, you know. He should probably try and have a last connection with his family.'

'Should he?' said Joel.

'Yes,' said Flora. 'You know. If he can.'

Joel looked unconvinced. 'More likely they're after his money . . . Oh yeah, Fintan just texted. Colton wants me to go and lay the situation out.'

'Well, be nice,' said Flora. 'I think he's going to be pretty upset. He seemed a pretty traditional kind of guy.'

'Did you like him?'

'Well, no . . . not exactly . . . but I felt for him a bit.'

'You like everyone. If you don't like someone that means they're pure evil. Come here,' Joel said as if noticing her for the first time. 'Oh my God, your breasts look amazing in that top.' He reached his arms around her waist, bent down and kissed her, and Flora couldn't help it, at this little promise of normality, of the chance to bask in his love. She sighed happily, reached up and took off his glasses.

'But I want to see you,' said Joel, whose eyesight was absolutely shocking.

'Yes, well, we tried that before, and then I found out how expensive your glasses are and nearly had a heart attack,' said Flora, putting them down carefully on the bedside table. Also, she figured the less he noticed at this point, the better – particularly a blue vein that appeared to be throbbing through the white of one of her breasts rather alarmingly.

Much as she hated Joel going away, she was never ever happier than when he came home, pulled off the expensive suits and ties he wore as armour against a world he found combative, and revealed himself.

Oh, she was due back at the café, but she didn't care. There had to be some upsides to running your own business. Slowly, she started undoing Joel's buttons, as he groaned in the absolute happiness of a man utterly content with who he is and what he is doing; and even as she did so she thought, Truly? Am I going to upset everything?

Afterwards, the jet lag looked like it was going to get to Joel; he was on the point of dozing off as Flora reluctantly got up to hop in the shower.

'Oh,' she said as if it was something she'd just thought of casually. 'You know, Lorna is thinking of moving back to the farmhouse in the new year. Tarting it up.'

'Mmm,' said Joel, half asleep. 'Why are you telling me?'

'Well, it's just . . . her place might be up for rent.'

Joel half-opened one eye.

'Oh,' he said.

Now he was awake.

'It was just a thought,' said Flora. 'If redevelopment does start here . . . '

They didn't say the unspoken: after Colton died. It was always there, underneath everything.

'Huh,' said Joel. 'Because I really like it here.'

'I do too!' said Flora, which was true – she did. 'But it's only one room.'

Joel looked at her.

'How many do you think we need?'

'Well, Lorna has three.'

'But even put together they're smaller than this one,' said Joel, which was undeniably true.

'Okay,' said Flora. 'Sorry to bring it up.'

Joel was wide awake now, and sat on the side of the bed.

'I have to get to Colton's anyway,' he said, looking for fresh clothes. 'You know ... I mean. Sorry. It's just. I've never lived with anyone before.' He thought about it and looked at her, trying to smile. He looked very young suddenly. 'Anyone nice, I mean.'

Flora's heart wanted to split in two. She loved him so much, but that damaged child inside him ... would it mend? Could it adjust?

She sat beside him.

'I realise that,' she said soothingly, and rubbed his back.

'It's ... I mean, you've always lived with about nine million people. And some cows.'

'Yes, that's exactly what farm life is like, well done,' said Flora.

'But. Things are a bit more difficult for me. I just ... if things are moving too fast ... '

Flora shut her eyes. Things were about to get a *lot* faster. A lot.

'That's okay,' she said.

He turned to her.

'You are happy, aren't you?' he said anxiously.

'Yes,' she said. 'Yes. You make me very happy. When you're here. I just like to be near you.'

Joel blinked, cheered the conversation was over.

'We'll get there,' he said, trying to be conciliatory. 'We will. You know how I feel about you … It's more how I feel about inflicting myself on you.'

Flora kissed him. 'Is Mark happy?'

'About moving in with someone? You just brought it up.'

'No! About them coming.'

'Yes. They're delighted. I think it means they're going to want you to cook a lot.'

Flora wondered if Mark could talk some sense into him. But on the other hand, it wasn't sense that was needed. Joel had been perfectly honest and perfectly clear. He didn't want to be rushed. That was entirely fair. But, she thought mutinously, if he would come charging off every flight he'd ever taken and demand to take her to bed immediately, she wouldn't be in this situation.

On the *other* hand, if she hadn't assured him that she was on completely reliable contraception …

Something rang at the back of her mind. Joel trusted her completely. To love him and keep him safe, possibly for the first time ever. She felt like she'd betrayed him on some ridiculous level; or rather, her body had let her down. Was he going to be strong enough to take it?

'Oh, baby,' she found herself whispering in the shower as she soaped herself down. 'Oh, baby. I am so sorry about all of this.'

Chapter Twenty

Fintan showed Tripp downstairs, both of them walking in silence, Tripp bright red in the face and furious.

'Well, good to meet you,' said Fintan in drawlingly sarcastic tones. Tripp grunted.

Joel had just arrived and popped his head around the kitchen door.

'Hey,' he said, pleased to see Fintan. 'How are things? I have a sheaf of stuff if . . . '

Fintan just nodded.

'Who the hell are you?' said Tripp. 'You look like a lawyer. Are you a lawyer?'

'I am,' said Joel suspiciously.

'Are you my brother's lawyer?'

Joel cast a look at Fintan, who nodded wearily.

Honestly, Joel had been expecting something like

this. He'd dealt with a lot of family-owned firms in his corporate career which were often bought up, broken up or swallowed whole by conglomerates. There was generally dissent between those who wanted to sell and other family members who had different views. It was never straightforward in his experience. Nothing involving money ever was.

And sure enough, so close to the end, here came the galloping cavalry – family pretending to be 'concerned' and worried about the fate of its richest member.

'Did you want to plan a meeting?' he asked politely.

'Will it cost me a fortune?' grunted Tripp. 'I'll get my own lawyer, thanks.'

'Is that something you're considering doing?' asked Joel as lightly as he could manage. Tripp sniffed.

'Oh, I imagine you've got this stitched up pretty neatly between you all,' he said. 'I imagine you've been cooking this up for a year or so, just to make sure his blood family doesn't benefit in any way.'

Joel didn't react, as Tripp was speaking the absolute truth.

'We simply followed our client's wishes,' he said quietly, and stared Tripp out through his glasses. He'd met plenty of men like this – all bluster and noise – and usually just waited for it to blow itself over so they could work something out.

Tripp halted.

'Well, as long as *he's* happy,' he said. 'I'll see myself out.'

The door banged behind him as he went back out into the freezing day. Joel and Fintan looked at each other.

'That guy,' said Fintan, 'is an absolute—'

'Colton upstairs?' said Joel quickly. 'Is he awake? Did he even recognise that guy?'

Fintan sighed.

'That's the problem.'

'What?' asked Joel. And Fintan explained about how Trip had energised his husband; woken him up. Was keeping him in the world at such great cost.

'God,' said Joel eventually. 'I don't know what to say.'

'Me neither,' said Fintan.

'So yeah,' he said. 'It's probably a good time to see him. Especially if Colton wants to hand over some money.'

* ❄

Upstairs, Joel knocked quietly and let himself in. He was, as Fintan had been before, entirely surprised to see Colton alert, his head up, unsupported, his neck turning around. He was still ghastly thin, obviously ill. But, in a very important sense, he was there; present.

'Hey,' said Joel.

'Hey,' croaked Colton, and Joel fetched him some water and sat by him to help him drink. 'Did you meet my brother?'

'I did,' said Joel tactfully.

'That fat fuck,' said Colton gloomily.

'Did he want money?'

'Sure.'

'Do you want to give him some? There's provision for that.'

Colton coughed, a horrible long hacking sound, and Joel found a pile of freshly laundered handkerchiefs and handed him one, then the water again.

'Dunno,' he said. 'If I give him a bit, will they want a bunch? Will that open us up?'

Joel folded his arms.

'It's certainly possible. If you make it very clear that there's nothing, that's harder to contest than you leaving something and them not feeling it's a fair slice of a pie.'

'When did I become a fucking pie?' said Colton.

'Sorry,' said Joel.

'No, you're right. Might as well be straight about it. Rather than Captain Fantastic downstairs, who thinks I'm going to live for ever.'

Joel didn't answer that. He made some notes on his legal pad then glanced up, thinking about what Flora had said.

'I'm only going to ask this once,' he said.

Colton cocked an eyebrow.

'Is this one of these questions that isn't really a lawyer question?'

Joel shrugged. 'I don't have a mom . . . '

Colton raised a cadaverous hand.

'Stop right there,' he said. 'I don't want to hear it.'

Joel nodded, and noticing how tired Colton looked, got up to leave.

'It's great to see you . . . more awake,' he said.

'I'm not giving that prick the satisfaction of dying while he's in the country,' said Coltan. 'That fuck.'

'Okay,' said Joel. 'Look, I'd better go. Do you want me to draw up a couple of alternatives?'

'Sure,' said Colton, his eyes losing focus. 'Cool. Bye.'

As Joel reached the door, Colton cleared his throat.

'Oh, and congrats on the baby.'

Chapter Twenty-one

It was a freezing day despite the sunshine. It had to be five degrees below zero, easily, with winds sweeping in off the Arctic, snow lying all around and more on the way. During the day this had been beautiful: dawn, shortly after nine-thirty, had been a frosted haze of pinks and golds, the geese flying low, the world on fire.

Now that it was cloudy and already dusk – apart from Colton's house, which was lit up cheerily – all the way around the headland to the Rock was utterly dense with darkness. The stars looked like huge chips of ice in the sky overhead, the half-moon sharp as a pin, but not casting any cold light.

Joel knew he should have taken the car back. But, speechless, he had headed back down the stairs, banged through the front door without saying goodbye to Fintan and had found himself outside in the biting cold needing to walk.

The snow was thick in front of his face as Joel stumbled out of Colton's house and down the path. It wasn't far to the Rock, just around the headland, but in this weather it was downright dangerous. Joel had never lived more than a block or so from an available cab in his adult life: if Fintan had been less distracted, he'd never have let him leave.

But Joel was so furious that he barely noticed the weather – the great flurries being thrown in his face as if from a vast hand, the ice stinging his long eyelashes, his glasses steaming up. He would have taken them off, but his eyesight was worse than even Flora realised: a legacy from long nights of reading secretly under the blankets and a succession of foster families that didn't prioritise eye examinations for the state-sponsored charges in their care.

His mind wasn't on the weather though. It was bursting with upset and confusion. How could she? How could she throw this on him? he thought. This was the problem. He had thought she knew him. That for the first time, he could draw back the curtain, let someone peep through, let himself become comfortable with someone ... and they go and throw this at him.

He had never, ever, ever thought about having children. He didn't know many – he worked with boys on the Outward Adventures, but only for a day here and there. Well, apart from Agot, who liked him precisely because he was utterly incapable of treating her like a child, and she didn't consider herself to be one, just a small adult.

He worried far too much about what his genes might unleash; what might come down from his father's side, from his mother's. The violence; the despair, the addiction.

He had had to fight incredibly hard all his life against his demons, always threatening to take over. What if a child couldn't do that? What if they were born under a darker star? He still didn't know if he'd got out from under it; he wouldn't put that on a child. Couldn't.

Flora would never understand. She was from a loving, slightly messy, but fundamentally normal family. But they'd never discussed children. He hadn't given it any thought, always assuming ... Well. He hadn't assumed anything. He hadn't thought about it. He'd just lived, for the first time in his life, for the moment. Getting to know someone. Opening up to someone in a way he never had before. Falling in love, even if love and being close to another person, open and vulnerable, as a concept was something that made him deeply and profoundly uncomfortable: he had rarely said the words to Flora. Although he did. Or rather he'd thought he did; or at least, he'd thought he might, maybe.

Joel felt his heart rate speed up and his breathing become slightly tighter, and so did his best to relax, to breathe in through his nose and out through his mouth the way Mark had taught him – to calm down, just in this moment – and the fresh, fresh air, bitingly cold, hit his face and he shut his eyes and stood still for a moment until he had a hold on himself.

The noise of the wind was absolutely unbelievable as he looked out over the headland. You couldn't see the lights of shore, or even the passing ships or distant oil rigs: the blizzard was up at full pelt, and it was like a living, moving thing, a swirl of a coat on the wind, a great, terrible giant striding over the world. Joel blinked, then turned around, suddenly frightened of the wildness of the strange place he was in, and then relieved beyond measure to see the lights of the Rock below, and stumbled down, his thoughts only on his frozen fingers.

Flora wasn't there. Some nights she let herself in; exhausted always from her early starts, he'd generally find her (unbeknown to him) having done her absolute best to arrange herself prettily (hair done, make-up on, wearing a pretty nightgown ordered from the mainland) to welcome him home cheerfully, instead nose-down diagonally across the bed, snoring gently, with *TOWIE* blaring on the TV.

It was a huge and entirely comfortable bed, and Joel never minded; in fact he was always delighted and jolted to see her there, so at ease, and he would crawl in and wake her up and . . .

Well. Anyway. She wasn't there. Which was good. Except it wasn't, because he needed to see her . . . No. He didn't. He couldn't.

He shrugged out of his wet clothes and took a shower. He should go over, but then they'd all be in the farmhouse, all those boys who looked at him like he was an alien creature. He knew Flora's brothers meant well, but their aggressively boyish teasing and farming ways reminded him a little too closely of some of the rural placements he'd had, and he knew he wouldn't truly fit in in a million years.

Flora seemed completely oblivious to this; she adored and argued with her brothers in equal measure. She seemed to have so much love, he thought, spilling out of her towards anyone she came across – baking it into bread, weaving it into the daily warp and weft of the life around her, where she knew everyone and everyone knew her, and despite people's foibles and follies, you were accepted because you were at home.

And he had so little. As if love were a tiny little pot, with the top screwed on, never to be opened or wasted, not a drop.

He switched off his phone. He didn't think he would sleep much, and he was absolutely right. What was he going to do? What were they going to do?

Chapter Twenty-two

Flora, on the other hand, after going home to see her dad and spending the night in her childhood bed – she'd texted Joel but had got a very brief message back from him saying he had a lot of work on, which wasn't unusual – had woken up in a good mood. She couldn't help it – she was just sleeping so well. Joel was home and he'd been pleased to see her, despite the not wanting to live with her thing, but that was … Well. They'd work out the details.

And they'd all woken to the most amazing world: the wind had dropped, the air was clear and snow blanketed the ground, reflecting the setting moon.

It was incredible. Snow didn't often settle on Mure; too much wind on their little rock. But here it was – Narnia outside their windows, pure and clear, the sheep snuffling around (they'd need taken in, and in fact she could see that Hamish and Innes had already taken off).

The old flagstone tiles were freezing under her feet as she scampered to the stove, and Bramble was disinclined to go and fetch the paper, having sniffed at the snow, attempted to eat as much of it as he could find, then changed his mind and decided to flop back in front of the stove.

But the kettle whistled merrily enough, and the boys hadn't had a bath yet, which meant she got first shot at the hot water – a joy in itself, even when she had to make the leap from shower to bedroom. She glanced at herself in the mirror. Her breasts were definitely fuller. She pushed out her stomach. It was truly amazing. To imagine. Growing in there. Her baby. Joel's baby. She swallowed hard.

And yet even that went out of her mind with the sheer joy of the landscape that fine morning. She crunched untrodden snow under her heavy lace-up boots, the barn dogs scuffling and playing, even as Innes whistled from yon high field. The low sun, which would barely creep above the horizon all day, nonetheless showed the promise of pink across the snow-deadened silence. Mure didn't have a lot of cars or planes, but it had tractors and cows that wanted milking and wind and crashing waves and seagulls and great fields of waving barley. It was never quiet.

This morning, though, it was like a world anew. The only sounds were the occasional high bird making enquiring noises and the shock of Flora's boots when she stamped through the fresh puddled ice in the farmyard. The chickens were still roosting; too cold and dark for them even to pad out to see what was going on.

Warmly wrapped in three jumpers and the beautiful Brora cashmere hat and scarf Joel had bought her in London, all covered in a down coat so big it was a little like getting inside a sleeping bag, Flora couldn't help find her mood lifting as she thought of the dusted cinnamon rolls they were planning that morning, that had been proving half the night and would make the entire place and in fact most of the street smell like absolute heaven. They were a bit of a faff to make by the time you'd rolled them all out, but they absolutely made their money back because it was basically impossible to walk down the street and not want one as soon as you'd smelled them. She made a mental note to add extra hot chocolate to the menu as they'd be overwhelmed by children if the snow held: they could slide down the hill all the way to the main street and be there, ready and waiting to dive in, cheeks aglow, eyes wide.

Would that be her baby? she thought. One day? Eyes glistening. Joel's dark eyes or her pale ones? And where would their daddy be?

She chided herself. They would sort it out. And here were Isla and Iona, swathed in so many scarves and hats it was hard to tell who was who, all bubbling over about the Russian sailors – who of course absolutely were not Russians or sailors and absolutely were not going to meet them down at the Harbour's Rest to play cards which apparently you could do when you didn't share a common language. There were almost certainly some other things you could do, thought Flora, but didn't mention them, and laughed aloud while bringing the tea urn to boil as Isla related accidentally trying to introduce Anatoly to her Auntie Jean while they were both a) pretending he wasn't Russian and b) rolling drunk on some wallpaper-stripping vodka he'd acquired from somewhere, and was topping up their Irn Brus with it while Inge-Britt played Candy Crush.

And that is how Joel found her, after his restless night tossing and turning in the huge empty bed at the Rock – her head thrown back in laughter, her cheeks pink, her hair shimmering down her back. Truly, he thought, she had never looked lovelier. There was a … He wanted to curse. Didn't they say that about pregnant women? A glow?

He remembered their conversation about moving. Of course she wanted to move. Of course she did.

It struck him that she could have easily demanded that he buy her a house; she knew he had money. Or that they get somewhere big and fancy. Instead she'd suggested going halfers on her best friend's cheap, tiny (to Joel's eyes) flat. Classic Flora. So even now, he couldn't think of her without smiling.

Her face turned towards him as he dinged open the door: she was both happy and – he saw now though he hadn't noticed it before – with a hint of wariness around the wide, clear eyes.

'Joel!' she said, beaming but blinking too much at the

same time. 'The tea is just boiling. Would you like some lovely clean water delicious fresh tea or that nasty coffee you like?'

Joel had retained a taste for burnt American coffee since his days of pulling all-nighters in law school. Flora pretended they had it in the back of the shop for lots of customers. They didn't; Inge-Britt had been throwing out an old burnt coffee machine and Flora had persuaded her to hand it over. The only person who ever drank from it was Joel. Flora kept it on all the time.

Joel shrugged. The two girls who worked there giggled as they always did whenever he came into the shop. He had absolutely no idea why. (In reality they thought he looked like someone from an American TV show – they'd never met many people who wore suits every day – and both fancied him madly.)

Joel didn't want to cause a scene. Not here, not now. Not ever in fact. He was utterly allergic to scenes, which was one reason why many of his ex-girlfriends had no idea he'd actually dumped them until after he'd done so.

But this . . . He looked at Flora. And she looked at him. And she knew at once that he knew.

Chapter Twenty-three

The stupid thing, Flora said, trying – and failing utterly – to turn it into a funny story for Lorna later – was that they couldn't even go outside as it was minus two degrees and filled with people out exploring the snow. The girls were in the Seaside Kitchen. Neither she nor Joel had their cars. They couldn't go to Flora's. It was, in fact, very difficult to have a private conversation on an inhospitable island with a small amount of people on it, all of whom know you and are also unbelievably nosy.

'Can I borrow you for a minute?' said Joel, and they went outside. The ice crackled beneath their feet, the cold a shock on their exposed skin. The sun was thinking about coming up further, but wouldn't for ages, so it was still half light at 8.30 in the morning. It was like being on the deck of a ship. Joel looked around, frustrated. Then he saw the ancient red telephone box. It just about still worked, but it was more there for tourists to get their pictures taken hanging out of it, and teenagers to get into mischief in, a fact that wasn't lost on Flora as he bundled her into it. In fact, for a single wistful moment she'd rather hoped that's what he had in mind.

Then she saw his face. He had purple shadows under his eyes which she knew to take for a warning sign. She checked to see about spotting those with Mark. He'd told her: make sure he doesn't lose any weight. Don't let him spend too much time on his phone. Keep him at home.

He pulled her gaze back up.

'Have you got something to tell me?' he said simply.

Flora felt like she'd been punched in the gut. She swallowed hard. This much anxiety couldn't possibly be good for the baby.

'Do we have to do this here?' she said. The phone box did not smell brilliant, to be honest. It still had the phone book chained in, though it had to be fifteen years old. Her mother would still be listed, Flora found herself thinking wildly.

'We have to do it now,' he said, his face tight.

Flora looked up at him, blinking back the tears.

'Joel . . . '

She couldn't figure it out. Lorna wouldn't have told him, would she? Surely not – she wouldn't have seen him. So would Saif let something slip? But Saif was so careful, so professional. She trusted him absolutely.

'How did you . . . ?'

'Coltan told me.'

Flora shut her eyes. Of course. Exactly what Fintan had been saying. Since Tripp was here, Colton had bucked up; had become more alert.

And of course this was the result.

'I thought . . . I thought he wouldn't . . . it was when he wasn't really talking . . . '

'So that makes it better?'

Flora realised how angry he was, how tightly he was trying to control himself. She no longer felt the cold in the small space.

'I was trying . . . I was trying to find the right time. Joel, I knew . . . I knew you'd react like this. I was just trying—'

'React like what?' he said immediately, and Flora knew she'd said exactly the wrong thing.

'Well . . . ' she started timidly.

'I'm *reacting*,' he said, 'to the fact that you didn't tell me about the single most important thing that might ever affect my life. That in fact you told other people before me. I have absolutely no idea how you thought I *might* react, but I can assure you, being left in the dark about something like this would probably elicit a pretty strong reaction in almost anyone. How long have you known?'

Flora hung her head.

'Six weeks.'

Joel was completely speechless.

'Jesus,' he said. 'How far gone are you?'

Flora's voice was quiet, steam coming out in the freezing cold.

'Ten weeks, eleven maybe?'

Joel blinked.

'Were you *ever* going to tell me?'

Flora gulped.

'I . . . I tried to talk about maybe moving in, but you didn't even want that. I mean, I thought that was a start . . . '

Joel was silent. He was thinking as fast as he could. Flora took it as hostility, as rejection, and she felt herself go red.

'It was a *mistake*,' she said, suddenly flaring up. 'I didn't mean to get pregnant. I wasn't trying to trap you or whatever the hell you think.'

'A baby,' he said, almost not hearing Flora at all. Neither of them was listening to the other.

The glass of the phone booth was becoming steamed up.

'I mean, YOU should have been more careful too,' yelled Flora.

There was a silence.

'Should I?' said Joel, still feeling oddly, terribly detached from the situation.

Flora stared at him in disbelief, then suddenly choked up with a vast, tearing sob, and before he could stop her, she pushed open the door and charged out of the phone box.

She ignored the early dog walkers and the incoming fisherman, and as she moved, Joel saw the tiniest hint of a belly under her layers and wondered to himself how he could have been such a blind idiot. He wanted to run after her but something stopped him – the idea of her being so furious at him. What had he done? What could he do?

Joel didn't register how upset he was. Emotions churning, almost without realising it, he picked up the receiver of the phone, and dashed it, hard, repeatedly against the metal call box, and when he looked up, she had completely vanished.

Chapter Twenty-four

Flora stumbled away, blinded by tears that thank goodness could be hidden by the sting of the sleet on her face
and the scraping cold. She rubbed her eyes, then opened
them again, staring out to sea. The clearness of the sky in
front of her – in contrast with the weather over the island
behind her – meant you could now see tiny dots on the
horizon that she knew were massive container ships of
one or two hundred metres long, vast football fields full
of Maersk crates.

It struck her as she stood on the harbour wall: how
many women had also stood here, a baby in their belly,
waiting for news, waiting to hear if their men would come
home from sailing the seas? She was the cliché now, she
realised, watching the waves pound the walls as the tide
would come in and the tide would go out and nothing on

the island would change very much. The seasons came and went, the lambing started, the cows were milked and babies were born – you made the right choice or the wrong one. That was just life.

But her life . . . her life was going to be different. She'd wanted everything, she supposed. And one mistake was going to ruin everything.

'COO-EEEE! Is that you?! I thought that was you!'

Flora didn't hear the voice at first, then when she did, she thought for a single excited moment that it was Joel's but of course it couldn't be. She went on ignoring it just for another second more, shrinking into the biting cold, in the hopes that she could escape – but that was one thing about Mure. Not a lot of escaping went on. For the first time since she'd returned two years ago, she missed the endless, overwhelming anonymity of London's over-crowded streets.

'FLORA! How are you?'

Flora blinked. It was Jan, Charlie's wife. She was wearing the largest, most neon yellow all-encompassing parka Flora had ever seen. It made her look like a lifeboat.

'Um, hi, Jan, how are things?'

As usual, Charlie was right behind her, smiling shyly.

'We were just coming to get some cake to celebrate!'

'Um . . . well, follow me,' said Flora, suddenly conscious of how freezing she was. Also maybe Iona or Isla could serve them so she could vanish into the kitchen and try and keep her tears out of the fruit cake.

The door of the Seaside Kitchen tinged as loudly as ever as they went inside.

'Guess what?' said Jan incredibly loudly. 'I'm going to need extra cake, aren't I, Charles?'

Charlie smiled that sweet slow smile of his and nodded his shaggy head. Flora blinked.

'Well, we have . . . '

She suddenly straightened up. It wasn't like Jan to be beaming and full of delight to be in the Seaside Kitchen. She normally slagged it off, if anything. What had changed?

She turned around slowly. And somehow, she just knew even before Jan opened her mouth. Something about the way Charlie was looking at his wife – not with the usual slightly hangdog obedience, but with something closer to awe. No. Please. No. Not now.

'You see,' Jan went on, 'we're having a baby!'

It was the hardest thing Flora had had to do for a long, long time.

'Congratulations,' she said.

She swallowed hard and looked at Charlie, who was bright red.

'Well done, Teàrlach,' she said quietly, and he grinned proudly.

'I told her not to tell anyone,' he said.

'Well, it's three months!' said Jan. 'Quite safe! I should think so too, I don't really hold with all this fussing, do you? It's only a baby! As long as you're fit and healthy you shouldn't have any problems!'

Flora tried to arrange her face into a pleasant smile but inside she was completely churning up. It was such a 'here's what you could have won' moment – if she had stayed with Charlie, if she had accepted his gentle, easy, all-encompassing affection. Rather than fall for someone for whom it was like squeezing blood from a stone. Someone who, ultimately, may not be capable of loving anything at all: not her, not the baby, not himself.

'Oh, Flora, you're *crying*,' said Jan with evident satisfaction. 'Well, you know, these things happen! We are *married*, after all!'

'What kind of cake would you like?' said Flora, rubbing her eyes briskly.

'One of each please!' Jan smiled complacently. 'One gets so hungry when one's pregnant, did you know? It's all those happy hormones all over the place. Of course I haven't been sick once. I'm just so lucky!'

And to be fair, thought Flora, putting cakes into a paper bag, she was.

'Joel is going to be so excited for us!'

'Mm,' said Flora as deadpan as she could manage.

'Of course he'll have to step up more to help us with the Outward Adventures ... although Baby naturally will be coming along too.'

'Is that what you're calling it?' said Flora politely.

'I don't see why Baby can't get used to the natural world all at once. I'll bind Baby to me in a natural way,' said Jan who as usual had a way of saying perfectly nice reasonable things in a bizarrely annoying way, blithely ignoring Flora's remark. And as usual, she looked enquiringly at Flora when she was presented with the bill.

'Even on such a special day?' she said.

Jan, from the richest family in the village, only came in on special days.

'Have you got your discount card?' said Flora, pretending not to have heard her. Of course she hadn't, but Flora plugged in the discount anyway, through gritted teeth.

The old ladies in the café couldn't hold it in any longer. A baby on the island was a great affair as the world had moved on and the young people had moved away, and the modern age swept through even Mure. A baby – and not just a baby but a baby from two old island families – really was a great event, and the knitters were up, threatening to knit before Flora could even get the ('Decaff of course! Do I need to tell you that?') coffees on the table.

Jan sat complacently, the centre of attention, as if she was the first pregnant woman ever to walk the face of the earth. Which, as far as Mure was concerned, Flora thought ruefully, she really was these days. Lorna would be delighted.

Lorna. She needed to see Lorna. She glanced at her watch. How could it only be nine o'clock in the morning? *How?*

She went through to the back kitchen. It was, in all honesty, as much as she could do not to call Innes and get him and Hamish to go around and beat some sense into Joel, no matter how awful a thought this was.

It wasn't just about him. It wasn't, it wasn't it wasn't. She bundled up her hands into fists, even as she could hear Jan shrieking with laughter in the next room, and felt more bitterly jealous and wretched than she could stand.

Chapter Twenty-five

'Lorna.'

Lorna sighed. She knew Flora had a lot on her mind, of course she did, and she was sympathetic, truly she was. But she was tired. Christmas was full on. They'd had another nativity rehearsal, and she was beginning to wonder about the wisdom of casting Ib as Joseph. Several of the other boys in the class had made nasty comments about it and she'd had to sit them down and talk about 'Words Matter' programmes and so on when frankly she wanted to knock all their heads together.

If Ib would unbend, just a little, and stop treating the other kids like the enemy, he would find his life so much easier – Ash had been much more open and therefore had settled in really well. But it was easier for him. Not only was he younger, with the easier way of forgetting situations than Ib – and certainly fewer memories of his mother – but also his natural personality was ebullient and affectionate; he was simply easy to get along with.

She knew that she needed to sit down with Saif and discuss Ib's difficult behaviour and attitude; maybe even explore taking him out of the play altogether. But that was . . . Well. A delicate problem would be one way of putting it. The fact was, whenever she was in the same room as Saif, she lost the ability to speak. And slightly started to drool. Which was a ridiculous excuse for not doing her job, or indeed never going to the doctor's again until she died of a completely treatable disease.

She sighed and sat down at her computer to draft an email.

Dear Dr Hassan,
   I LOVE YOU

Nope. She deleted.

Dear Dr Hassan,
   I wanted to briefly discuss . . . HOW MUCH I

Lorna sighed. This was ridiculous, and she had an absolutely massive pile of marking to do.

Dear Dr Hassan,
   I just wondered if you have five minutes to discuss Ibrahim's progress with me.

Her mind strayed instantly to what she could wear – that pretty rose-sprigged skirt, maybe, which swirled . . .

And she was lost in a reverie, and then the phone rang and the moment was lost and the email never sent, and the meeting never had, which could have saved a lot of trouble.

*　*　❋

'LORNA! Are you finished? Are you finished? I need you!'

'Flora? Calm down!'

'I can't calm down! I've had to be calm all day! And smile at people and laugh and pretend I am fine when I am EVER SO NOT FUCKING FINE.'

'Is the baby okay?'

Lorna flinched and glanced around in case Mrs Cook was next door and could hear her. She repeated the question, but whispered it this time.

'Oh yes, no, I don't know. Can you meet me? Like, now?'

'I've got to finish up.'

'Soon? Please? I have millionaire shortbread.'

Lorna blinked.

'Please,' said Flora.

'I'm on my way,' said Lorna.

The Seaside Kitchen was closed up for the night: a warm sweet smell of cake and coffee lingered on the air, the tables were clean with the chairs up on them for mopping the floor in the morning.

Lorna and Flora sat in the cosy back kitchen by the

stove, both hoovering up millionaire shortbread for different reasons. Flora let the tears fall as she told Lorna about her dreadful morning with Joel.

Lorna blinked.

'And he hasn't called all day? Hasn't been back in?'

Flora shook her head.

Lorna sighed.

'Are you sure?' she said to Flora. 'Are you absolutely sure he isn't just a nobber?'

'That's what Fintan says,' sobbed Flora. 'That's what everybody says!'

'Do they?' said Lorna.

'I promise, though, he isn't. And anyway, it doesn't even matter if he's a nobber.'

'If . . . ?' said Lorna dubiously.

'I'm still carrying his stupid nobber baby.'

Lorna blinked again. 'I know this is hard to ask but do you really have to . . . ?'

Flora shook her head.

'I know what you're going to say. And, Lorna, I'm thirty-one. I'm ready. It wouldn't be for everyone. But it is for me. I just didn't want to do it alone.'

This brought on another flood of tears. Lorna, like all teachers, never went anywhere without a packet of Kleenex and patiently handed them over one by one.

Suddenly there was a knock at the door. The girls looked at each other, Flora with hope flaring in her eyes.

'Maybe he's crawling through the snow begging forgiveness,' remarked Lorna. 'On his hands and knees.'

'Don't joke,' said Flora, swinging herself down from the stool she was perched on. That wasn't Joel's knock, anyway. Was it? Anyone else – literally anyone else – would just have marched straight in. The door wasn't locked.

A man was standing on the other side of the glass; Flora registered immediately that it wasn't him. Of course it wasn't him – she'd known it wasn't going to be him; there was no point being disappointed now. She stepped forward and turned on the light.

'Delivery,' said the man in a bored tone of voice as she answered the door. He was holding up the largest bouquet of flowers Flora had ever seen.

You couldn't get flower delivery on the island; there just wasn't the economy for it. To get flowers delivered you had to order them well in advance to get them sent over from the mainland. It cost a fortune; nobody ever bothered. To get them on the same day must have been astronomical. The last time they'd had bouquets had been ... well, Colton and Fintan's wedding, she thought sadly. Then, when spring came around, the hills thickened with daffodils, crocuses and bluebells as far as the eye could see and the idea of anyone picking a flower seemed strange and sad. Why would you? Flowers were as much a living part of the glorious world around them as the bees which depended on them in the thick, pinkening field of wind-blown barley. Mure folk tended to view bunches of flowers the way some people see animals in a zoo: out of their natural habitat, their life and freedom taken away.

Here were hothouse roses in pink and white, great thick stretches of ivy and trailing narcissus. It was a very impressive bouquet.

'Thanks,' said Flora flatly, signing the chit. The man looked up.

'Any chance of a cup of coffee before I take the ferry back?' he said hopefully.

'No!' said Lorna's voice from the back. 'She's tired and had a big day!'

'I don't mind . . .' started Flora, but she realised quite quickly that she couldn't trust her voice. She slumped back down, the huge bunch of flowers overshadowing her completely.

Lorna and Flora watched the man turn to go. Then Flora gave Lorna a look, and she instantly scooped up the leftover pieces of millionaire shortbread and stuck them in a bag and ran out after the very grateful chap.

Returning to the Seaside Kitchen, Lorna locked the door behind him then wandered over.

'Well, he's sorry for something,' she said brightly.

'Buying flowers is easy,' said Flora. 'In fact, if I'd been one of his exes I wouldn't have had to hold out for flowers. He'd probably have bought me some diamonds or something.'

'Mmm,' said Lorna.

'Coming to talk to me. That would be the hard thing to do.'

And then she picked the entire lot up and went to dump it in the bin. She turned to Lorna.

'Sorry ... would you like them?'

'Actually,' said Lorna, with a longing look. She'd never seen such an overwhelming bouquet. 'They would look lovely in the school ... '

'Fine.'

Flora handed them over, didn't even notice the little card with the message that tumbled out behind the counter and came to rest between the saucers. Lorna picked it up.

'What does the note say?'

'I don't care,' said Flora, lying through her teeth.

'Can I read it?'

Lorna opened it just as Flora grabbed it from her fingers.

'I'm sure it says, "Let's have a lovely baby and make a family together",' said Lorna encouragingly.

Joel had agonised for so long about the message on the phone that the girl chewing gum on the other end had nearly given up on him. In the end he'd gone for the simplest, most honest response he felt at that moment. Because he was – if we were being charitable – very, very new to all this, and if we were being not so favourably inclined towards him, we might say just an idiot.

'"I'm sorry"?'

Flora burst into a fresh barrage of sobs. 'He's *sorry*. For getting me up the duff and ruining my life and leaving me!'

'It doesn't say he's leaving you,' said Lorna pragmatically. 'He's probably just sorry for how this afternoon went.'

Lorna was one hundred per cent correct about this. Flora was having hormone issues.

'You've changed your tune,' said Flora. 'You were the one calling him a nobber five minutes ago.'

'I know,' said Lorna slightly regretfully. 'But nobody's ever sent me pink roses before.'

Flora blinked.

'No, me neither,' she said crossly. 'I would have thought I would have enjoyed it more.'

'He's trying,' said Lorna.

Flora stroked her stomach thoughtfully.

'Then he should have written, "I'll try",' she said.

Chapter Twenty-six

Innes was having a tiring day. Firstly, Eilidh, his ex, had been on the phone. He couldn't quite figure it out. He knew she'd find it hard having Christmas without Agot – who wouldn't? But she kept talking on and on about what a great time she was having and how she'd been learning to cook and how she'd started Pilates and lost weight and everyone told her she looked great all the time.

Innes was completely bamboozled as to why she was telling him all this.

'So I thought I'd just bring Agot over . . . obviously, very late. I wouldn't like to miss the last ferry! That would be *such* a disaster,' she said with a giggle he hadn't heard for a long time.

'Aye,' he said cautiously, keeping an ear out for Agot who was supposed to be decorating the Christmas tree.

They'd got all the old boxes down from the loft as usual: the same lights their father had bought, with the extra bulbs, in the little flower shapes; bits of old moth-eaten tinsel; Christmas baubles made by generations of not particularly artistically talented MacKenzie children. It would not have occurred to any of them to make the tree fancier than it was: it was the Christmas tree, and that was that.

He could hear Agot and her little friend Ash repeating something they seemed to find frightfully funny about being IN and IN and IN and IN and he couldn't figure it out at all, but they were laughing, which would do. Ash thought Agot was the funniest person on earth and she liked him to follow her around as her own semi-permanent audience so they really were the best of friends, with Ash successfully avoiding the frightful feuds Agot occasionally started up with other completely innocent children who had committed the terrible sin of, for example, owning a slightly fluffier pencil case than she did.

He hung up on Eilidh, still puzzled, and went and had a look at the children just in time to see Agot hang the fourteenth bauble on the same branch of the beleaguered tree, and the whole edifice nearly crash down on top of them. He scooped up both children just in time, reminded Ash it was time to go home, which immediately brought a fervent storm of protest from both of them, and finally calmed matters by rashly promising Agot chips if she could keep quiet for ten bloody seconds.

In Agot's defence, it was about nineteen seconds.

Tripp Rogers was also having a confusing day. This was not a particularly unusual state of affairs for him: both of his ex-wives had confused him utterly, as did people who didn't like football, beer and the 'way things were'.

But this needed a bit of sorting out in his head, and he was sitting in the Harbour's Rest trying to figure it all out.

Honestly, he had expected Colton to put up a bit of a fight. Well. He hadn't expected anything like what he'd gotten, that was the truth of it.

Tripp sighed, thinking of the time recently he'd caught his mother crying over the old family albums. Or the resentment he'd built up about his faggy brother who had made a fortune and meanly never shared any of it. He'd realised he'd been thinking about Colton, on and off, his entire life; they all had, even his sister.

And Colton hadn't been thinking about them at all. He'd just got on and done it.

So all this time they'd imagined him plotting against them – laughing at them all in his big house, like Scrooge McDuck; deliberately buying companies and travelling just to show those he'd left behind a thing or two. He hadn't done anything like that at all. He'd simply snipped them out of his life. He'd got married without giving a whit as to whether their parents were there – Janey, on the other hand, had nearly given them all a nervous break-down with her wedding preparations, both times.

And now, at the very end of his life, he'd deliberately come here to die among these weird-sounding people who appeared to think were his real family, in the middle of nowhere in the freezing cold, and if Tripp hadn't stopped by, they wouldn't have known anything about that either.

It was far, far more hurtful to know that, instead of being hated and resented, they had simply all been forgotten.

He would have to call Mom. But he couldn't bear to make this conversation. Inge-Britt brought him over another whisky – he'd asked for Jack Daniel's and she'd looked at him like he was a maniac and brought him something called Lagavulin. He'd simply have to.

Oh God. And they'd have to sort out Pa another way. Hell, he'd probably end up living with Tripp, which was the last thing Tripp wanted. He'd always been closer to his father, but as it turned out, particularly as his mind was starting to go, his pa was a bit of a mean sonofabitch after all. Colton hadn't been entirely wrong about that.

This didn't sit right with Tripp. It didn't sit right at all. He thought again of his mom, fretful and unhappy in her own age. In fact, the more he thought about it, the more he thought she might have been fretful and unhappy her entire life. He wondered if she'd been happy married to his loud, overbearing pa. Maybe not. It had never even occurred to him.

But that was just families, wasn't it? he thought. Families were always complicated. They never just got on. That was for the movies.

He considered it some more. Nobody was perfect. But it was pretty hard to think of them, not knowing their only son was dying until it was too late. They deserved another conversation, didn't they? Didn't everyone deserve a second chance? One last chance to say goodbye? A little comfort in their old age.

It occurred to Tripp suddenly that when he'd arrived here he thought it was Colton who needed a second chance, to stop being such a rich douche all the time.

Now he wondered, just in a tiny deep part of himself, if maybe it was his parents who needed a second chance. Or all of them.

Tripp Rogers was not a man given to much introspection. It must, he thought, be the wild wind and the snow outside and the fact that there was absolutely nothing as far as he could tell – not a bowling alley, not a golf course – here to do. Picking up a book would not have occurred to him.

Inge-Britt smiled over at him sympathetically.

'Hey, got anything to eat?' he asked. He'd no idea what time it was – it was always dark, apparently, and he was still jet-lagged, but his belly was telling him he was hungry.

'Just crisps,' said Inge-Britt, which, it transpired, meant chips and he wasn't going to get satisfied from those.

'You should remember to go to the Seaside Kitchen,' she said. 'It's great, the food there.'

Tripp harrumphed.

'I'm banned from there.'

'*Banned?*' said Inge-Britt. 'From the Seaside Kitchen? I wouldn't have thought so. Flora's lovely.'

'Yeah, I don't know why.'

Inge-Britt looked at him.

'. . . I just asked after some faggy guy . . .'

Inge-Britt stared at him.

'You mean Fintan?'

Tripp glanced to the side, conscious that he'd made a terrible mistake.

'Uh . . .'

'Out,' said Inge-Britt. 'Settle your bill, and then out.'

'But there's nowhere else to go!' whined Tripp.

'Not my problem,' said Inge-Britt. 'We tolerate quite a lot round here. But not arseholes.'

✶ * ❄

It was freezing outside. Tripp eyed up his huge car and wondered mournfully if he could sleep in it. Throwing himself on Colton's mercy wasn't even an option; he assumed the answer would be no. Or if it was yes, it would only be so Colton could look down on him. That's how he would feel if the boot was on the other foot.

Also he could smell food, definitely somewhere. He buried his hands in the pocket of his parka and followed the scent of fish and chips down to the harbourside.

A small girl was standing in the doorway of the shop. Tripp didn't have kids – neither of his marriages had lasted quite long enough, which was a relief, although he'd still ended up having to pay them both enough. The girl had her arms folded, and hair that was almost pure white.

'YOU HAVE TO WAIT BEHIND ME,' she announced.

'All right, little lady,' said Tripp, happy to meet someone he probably wouldn't offend.

'Agot, stop being a hellion,' said a pleasant-sounding voice, and a tall brown-haired man, who looked slightly familiar, stepped out from behind her.

'Sorry,' he said. Then he looked at Tripp and blinked.

'ATTI FLOWA IS TIRED AND NO DINNER,' explained Agot patiently, and Tripp thought about the name Flora, and his tired brain put it together. Christ on a bike, was this entire family the only people on this godforsaken island?

'Well, that sounds like a good reason for ... whatever this is.'

'It's fish and chips,' explained Innes. 'But you can have haggis if you like. Or a saveloy.'

Tripp blinked again, confused. None of that had meant anything to him.

'Would you like me to order for you?' said the good-natured Innes, who was used to Americans looking confused in the chippie, and Tripp said yes, and Innes ordered him haddock and chips with extra crispy bits and plenty of vinegar and a large bottle of Irn Bru, and Tripp was so hungry he started eating it then and there, whereupon of course Agot wanted to eat hers, and Innes being Innes let her, so they ended up in conversation and, unaware of the gossip or problems, Innes gathered that Tripp was here to visit his brother, and somehow – this was unusual, particularly in December – there wasn't any space at the Harbour's Rest for him and so he ended up offering him a place to stay for the night.

Chapter Twenty-seven

Flora only wanted a hot bath and an early night when she arrived home. Rather to her consternation, there was more noise than usual in the kitchen. Agot was shouting at someone.

'YOU NOT COWBOY,' she was saying.

'That's right, little lady,' another American voice was saying. 'I'm not a cowboy.'

'YOU NOT COWBOY.'

Wearily, Flora put her head around the door. It was not the American voice she was looking for. In the kitchen was her father by the fire, Hamish sitting opposite him playing Jenga by himself, Innes opening the post and Fintan by the kettle looking annoyed about some-thing – i.e. a fairly normal scene. But down on the floor was a furious-looking Agot talking to a stout man Flora recognised immediately as the man she'd thrown out of the Seaside Kitchen.

She raised an eyebrow at Fintan immediately, who shot her a look back.

'Fintan, can I have a word?' she said loudly.

'Talk to Innes,' said Fintan. 'Anyway, nobody thought you were coming home tonight.'

Innes looked up surprised.

'Joel's just got back. I assumed you'd be at the Rock.'

'KISSING!' shouted Agot gleefully.

'But . . . !' said Flora.

Fintan looked at her wearily.

'Flora,' he said. 'He's family.'

Tripp stood up and put out his hand formally.

'I'm sorry for what I said earlier, ma'am,' he said.

'Are you?' said Flora. 'Or are you just looking for a place to stay?'

'Your kind brother did show me the best and only fish and chips I've ever had.'

Flora sniffed.

'Did you get some for me?'

'Oh God, she's hangry,' said Innes.

'HANGRY!' shouted Agot mischievously.

'Right,' said Fintan. 'I'm off. See you later. There's a stroganoff on the stove, sis.'

'Kiss Colton for me,' said Flora wearily. She meant to add, 'And kill him for telling Joel about the baby,' but perhaps this wasn't the time.

Chapter Twenty-eight

It was 4 a.m. in New York. Joel had to stop doing this to Mark; he wasn't getting any younger, and one of these days he'd give him a heart attack. At least, that was what Marsha thought as soon as she realised who was making the telephone blare beside their bed, only the language she used was rather saltier.

'I'll take it out in the sitting room,' said Mark, rubbing his eyes, but it was minus seven outside in the snowy streets of the great city, and even their modern penthouse had cold floors.

'No, it's all right,' said Marsha, fumbling for the bedside light and pulling on her glasses. 'If it's Joel, can I listen in?'

'She's here,' said Mark, in a sleepy voice. 'Can you still talk?'

'Yeah, yeah, I guess . . . yes.'

Marsha blinked.

Mark obligingly put out a large arm in their flowery sheets, and she leaned into his comforting, incredibly familiar hairy warmth and laid her little, birdlike head on his chest so they could both listen without putting on the speaker, which neither of them knew how to work.

'Joel?' said Mark.

'Uh,' said Joel uncomfortably. He was back at the Rock, pacing the empty corridors as his own room had seemed to be closing in on him. 'Uh, something happened.'

'Okay,' said Mark in that slow comfortable voice. 'Okay, Joel. I see. Now, are you calm? Are you breathing properly?'

Joel took another deep breath in through his nose and out through his mouth.

'Yeah, man. I'm trying.'

'Okay. So. What's the matter?'

It was odd: after years of very sporadic contact from Joel, the last year or so had been such a seismic one for him emotionally, they'd somehow become much closer. On the surface, Joel looked so professional – smart, fit, together. Only a very few people knew how deeply troubled he was; how hard he had to work to hold together that persona. And being in love for the first time was exposing all the cracks to the air.

Mark very much believed in exposing cracks to the air. He thought that was the only way anything started to heal.

'It's Flora,' said Joel, not quite able to believe he was speaking the words. Marsha looked concerned.

'She's . . . she's pregnant.'

159

Mark cautioned Marsha to silence. Then, very quietly and carefully, he held the phone far away from his ear. He and Marsha turned to each other deep in the marital bed and mouthed 'YEEEEEAHHHHH!'

Trying their best not to giggle, Mark emphatically shushed Marsha, threatening to put his hand over her mouth, then straightened up his own face, wriggling his jaw to make sure he retained a suitable tone of voice.

'I see,' he said, and his bland tone would have fooled anyone in the world. 'And this is . . . ?'

Joel found himself staring out of a huge window at the end of the corridor, over the pounding sea. He could see too his own reflection in the spotless glass.

'I . . . I . . . '

There was a pause. Marsha was doing a silent victory dance in bed.

'I'm not ready.'

Mark left the silence hanging.

'Why not?' he said eventually.

Joel was frustrated.

'Well. You know how it is, because the last time I looked in my family, there was a bit of a tendency towards murder?'

Mark let that sit there too. Then:

'You think babies are murderers?' he said.

'*No*,' said Joel. 'I'm sure nobody thought Hitler was a murderer. When he was a baby.'

'So Flora is going to give birth to Hitler?'

'This isn't funny, Mark.'

160

'And does Mure raise a lot of murderers, would you say?'

Joel sighed.

'We've been … we've barely been together five minutes …'

'JOEL!'

'Sorry … that must make me sound like a dickhead.'

'I can't remark professionally on that,' said Mark as Marsha nodded emphatically in the bed next to him.

The line crackled the thousands of miles across the great Atlantic Ocean, over across the wild miles of water, far above the chugging tankers, the whales and all the concerns of the deep oceans of the world and between the tiny, tiny, tiny islands of Mure and Manhattan, under a dark sky. Joel looked out again. At last a line of pink was marking the dawn, at nearly 9 a.m., across the water. It was fearsomely cold, but the sky was lined with rose-gold tones. Freezing out there, ice thrown in your face – but very beautiful.

'How's Flora?'

Joel screwed up his face.

'I'm not sure I handled it very well.'

Mark could feel Marsha rolling her eyes next to him.

'Tell Marsha to stop rolling her eyes,' added Joel.

'I'm saying nothing,' said Marsha loudly.

'You know, women can feel very fragile during pregnancy.'

Joel snorted.

'There's nothing fragile about Flora. She's the strongest person I've ever known.'

'Do you really think that?' said Mark. 'Or do you need her to be that? To fix everything you feel is missing in you?'

Joel bit his lip crossly.

'Well, exactly,' he said, sounding like a child. 'If I'm wrong about that then I'm in no fit state to move on to … to all this.'

'A baby,' said Mark softly. 'It's not "this." It's everything.'

He was conscious now of Marsha moving away from him, staring out of the window silently. Their inability to have children had been the only blot in what had otherwise been an extremely long and contented marriage, and the soreness had never quite healed.

Joel leaned his head against the window.

'What if I can't do it, Mark? What if I can't be a dad, can't handle it?'

'You've managed everything you've ever tried,' said Mark.

'Yes, because I can control me. You can't control a child.'

'He's up on the parenting lore already,' said Marsha, and Mark hushed her.

There was a pause.

'Anyway,' said Mark. 'The baby doesn't matter.'

Joel blinked, took his glasses off and rubbed them.

'What?'

'The baby doesn't matter.'

'What the hell are you talking about? This is all that matters.'

'Not today. There's no baby today. All that matters today is your girlfriend.'

Joel paused.

'Joel. Tell me you at least call her your girlfriend?'

Marsha made a groaning noise.

'Well. I mean . . . '

'I've said it before,' said Mark, 'and I love you, but sometimes I worry whether you deserve this girl . . . '

There was a long pause.

'I want to,' said Joel finally.

'Good,' said Mark. 'Look, Joel. You can deal with this. I promise. Any of it and all of it. Don't do anything rash. Think about any decisions that have to be made. Today, all you have is a girlfriend. Who needs care and attention. Baby steps – one at a time. One day at a time, one breath at a time. That's the only way anyone gets through anything, okay? And call me in the morning. My morning, not your morning.'

Joel made a non-committal noise and hung up. It was strange: they seemed completely unsurprised, and had just assumed straightaway that it would work out, that he and Flora would even keep the baby, that it would be okay. This was a new thought to him.

Chapter Twenty-nine

Literally the last thing Flora felt like was entertaining an unpleasant stranger. On the other hand, it helped a little. Otherwise what was she going to do – sit in her room with the door closed, crying?

Agot was standing in front of her father, mutinous.

'HE NOT COWBOY, FLOWA,' she was saying crossly.

'I don't think he said he was one,' said Flora mildly, going to the stove. Thank God, Fintan – who couldn't bear fried food – had indeed cooked something up for her: the stroganoff smelled rather magnificent and the miraculous wonder that was microwaved rice had finally made it to Mure. And winter chard would work as a vegetable, however much Agot turned up her tiny nose and repeatedly made the urgent point that it was HOSS FOOD, ATTI FLOWA, NOT PEOPLE FOOD.

Tripp stood there, running his hand up and down his hat unhappily as Flora walked past him.

Eck looked up from the fireside, where he had been snoozing in front of the racing pages. He never really paid much attention to who traipsed through his kitchen.

'Come sit.' He nodded at Tripp. 'Flora, get another glass please.'

Flora brought another glass with bad grace and poured out whisky without offering any water with it, which actually suited Tripp just fine.

'How was it seeing Colton?' she asked eventually, unable to bear the atmosphere in the kitchen. Fintan, trying to leave, glanced over.

Tripp shrugged.

'Ah. Well ... I mean ... '

'Why did you come?'

Tripp blinked.

'Well. He's family. I mean. We haven't seen much of him over the years ... '

Flora sniffed – she couldn't help it. Agot immediately tried one out too.

' ... but we follow him. In the papers and so on. And when we saw ... that he wasn't around much ... '

'You came looking for his money,' said Fintan tersely while putting on his scarf and gloves.

Tripp put down his glass.

'That was part of it, yeah,' he said. 'But his mom wants to know ... she just wants to know he's okay.'

'Well, he isn't,' said Fintan shortly.

'I can leave tomorrow, man,' said Tripp.

Fintan heaved a great sigh.

'No,' he said. 'You don't have to do that.'

There was a long silence disturbed only by Agot practising her haughty sniff, which was clearly about to become an important part of her repertoire.

'It's just . . . '

'What?' Fintan looked up, critical and hopeful all at once.

Tripp shrugged.

'I think . . . if it was possible. I think Mom . . . I mean, Pa can't really tell much of what's going on at the moment. And him and Colton. They never saw eye to eye, not really. But Mom . . . I mean. She was pretty much . . . '

These words were hard for Tripp to say.

'I mean. Pop was a tough character, you know? He wanted things done his way. And Colton, man . . . Colton won't do anything anybody's way.'

Fintan half smiled at that, because it was so true.

'And Mom . . . she just went along with it. Even if . . . '

His voice trailed off.

'Even when maybe she shouldn't.'

He looked up.

'I think . . . I think maybe she'd like to see him, one last time? By Skype maybe? Or a phone call?'

Fintan looked mutinous.

'Well, you'd need to ask him.'

'And he'll tell me to go screw myself,' said Tripp.

'And this isn't going to change his mind on the money, if that's your plan.'

'Come,' said Flora. 'Everyone sit down and eat.'

'THAT HOSS FOOD, ATTI FLOWA.'

'Innes, tell Agot to come to the table.'

'She's had chips already,' said Innes, looking uncomfortable.

'Well, that's not right, is it?'

'I didn't think you were coming back tonight!'

'I cook also!' said Fintan. Innes sighed.

'Agot, if you don't come to the table, no nativity play.'

Agot jumped up as if shocked and ran to her chair.

'She's not in the nativity play!' said Flora. 'Hang on, is she?'

Innes shushed her. 'She thinks she is. Got the angel costume and everything. I'm going to let her sit by the stage and do the actions. I'm sure Lorna will say it's fine.'

'That doesn't sound remotely fine! What if she gets on stage?'

'I ANGEL IN TIVITY PLAY,' said Agot stoutly.

'Well, would that be a problem?' said Innes weakly.

'Yes!' said Flora. 'For every other parent trying to get a shot of their beloved child doing their actual nativity role without a small shiny monkey climbing all over it!'

'Are we still doing the party here?'

Even though it was the last thing Flora felt like doing this year, the annual party had been held at the MacKenzie farm since time immemorial and she didn't feel like denying a) all the island's children – without business brought in by the island's young families, the Seaside Kitchen wouldn't keep going through the wintertime, and b) Lorna, who otherwise would have to have it in the school gym hall and then stay there for sixteen hours afterwards trying to get the school back in order.

'Yes,' said Flora in a downbeat tone. 'And I'll need all hands on deck.'

'I'll be at Colton's,' said Fintan immediately.

'Well, when he naps you get back here and do sausage rolls,' said Flora. 'Hamish, you can organise the squash and don't make the mulled wine too strong otherwise the grown-ups forget they've even got children and we find them all asleep in the hay barn.'

At least one MacKenzie said this every year but to no avail. People worked hard on Mure; many held down two or three jobs just to keep the island turning. Tourism, fishing, firemen, farming – it needed to be done, and there weren't enough souls on the island to keep it all ticking over. So when the chance came to take a small amount of time off, they grabbed it with both hands.

'All right, all right,' grumbled Fintan.

'I can help, maybe,' said Tripp.

'Yes, perhaps you can poison the minds of the children,' snapped Fintan.

'Stop it,' said Flora. 'We're at dinner.'

'I didn't ask him to stay!' protested Fintan, halfway out the door.

Eck cleared his throat. This was unusual: it meant he had something to stay. Eck cleaved to the old ways:

his forefathers had eaten their plain meals in strict Presbyterian silence, the kirk being suspicious of pleasure at the best of times. It had been one of the many things he'd adored about Flora's mother – her joy in food and family and mealtimes and laughter and all the things he'd felt were missed from his own upbringing. He still wasn't much of a talker though.

Everyone automatically faced him as he sighed and fingered Bramble's soft head under his fingers.

'Ach, ah was thinking richt noo,' he began. Tripp screwed up his face trying to understand.

'Colton is oor family noo.'

Everyone nodded heartily at him. It had not been easy for Eck, his youngest son marrying a man. He had coped surprisingly well.

'So. We respect his wishes. But . . . '

Flora and Fintan traded glances.

'I don't think your mither would have turned away brethren.'

Suddenly Flora found herself staring hard at her plate. When her mother had been dying, she had found it overwhelming; had wanted nothing to do with Mure, or anyone in it, and had come to deeply regret it.

'So,' he said.

Then he got up from the table and retired the few feet to his seat by the fire, Bramble cheerfully accompanying him the four paces, then collapsing as if exhausted back onto his slippers as Eck picked up his whisky glass once more.

'What does that mean?' whispered Tripp to Flora.

'It means you can sleep on the sofa, apparently,' said Flora.

'NOT AGOT BED,' came a small voice, fresh from yet another failed attempt to get Bramble to eat the vegetables she'd pushed under the table.

Chapter Thirty

When the day of the nativity play finally dawned – the snow was resting, but it was cold and bright – at first, Saif didn't notice the whispers.

He found a seat next to Jeannie, whose kids weren't even in the nativity play any more, but who just liked coming anyway. In fact, as he looked round, he realised that the entire island was there whether they had children or not. Flora was hosting a party at the farm afterwards; her mother had used to do it, he'd heard, back in the day when Flora and the boys were at the school (Hamish was always the donkey and happily carried whoever was playing Mary, which to Flora's fury had been Lorna one year and a girl actually called Mary the next. She could forgive Lorna, who had been very fetching in the pretty blue dress, but Mary MacArthur was patently cheating and that was that. Being of bossy demeanour, Flora was normally the narrator, and not pleased about that either. Fintan was always the Angel Gabriel; Innes the inn keeper.).

Saif nodded to Flora, who was right in front of him, wondering as he usually did why it wasn't totally obvious to the rest of the world that she was carrying a baby. Her frame had widened, her breasts were bigger and her stomach rounded. People never noticed what was right under their noses. He wondered where Joel was. Next to Flora was Agot, who was clearly furious not to be involved in proceedings. She was wearing something strange (it was, in fact, Fintan's old angel costume) and muttering, 'STICKY STICKY STICK STICK' in a tone just loud enough to be irritating and just quiet enough that she was getting away with it.

'What actually happens?' Saif whispered to Flora.

'This is going to be weird, trying to explain the concept,' Flora said. 'Well. Right. Okay. You know Mary was a virgin ... Oh God, that really does sound weird. Well, Joseph and Mary had to go to Bethlehem for, like, a survey or something and they couldn't get a hotel. So they had a baby in a manger in a stable but there was a star thing and shepherds and kings came to visit.'

Saif nodded his head. He knew that much.

'And that's what you're doing? Acting it out?'

'Um. Yes,' said Flora. 'It's nice.'

A small wailing child dressed as a sheep wandered past with a black nose and a loo roll tube filled with cotton wool for a tail. Saif blinked.

'There are also shepherds,' said Flora.

'Ah,' said Saif.

Lorna came out and Saif automatically crossed his arms over his chest. Flora glanced at him. He had absolutely no idea he did that, she was sure. It was his way of protecting himself; not betraying the way he actually felt. Flora glanced at the stage. Sure enough, there was her friend doing what she always did: glancing quickly so she knew where he was in the room – in every room – then pulling her eyes away so she didn't betray herself, or at least any more than the light rose blush stealing over her cheeks did. Honestly, thought Flora. The pair of them. And then she reminded herself not to fall asleep; she was absolutely knackered after preparing for the party. The boys had helped. Kind of.

'Good afternoon, ladies and gentlemen,' said Lorna, 'and thanks for coming. You know we appreciate it.'

Everyone harrumphed cheerily. It was a well-known fact that the nativity play was an utter gouge – £5 a ticket! And, once you were in, £1 for a small plastic cup of diluted orange juice, £1 for a plain biscuit or £4 for a hot plastic cup of very weak mulled wine. It was the school's major fundraising event of the year, and they needed every penny.

'The children have been working very, very hard for today, so I hope you enjoy it, and a very merry Christmas to you all!'

There was much clapping as, doing the best she could, Mrs Cook started up 'Little Donkey' on the piano,

173

accompanied by some fairly risky recorder playing from the top group and some very enthusiastic bell-ringing, which was rapidly hushed for coming in too early.

Then two figures came across the stage. Hamish would probably have happily volunteered to be the donkey again, but those days had gone and now wee Alice-Elizabeth MacKay, who was related to ninety per cent of the village, all of whom sent up a massive cheer when she appeared in a wildly ridiculous, sent-for-from-the-mainland blue-and-white 'Mary-style' ballgown, walk behind a stuffed donkey. And behind that was – and everyone immediately went quiet – Ibrahim, walking slowly on bare feet, with his head down.

Even though he was still small for his age, he stood out against the tiny Alice-Elizabeth MacKay. And he was wearing – what was he wearing?

Saif leaned forward, aghast, as everyone else pretended not to be looking at him for his reaction. He was wearing a bizarre tea towel on his head and— Was that meant to be a dishdasha? Is that what they thought it looked like, or what it was, or what it meant?

Saif's face grew hot. In Syria they had plenty of robes. For formal occasions such as family weddings, the boys would wear neat thobes, beautiful, embroidered garments Amena chose with her own mother, or family heirlooms passed down.

Not ... not this ridiculous smock thing that looked like someone had hollowed out a potato sack. Saif felt his face grow hotter with fury; his skin felt like it was itching all over. Is this what they thought of his little Middle-Eastern children?

Ib wouldn't catch his eye. He too must be remembering: occasions – proper, ceremonial special occasions – at home. Not this ... this ... travesty.

The children suddenly realised there was something wrong with the atmosphere in the room. Lorna, who had worried so much and worked so hard to figure out how to do what was right, also suddenly realised that whatever she felt for Saif, however difficult it was to be near him, she should simply have done the easiest thing there was to do – asked him. She thought of the email she hadn't sent and cursed herself.

She stared at his stricken face, but couldn't catch his eye. Meanwhile, Ib, onstage, his accent still heavy, forced out in a deadpan:

'Please help. My wife to have baby. Do you have room?'

The donkey was wheeled away and Saif gasped as he realised the tiny girl on stage actually had a cushion up her robe to make her look pregnant. It was grotesque.

If his son hadn't been on stage and the eyes of the town upon his response to what he saw, he would have got up, grabbed his sons and walked out.

Worse was to come. Ash, looking – to most of the crowd at least – absolutely adorable with his huge eyes and tiny body and still weak leg, limped out as the innkeeper.

Ash stared at the audience, all words forgotten, caught his father's eye – Saif didn't realise quite how grave his expression was – looked at his brother, who still had his face staring at the ground, and suddenly looked as if he were about to burst into tears. Lorna hung back, ready to run on and rescue him if need be. Normally when a child forgot their lines there was indulgent laughter from the crowd, but not today; today you could hear a pin drop. Somebody sniggered and Saif felt his entire body go stiff.

Suddenly Agot stood up from the audience before Flora could stop her and hollered:

'I'S HAVE NO ROOM AT THE INN!'

They had been practising Ash's lines together very seriously the last few times they had seen each other.

Ash's face lit up.

'I'S HAVE NO ROOM AT THE INN!' he said in his funny little accent – half Syrian, half Scots – and the entire audience clapped and laughed and cooed and Saif sat, stewing, furious, as they patronised his family. What had they been *thinking*?

* ❋

Even twenty little ones lisping 'Silent Night' – something which normally could bring a tear to the eye of an iron horse – managed to move Saif, who was unfamiliar with the song and found lyrics hard to understand in English so he wasn't really listening, just sitting there, his ears burning.

He hadn't really thought so much about where he was sent to begin with. Anywhere, he didn't care. Anywhere that was safe to bring his family. Anywhere he could put his children to bed without expecting to wake in the night to the sound of bombs and his house being blown up. Both sides to him were equally incomprehensible, the issues utterly muddied. So when the British government had taken him in, he had been grateful in the abstract but hadn't really cared where he was sent; he had only cared about getting his family back together. English, French, wherever.

And yet over time – after first barely noticing anything apart from an array of old ladies who looked very similar, with an array of minor complaints that he often wasn't exactly sure warranted his expertise – he had gradually started to open up to the reality of the world he now found himself in. Its beauty, the shocking speed of its weather, the way the clouds danced on the horizon, the fresh smell of the sea, the shocking icy water – the best he'd ever tasted in his life.

There was also the kindness and chattiness of the people, which reminded him of home; the warmth and hospitality, which he rarely took up but was glad was there. And of course, Lorna's friendship, which had led him to an appreciation of the community he lived and worked in.

He had let his guard down. And he knew it. Here was the proof. They were still such outsiders. They were still figures of absolute strangeness and fun.

He stayed in his seat, a pasted grin on his face; the crowd had dispersed in various directions. Flora shot him a worried look and whispered, 'The boys were great,' which didn't seem to register at all, but she'd had to hare after Agot who, the moment Lorna had left the stage, had jumped up and appeared to be about to lead everyone in a communal dance.

* *

Ib was furious backstage.

'They think we're funny! That we wear tea towels on our heads!' he was shouting in Arabic. The other kids were giving him a very wide berth. Saif had gone back to find him once people had started coming up to him – they'd read his expression and retreated fairly quickly.

'It's okay,' said Saif in English. 'It's just a story.'

'IS NOT STORY!' said Ash. 'IS TRUE! BABY JEEBUS COME.'

Saif wrinkled up his face and rubbed his eyes. Ash was beaming.

'I was good, *Abba*?'

'It was all stupid,' said Ib bitterly.

Saif put his arms around his younger son; Ib was keeping a safe distance, having pulled off the tea towel and thrown it on the floor as the other children scampered into the adoring arms and videotaping hands of their families.

'You were very good,' he said, and Ash beamed.

'It was STUPID,' said Ib dangerously loudly. 'And you're a stupid baby!'

Ash's face crumpled. Fortunately Agot turned up just at the right moment.

'ASH! ASH! PARTY!'

Like all six-year-olds, Ash's moods turned on a dime.

'Party?!'

'Party now!'

He turned to look at his father.

'I go party,' he said, nodding emphatically in an attempt to get his father to nod along, and he took Saif's hand in a proprietorial fashion.

'MY HOUSE PARTY.'

Saif blinked. Ash was ... he was happy. Ib ... not so much.

'Ib. Go with Ash. Make sure he gets down okay.'

'I don't want to go to a stupid party with stupid babies.'

'Just go,' he said. 'I'll join you in a minute.'

In fact, he wanted to leave the kids to have fun at the party while he had a few very choice words with the teaching staff. He'd pick the kids up later. They didn't need to see that. Neither could he deny Ash what he wanted most in the world: normality. To do what everyone else was doing. His own fury and sadness didn't mean anything to a six-year-old being offered a piece of cake and some fizzy pop, and even in his high mood he wouldn't have dreamed of denying the little boy.

* ❄

Most people had left the school by now, rubbing their hands together at the thought of the MacKenzies' annual Christmas hoolie. It was normally a good one. Shouts and

179

laughs and overexcited adrenalised children scampered and ran down the hill. It was already pitch-black at 4 p.m. As usual, the village council had voted against a large communal Christmas tree, using the money instead to hang lanterns and bulbs all the way down the steep hill to light the children's way home. Even in mid-afternoon in December, it was hard to see your way, and so there were jolly lights, twinkling in the trees like a sparkling rope, and the children loved them.

Various parents were still helping out – putting the chairs away, scraping up the bits and pieces of costumes and books – and Saif tried to look inconspicuous even as he was still churning up with anger and upset.

Chapter Thirty-one

It was in the gym that Lorna found him, eyes burning.

Eventually, the helpers drifted off, too tempted by the warm lights and the sounds of music starting up from the farmhouse down the hill. Saif, being a conscientious sort of man, was just putting the last of the chairs in the corner of the room-cum-dining hall when Lorna walked round to switch off the lights. She turned them off in the hall by accident, not realising Saif was still inside until he called out, 'Lorenah?'

The brilliant moonlight cast itself across the room, changing the dusty old hall into something twinkling and rather magical as it caught the tinsel and the shimmering backdrop of the starry nativity and all the glittering decorations the children had made hanging from the ceiling.

For some reason, Lorna didn't immediately turn the lights back on. Instead, she felt a twist of excitement in her stomach and took a step into the room, not quite able to help herself.

'Hello?' she said as if she didn't know who was in there.

As *if* she wasn't aware, every waking moment, of exactly where he was. As if she didn't know when surgery hours were, or the exact moment his shaggy dark head would appear over the crest of a hill with the little ones of a morning.

She took a deep breath and stepped in the room. She owed him an apology. It had been insensitive and inconsiderate. She had thought the boys would like it, but instead she could tell he found in inappropriate. Upsetting him had been the last thing on her mind. If anything, she had hoped he might be so thrilled with how the boys performed, how central to the school and the performance they had been . . . that he might . . . that he might have been pleased with her. She winced at her own naïveté.

'Saif,' she said. 'I am so sorry. I thought the boys would enjoy being in the play.'

He turned around.

'What . . . what did you think? That they would be good brown little boys? Is that what you thought? We will look the part and be good little Christian boys because you are in charge of what my boys think now! And you are in charge of what they believe! Is that your way? Is that what you want?'

Lorna took a step back, upset, but having known on one level that this was coming.

And she sensed somewhere deep within her that this rage was not just about the boys. But she also had the awful, self-betraying flutter of happiness about having his attention on her, even if it was rage. Well. Hate was an emotion, wasn't it? The only thing she feared from Saif was total and utter indifference.

She looked up at him.

'I'm sorry,' she said. 'I got it wrong. Totally wrong. I should have spoken to you about it.'

'You should have. You *should* have.'

'I know,' said Lorna. 'I . . . I wanted to. I couldn't.'

He stared at her furiously.

'And why not?'

And they both knew, right then, that they had gone too far. Saif stepped back and let out a huge, long sigh.

He stood, stock-still in the moonlight. Lorna still hadn't turned on the light, though at this point couldn't have said why not.

Saif stepped further back and tried to change the subject.

'Ash,' he said at last, trying to tone matters down a bit. 'Ash, I think he was very happy.'

Lorna blinked.

'I think he was too,' she said.

'He is so happy here,' said Saif. 'I worry . . . I worry that he forgets that this is not his real life.'

There was a long silence. Finally:

'Are you sure?' said Lorna very softly. 'Are you sure this isn't your real life?'

* ❋

It was, in their defence, a very beautiful night: thick snow on the old school roof; clear, clear stars in the freezing air. If you were to ask me, I would blame the fact that it was getting so close to the longest night of the year. The deepest moment; the ancient turning of the old year into the new; the very changing instant.

On Mure, midwinter had been celebrated long, long before the Christians had arrived in the northern lands; way back as long as there had even been people, they had marked with standing stones the position of the heavens, and the changing of the seasons, and the very centre of the dark.

Midwinter is a far deeper, wilder magic than Christmas. It began before religious divisions and is older than religion itself, beyond nativities or other portrayals. Midwinter is a human concern rooted in the earth and the body, not the heavens and the soul.

Lorna took another step forward then, into the dark. Saif stayed where he was, beside the chairs.

He did not head towards the light switch, or make a joke, or do anything someone might do under normal circumstances. Because, in an instant, these were not normal circumstances. A moonbeam illuminated his dark shining hair. His trembling hands.

Saif stood still. It was the moonlight, Lorna told herself, feeling the breath quicken in her throat. Somehow that makes it okay. In the moonlight nothing else matters.

She opened her mouth to say something more, then decided not to. Because suddenly there was a spell in here and she didn't want to break it and she didn't want it to go away and . . .

All at once, Lorna found herself compelled to move, because if she waited, she realised she would think again, would change her mind, would never, ever know.

And from nowhere and with no expectations, on a day that had started like any other – namely in Lorna's case, with a deep low ache of a passion for someone she never felt she could possess – suddenly, out of the blue she found she was running full pelt across the wooden gymnasium floor and into his arms – and he was there, equally to meet her, seizing her fiercely, his arms on her arms, his strong fingers grasping her and then, roughly, his mouth was on her mouth and he was kissing her at last with the pent-up passion of what felt like eternity; and she kissed him back, completely unconscious that there were tears running down her cheeks, because the space between them was finally filled. And now he was trailing his hands up her face and through her hair as he kissed her, and then he was cupping her face and tracing his fingers over her forehead as if she was the most perfect thing he had ever known and a huge wave broke over her, and she was at once absolutely and completely desperate for him, pressing herself against him shamelessly, completely unhinged as she immediately started pulling on the buttons of his shirt, desperate to feel his chest pressed against hers.

The ludicrousness of their surroundings, the utter inappropriateness of the situation – it didn't stop them. Nothing could.

Except for a pile of gym mats.

They crashed over the pile onto the floor and Lorna gave a shocked cry of surprised laughter, which cut off when she realised how quickly Saif had stopped laughing, and now how seriously he was gazing at her from his knees, as if he had barely noticed them fall. She could live in those dark eyes for ever, she thought. And she stood up, and he didn't take his hungry eyes off her; she grabbed his hand and helped him up.

'Come with me,' she said urgently, her voice low.

Outside the night was so clear, so quiet. Freezing, or a degree or two under. There was nobody around. Lorna locked up as quickly as she could – her hands fumbling the locks over and over again – conscious that time was important, that if she stopped for too long one or other of them would come to their senses; Saif would feel too guilty or something would go terribly wrong.

She practically pulled him into her little red car. It wasn't far to walk but she normally had piles of marking and materials that were heavy to carry, and the track was often muddy. There was nobody about, and although it was only just after four in the afternoon it was, of course, as black as midnight.

Neither of them said anything, their breath like smoke in the frosted atmosphere. Lorna was breathing quickly. She turned on the ignition and immediately the radio started up. BBC nan Gàidheal was playing, of all things, 'Oganaich Uir a Rinn M'Fhagail', a lament for a lost lover which also happened to be one of the most erotic pieces of music in all of the Celtic canon.

Saif wouldn't understand the words, she thought, glancing at him, that beautiful strong profile – but nobody could possibly ignore the significance of the rising, imploring melody; the driving strings and yearning, pulsing beat: it was universal. She put her hand up to still the music, but his hand was already there and took hers away and so they let the music play. In the dim light of the car, he gently caressed her face as she leaned into his large, strong hand with its long fingers; then, as the car started to move, and she tried desperately to focus on the road, he lightly brushed his hand down until it was just skimming the curve of her breasts through her dress and she found herself trembling even harder, her pulse thudding through her, and she grabbed his hand, which was freezing, and placed it right on her breast, which was not, and they both gasped.

'I'm going to crash the car,' she murmured.

'I fix you,' he said, and she looked at him and saw the glint in his eye – the wicked, laughing, teasing side to this very serious man that so few people saw – and just as she had thought she couldn't possibly want him any more, she absolutely did, and she found herself – entirely out of character for her – grabbing his hand once more and practically throwing it down where it was even warmer, where her skirts met the top of her thighs, and when he wasted no time, and gently but firmly took hold of her there, she closed her eyes and very nearly did crash the car.

They fell, tangled up, upstairs into the little apartment. It was so cosy and warm: the fairy lights were lit, the fire damped down even as Lorna stoked it back up and the curtains were drawn, Milou snoozing. Lorna's perfume was on the air, maddening Saif beyond endurance, and although the rational part of Lorna's brain said she should wait, slow down, she couldn't, not at all. To hell with it.

She couldn't wait and she couldn't stop – not when he was finally here, in her house, in the empty bed that she had dreamed he was in for so long – and she could finally do what she had wanted to do pretty much since he'd stepped off the boat, downtrodden, in desperate need of a haircut, his eyes the saddest thing she'd ever seen. She needed to pull off the doctor's tie, undo the buttons of his fresh white shirt to reveal the golden chest covered in dark hair that she'd dreamed of so often. He, in his turn, kissed her deeply, buried his head in her neck, coiled his hands deeply into her thick red hair and, almost without realising how it had happened, they had both staggered into her bedroom and onto her bed.

She expected things to continue to happen very quickly then, their tumult was so great. Though she had managed to scramble to the bathroom to find her diaphragm, everything was a blur and her heart was racing. But when she was back in the room, when she was finally lying beneath him completely naked, everything changed.

He propped himself on his elbow, his shadow over her, utterly in control. The only sound in the room was their heavy breathing and the crackling of logs in the fireplace next door. Then he took his left hand, and began to trace it, painfully slowly, down her pale body, tracing its curves, both of them fixated on where his hand was going. He caught her hand in his, their fingers interlocked, and drew both down together all over her as she gasped and felt goosebumps rise up on her skin.

Lorna desperately wanted things to happen faster, but with a faint smile at the corner of his lips, Saif shook his head a little and continued with exactly what he was doing, tracing his hand along everywhere it wanted to go – sometimes with more force, sometimes with less, now with his mouth – until he had the entirely pleasurable experience of seeing Lorna squirming, helpless beneath him, unable to focus, caught up in an agony of pleasure withheld. Lorna herself was in awe of this power he seemed to hold so lightly, and he continued, precise and unhurried, even as his own breathing grew thicker and more ragged, even as she was gasping and starting to make high-pitched noises that threatened to turn into screams, never stopping the maddening stroking.

Lorna arched her back towards him, and he, still slowly, moved until he was lying on top of her, his hands gently taking her wrists and moving them above her head; his mouth and beard were on her neck, moving lower; his chest was pressing against hers; and by the time he finally lifted himself to enter her, she was already so unbelievably wound up that the second she felt him push in between her damp thighs, she found herself already on the brink of coming – and then, as she felt him thrust inside for the first time, she did so, incredibly quickly and crashingly hard, shouting out loud – it was like nothing she'd ever felt before, not with anyone, certainly not the first time . . . and she collapsed back onto the bed, overwhelmed and tearful as he burst out laughing in joyful amazement. But he had only just begun, and was in no mood for stopping. He scooped her up again, whispering all the time in her ear – endearments and encouragement in his native language, and her name, over and over again.

She was now roughly upright around him, sitting up, her knees locked behind his back, so he felt fully in her a different way and he held her so close that as they moved together she found herself building once again, and now – this was unprecedented – she felt herself, more and more, bright red and groaning, sore and ecstatic at the same time, her body quivering, sweating hard, as he heaved her fiercely up and down. Saif felt himself desperately inside her skin, driven mad by the vivid, bright red shock of her, her sharp fingernails pressed into his strong back, and he roared suddenly and pulled her incredibly tightly towards him, plunged her down, and she squeezed her eyes tight and came again, rode it out with him, yelping and whimpering; and by the time she came back to herself, the bed was a tumbled mass, her breath was a ragged sob and they found themselves staring at each other as if neither could believe the other was real, and the world glowed rose and gold.

Chapter Thirty-two

Neither could believe it was only 6 p.m. Never in her life had Lorna wanted more never to move again; to stay, cocooned, safe in Saif's strong arms. Neither of them could speak: it felt so huge, like more than the world could bear.

She wanted all of it, everything to disappear. She wanted to stay under the covers, in her snug sanctuary, building a little world with him – a den that would belong to them and nobody else for ever – to stay there until the end of time; to kiss him until she had had enough though it was the one thing she knew absolutely that she would never ever have enough of and, she could tell, under the covers, that he hadn't either. She turned to him as she felt him stiffening again, his eyes burning into her, and moved to kiss him, feeling the delicious pain of her tender lips over his bristles . . .

But the outside world wasn't going anywhere.

'I have to go,' he said, his voice full of regret. 'The boys ... Oh, my darling ... '

He kissed her again and she pressed herself against him, knowing in her heart that she too would be missed any moment now; that everything could fall apart – would fall apart – as what they were doing was inappropriate at best.

Oh, she could not bear it! She could not tear herself away from the sweetest thing she had ever known.

They clung to each other wordlessly, and just as things started to get completely and utterly out of control again, Saif's phone in the next room started to buzz quite insistently, and he had to jump out of bed and it felt like she was being ripped apart.

A word from either of them, she knew, would break it. It would break the spell. The question, as she sat up, that she couldn't ask: would he? Would they ...?

He leaned, so tall in the doorframe, staring at her, his eyes full of emotion as she gazed back at him. He was the most beautiful thing she had ever seen in his life, standing there, clutching his phone.

She tilted her head to the side, shooed him away. He moved forward, kissed her deeply, then turned away and pulled on his shirt. Watching him dress was agony. She wanted to tug on his sleeve, pull the shirt back off those arms, reverse time, put him back in her embrace, never move ...

'I have—'

'Sssh,' she said. She was in a dream, she decided. A magical, wonderful dream, and their words were going to break it, one way or another, and so he kissed her once more and then he left, and she wept with the glory of it all, and the fear of what would come.

* * ❋

The party of course was buzzing, in full swing when she turned up. Every family in the village was there as well as many of the childless farmers whom Flora always invited along because they didn't deserve to miss out on the fun. It wasn't their fault so many of the women of the island moved to the mainland so they wouldn't have to be a farmer's wife. Nobody pretended life on Mure was easy.

But on nights like tonight – the frost burled hard in the furrows of the earth, the stars glittering bright above and the farmhouse a glowing haven of golden warmth, food, music and fraternal feeling, and Christmas coming, and work stopped for a little while – well . . . Then you might indeed feel as Flora did when she was looking hopefully around for Joel. Of course he was not here tonight. She hadn't heard from him since the flowers. He must be sitting at the Rock, on his own, brooding, which only made her more furious.

Saif was full of apologies for being called out, leaving the children in her care, but she waved it away. The island's children were everyone's children after all; it was never a case of favours done and owed, never. It was odd of him even to apologise.

Then she saw, ten minutes later, a rather quiet, rattled-looking, frightfully pink Lorna slip in. And before she even checked Saif's face – who took a terrified glance sideways and didn't even turn around whereas normally, of course, the very least he would do would be to greet the woman who was teaching his children – she knew.

She kept a social smile on her face as she left Saif and told him to help himself to punch, a concept he found both peculiar and revolting, and sidled up to her friend.

'So where have *you* been?' she said, proffering a glance of prosecco with a conspiratorial grin on her face.

'Just tidying up the school,' babbled Lorna. 'It was such a mess after the nativity! Streamers everywhere! And so much fake snow! Oh my goodness, it really needed a good going over! Took for ever, you know what it's . . . '

Lorna hadn't even had a shower. The idea of washing him away, the scent of him on her skin – she wouldn't ever do that. Didn't ever want to do that.

'Also, did you just shag Saif?'

'WHAT?'

Flora thought Lorna's head was going to explode as she grabbed her hand in an incredibly schoolmistressy way and guided her outside into the frosty air. The cold hit them both.

'What did you just say?'

'Oh, just something to which your reaction just

confirmed a very mild suspicion I had due to you two being the only people in the village not here until now and arriving late within two minutes of each other and both of you being bright pink and also both of you being in love with each other?' smiled Flora, for once merry and full of mischief, her own troubles temporarily forgotten. Frankly she was just incredibly relieved that someone else had problems she could fixate on instead of her own. She took Lorna's arm.

'What did you do?'

'I thought you knew everything?'

'Took a guess. Your face though.'

'Oh God,' said Lorna in a panic. 'I could lose my job. So could he. Oh God, Flora, please '

Flora shook her head. 'I only guessed. I'm sorry. Pregnancy intuition, I think. As in everyone else managed to get absolutely steaming in about half an hour and I'm the only one with a clear head.'

As if to prove this, Ranald MacRanald's dad, Ranald, came lurching up and shook Lorna's hand, pumping it up and down and telling her she was the best teacher in the world, from a grand total of the two teachers he had ever met before, having been born and bred on the island, then staggered back inside again.

The girls stared at one another, Flora's jolly mood dissipating as she saw Lorna's face.

'Is it not okay?' she said.

'Oh God,' said Lorna, turning bright pink and trying not to cry. 'Oh God, Flora, you can't imagine. It was

amazing; incredible. It was ... it was different to anything ... I can't explain.'

Flora thought of Joel, his ferocity and hard body in bed,
and thought she did understand.

'So what's the problem? People will get used to the
idea. I mean, it'll be weird to start with, but ... '

Lorna shook her head.

'Oh God, I don't know. I really don't. I don't know if
he ... if I ... '

Flora hugged her.

'Was it worth it?' she whispered in Lorna's ear.

'Oh God, yes,' said Lorna fervently.

'Well then.'

They went back in out of the cold, where Lorna meant
to say quick goodbyes to the other parents then head back
home – alone, she supposed, but who could say? – having
put in the requisite appearance.

Instead she found Ash, with his best friend Agot not
far behind him.

'MISS LORNA,' he hollered cheerily. Her heart
fluttered. Oh God. What she'd done with his father ...
She glanced around. Sure enough, there he was, leaning
against the larder door, half in half out of a conversation
with Colin the local policeman and Alan who ran the
RNLI as they discussed winter survival exercises. Only
he clearly wasn't listening. He was staring at her in a way
that burned right through her; in a way she thought must
be immediately clear to everyone else in the room, as if
there were heat lines coming off them both. She met his

burning gaze and flushed and immediately wanted to drag him off to the nearest bedroom and . . .

'MISS LORNA!'

'Yes, Ash,' she said reluctantly, kneeling down. The little boy's eyes were wide; he was still obviously slightly overexcited from the nativity play, and the whole of Christmas happening around him. She knew that Mrs Cook had been gently trying to elicit from Ib where they had been the Christmas before without any particular success so far. It felt all sorts of wrong to be talking to the child of the man she'd just been naked and utterly shameless with. Coupled with the fact that if she was talking to Ash, Saif would be watching them. She felt herself flush bright pink. Saif caught it too and almost swore, his desire for her was so strong. He wanted to tear across the room, grab her away from Ash, whisk her off . . . These were terrible thoughts, he knew. But he had them nonetheless.

'So he said, if you need an extra man . . .' Alan was saying hopefully, and Saif nodded vaguely, which Alan took as an agreement to do what he'd been talking about for the last half hour, namely for Saif to join the RNLI crew, which was to surprise Saif utterly when he started to get the letters about it as he didn't recall a single word of the conversation.

It tells you everything you need to know about Saif that he attended the courses, took the exam, joined the local lifeboat crew and proved a brave and stalwart member of the team as long as he lived there, without

198

ever letting on that he hadn't remotely wanted to do it in the first place.

'They has a tree inside!' Ash whispered to Lorna.

At first Lorna couldn't work out what he meant. She glanced around. Of course he must have meant the fir, which arrived on the overnight boats from Norway without fail every year. It took up half the kitchen, being miles too large for the space, but was a wonderful tree nonetheless (Lorna's own tree was small and chic and had tangerines and real candles). No designer nonsense for the MacKenzies' tree. It was covered in terrible old angels and baubles, obviously made by various MacKenzie offspring down the years – none of whom had ever been notably burdened with artistic talent – strands of multicoloured lights Lorna was sure she remembered from the nineties, the occasional real trinket – carved driftwood boats and Celtic symbols from years gone past – and mounds and mounds of gaudy tinsel.

'Lots of people do, Ash,' she said.

'It's *beautiful*,' he said, eyes wide.

Lorna smiled.

'Well, yes,' she said.

He turned to look at her.

'I thought tree was for school? And TV?'

Lorna blinked at him.

'Don't you have a tree . . . ?'

She realised instantly how thoughtless and ridiculous she was being. Why would they have a tree? Why would they have been in anyone else's house to see them? Her heart melted for him and she took his out-stretched hand.

'Well,' she said. 'Some people like to have trees in their houses.'

'I would like tree in my house,' he said dreamily.

'Well, speak to your father,' she said. Ash turned to wave at his dad, who was still staring at them, and Lorna felt her heart lurch. She couldn't help it. She had to get Ash out of the way. Just for the moment. She couldn't deal with him right then, fond of him as she was.

'Come here,' she said to Ash, who had turned his attention back to the tree and was looking at it like he couldn't believe it existed in real life.

'I COME,' shouted Agot, grabbing her other hand. And Lorna led them both over to the tree.

'Now,' she said. 'Lie on your backs and put your heads underneath the branches.'

They both obeyed her unquestioningly, their little feet poking out from under the ends of the branches as they gazed upwards through the fir's thick foliage, the lights glimmering and dazzling their vision. She could tell by their *ooohs* and *aaahs* that this had been a good idea and left them to it as more and more little ones were coming over to do exactly the same thing until there was a little line of boots sticking out in a perfect circle underneath the tree and a fair amount of giggling and whispering. Lorna started to worry that they'd knock it over, though old Eck was watching them all from the fireside with a smile of genuine happiness on his face.

Then, heart thudding, she looked up again. She realised that somewhere inside she had told her heart a lie: she had promised herself somehow that if she had one chance – one hour spent with him – then that would be okay; that it would somehow be enough. She could get him out of her system; get on with her life.

Now she saw quite clearly that that was an absolute load of nonsense. That in fact the smallest taste had made her absolutely starving for more.

Flora was there, refilling her glass but actually pulling her on the sleeve.

'I just … Don't take this the wrong way,' she said. 'But I just wanted to say, if you guys want to keep this secret, you have to stop ignoring everyone else to stare at each other like you want to eat each other up. I mean it, honestly, it's gross. It's putting people off their mince pies.'

Lorna nodded.

'There's a million parents here and I'm only telling you this out of kindness, but I think they would all like you to tell them how awesome their child was as a sheep.'

Lorna sighed.

'I know.'

'God,' said Flora.

'I know,' said Lorna. 'It's such a mess. Such a gorgeous mess.'

'Oh no,' said Flora. 'I was thinking about how in a few years this is going to be me.'

Flora looked round. The village did – it was true – look happy. Everyone was there. Well, almost everyone. Jan was in the corner ostentatiously rubbing her stomach and holding court to the old ladies. Hamish was trying to start a conga line as always. Even Tripp was here, furiously apologising to Inge-Britt who, Flora knew, wouldn't be able to be angry with him for long; there were men on the island who'd been banned from the Harbour's Rest half a dozen times. Fintan had popped in, then whisked off again. She wished for a selfish moment that he wasn't so distracted. They were the closest in age and she would have liked his advice about now. Or her mum's, of course . . . She quickly grabbed another plate of warm vol-au-vents and went to offer them round. Tripp swooped in and grabbed them.

'You don't have to do that,' she said.

'Oh no, I don't mind,' he said. 'Good way to meet everyone.'

Flora eyed him narrowly. He must be trying to butter them up to try and influence Colton. Well. It wasn't going to work on her.

'Thanks,' she said nonetheless, handing them off and turning round.

Lorna did just about manage to get around all the parents. And it wasn't until everything was winding down as the very little children, buzzed up on far too much sugar, were starting to get very fretful – that people began to drift away. Ash of course never wanted to leave Agot, who was staying there, and they were soon ensconced in the front parlour, watching *Moana* at full volume, as apparently *Frozen* was only for babies now.

Lorna knew she should go. She couldn't bear to leave alone, but she'd have to. She watched Saif trying to chivvy Ash out and wanted to go to him … but there were still parents circling. On one hand, it was perfectly natural to chat to the parents of the schoolchildren. On the other hand, how could she stop herself from grabbing him … ? Though it was normal for the local doctor and the local teacher to talk about what was going on in their community. But she wasn't entirely sure she could stop herself from simply sinking into his arms; whether she could even be close without going completely crazy.

She hugged Flora, kindly didn't ask about Joel as everyone else had done and didn't have to listen to Flora lie that he was working, and retreated to her car. She couldn't be around him, and she couldn't be around anybody who wasn't him, that was for sure. She would go home, and curl back up in the bed they had both been in, and hold the sheets he'd coiled her in, and hope and dream of it happening again. Because it would happen again, wouldn't it? Mustn't it?

The cold air was freezing and hurt all the way down to her lungs as she fumbled towards the car. He caught up with her just outside.

'Lorenah.'

He never could pronounce her name. She flashed back suddenly to the first time she'd ever met him. It had never crossed her mind that he was attractive – he had been so thin, in desperate need of a haircut, so broken down and timid. She had said, 'Hi, I'm Lorna,' and he hadn't been able to pronounce it, which was slightly ironic given all the Eilidhs and Tadgs he was about to meet, and said 'Lorenah?' and she had felt so awkward and sorry for him then that she couldn't bear to correct him and had smiled and said, 'Yes, exactly,' and he had called her that for evermore, and now she liked it more than her actual name.

She turned; he was very close to her at the car. She fought the impulse to pull him to her, right there, with people in the house behind her. But it was hard.

'Yes?'

'I have to . . . I don't know . . . '

His confusion was so obvious she felt better immediately: she wasn't the only one who felt in consternation about the whole thing. She wasn't some passing fancy.

'Can you . . . ?' she started urgently.

'I will . . . '

Lorna glanced around.

'Can you come . . . ?'

'Not tonight,' he said, in a deeply regretful tone. 'But I will find . . . '

The ludicrous impossibility of the logistics threatened to overwhelm Lorna, but she was too relieved that he was keen to continue to discuss it. Talking was for another time.

'Kiss me,' she said breathlessly.

'I can't,' said Saif. 'Because if I start . . . '

'Start!' It was an order.

He moved closer, just as Lorna's phone rang. She glanced at it. It was Flora and she didn't have to pick it up to know exactly what her friend was going to say.

'Go,' said Saif, and she nodded. He briefly, very briefly took her chilled fingers in his hand and drew them to her lips, and even that was enough to make her shudder. She yearned to linger but knew she could not and, with the deepest regret, let him open the car door for her.

'Go in,' she hissed. 'Someone will see. And you'll get cold.'

'You can warm me.'

'Oh yes,' she said. Then to try and stop herself, she got into her car and drove away, back to the little apartment with the tangled sheets she could not bear to change. Instead, she wrapped herself in them, in the sense of him, full of utter joy, and drifted happily off to sleep trying to pretend he would be there when she woke up.

☆ * ❋

Back at the old manse, Ash stared up at Saif, who was miles away.

'*Abba?*'

'Mmm?' said Saif, still in shock, truly, at how the night had unfolded. After so long . . . after so very long . . . it had been almost too much, too intense; the colours of her so bright. And something else creeping in too: deep guilt that he was refusing to allow to take a foothold. He did not believe, surely, that the universe could deny him a little happiness. But that was so selfish too. He sighed. Amena wasn't the only women he'd ever slept with. But he had been married at twenty-two; a boy, truly. Now, as a man, knowing what he knew, with everything he'd been through . . .

He hoped fervently that she had enjoyed it as much as he had. Then he remembered the thin trail of sweat that had run from her neck, all the way down- between her breasts, all the way down her stomach. The tears in her eyes; the colours that flushed her skin.

No, he did not think it had been a disaster. But . . . but . . . how? How could he square this with everything he had to do; everything he needed to do? The fact – the absolute undeniable fact – that he was still married to someone he loved very much.

Oh dear.

'*Abba!*' said Ash more insistently. 'I want a tree.'

Saif blinked.

'What kind of a tree?' There were almost no trees on Mure; the wind levels didn't let them grow. Saif was completely bamboozled.

Ash rolled his eyes.

'A Christmas tree!'

Saif realised he meant the things springing up around the place, but had absolutely no idea how to get hold of one.

'All right, okay,' he said to get Ash to settle down. 'Now go to sleep, please.

And for once, obligingly, both the boys did, worn out by the day, the play, the problems with the play, the party, which had mostly – but not quite – fixed it.

Saif was worn out too, but he didn't have a hope of sleeping. He wandered to the front, considered looking outside to see if he could crane his neck down into town all the way to Lorna's little flat. But he couldn't, of course; he knew that. He was being ridiculous. But being there . . . had made him so happy; happier than he could remember being since . . . Well. For a very, very long time. He wanted to be back there more than anything. If he closed his eyes, he could just about see her hair tumbling in the firelight.

He glanced at his phone. He wasn't on call that night – it was old Dr MacAllister's turn – but it was a quiet night in general: no babies due, no complications expected; old Felix in the north recovering well from his heart surgery.

His bravado of earlier had faded. He knew, just balancing slightly out of view, there were the doubts, the regret, the sadness, all waiting to pounce on every sleepless night.

But he was not going to let them in. Not yet. He was going to revel for just a little longer in the memory of her; how she had felt better than he could ever have imagined; how extraordinary it had been; how glorious she had looked, spread beneath him, every inch of her.

The guilt could wait. But he knew it was out there in the shadows, waiting to pounce in the dark. That he had betrayed his wife; that he had betrayed his children, his family, his marriage – everything he had ever dreamed he stood for.

He felt cross and defiant, and for the first time in fifteen years, he wanted a cigarette. Why did everything always have to be harder for him?

Then he realised he was being self-pitying, and turned to go to bed.

He had to take his life as he had had to take it for the last five years: to have no expectations as to what each day would bring. In fact, to expect nothing. To grab joy if he could. To hold fast. To try never to be surprised.

In this latter aim, he was about to be proved very, very wrong.

Chapter Thirty-three

It wasn't a notable phone call. Saif had not even realised that since the boys had returned to him, he had stopped jumping every single time the phone went off. Of course, it was always in the back of his mind. But somehow he hadn't been able to be quite as desperate as he normally was to answer it now; he wasn't running at quite so high a pitch. His guard was down.

He should have known.

'*Abba* very happy today,' Ash observed at breakfast time as Saif had heated up the porridge they adored and, as usual, tried to ration the golden syrup, a mostly pointless exercise that generally ended up with Ash licking his sticky hands like a baby bear.

Ib glanced up from the comic he was reading.

'I'm happy every day,' said Saif, emptying his coffee

cup. But it was true: there was a little smile in the corner of his mouth that he couldn't seem to get rid of, like a twitch.

'Also, Santa Claus,' said Ash. 'I have a letter for him.'

'You can't write!' said Ib viciously.

'I'S CAN!'

Ash jumped up and retrieved a faintly grubby piece of folded paper from his school bag. There were letters on it. They were completely incomprehensible, and mostly went from right to left, but they were there, which Saif took as evidence of progress of sorts and Lorna had said in his last assessment wasn't notably worse than some of the locals. Thinking about Lorna again he had a sudden flashback to the look on her face as she'd lain, spread out beneath him on the bed, and it made him blush, so he concentrated hard on the paper.

'What does this say?' he said. 'Could you read it for me?'

'*Abba* can't read,' asserted Ash confidently.

'Nobody can read that nonsense, you baby,' said Ib.

'Ibrahim! Stop it!' ordered Saif. 'Ash is trying, and I hope you're trying too.'

Ib shrugged. He understood everything in class and was performing very well in mathematics and anything science-related – just as his father had. When it came to English and writing things down, he wasn't remotely motivated or interested; his spelling and grammar were atrocious, and truth be told, he wasn't doing that much better than Ash, although he could read in English now.

'Who cares?'

'Everyone,' said Saif. Next year, assuming they were

still here, Ib should have to start weekly boarding at the secondary on the mainland. Saif was dreading it – he couldn't bear the thought of sending his boy away when he had only just returned. In fact, he was planning on keeping him back another year but didn't quite know how to break it to Ib.

'If you can't learn to spell properly, you won't be able to move up a grade,' he warned, and was somewhat comforted to see Ibrahim shrug as if he didn't care. Keeping him back a year would punt the problem down the road a little; he remained small compared to the other boys too.

He was just thinking he should discuss it with Neda, their social worker on the mainland, when his phone rang and it was her. Pleased, he picked it up and said a cheery good morning, but Neda's tone was grave.

'Can you talk privately?' she said.

Saif frowned at the boys, who were kicking one another under the table, and moved into the next room, his heart pounding suddenly.

'What?' he said. When he was nervous, he often became brusque without necessarily realising it.

'You need to come to Glasgow.'

'What? Why?'

'I can't tell you over the phone, I'm afraid.'

'Is it Amena? Something about Amena?'

He remembered the last time. It had been the Home Office who had contacted him, not the social work department, although he had long given up attempting to work out the vagaries of the British government departments.

He was grateful, that was all, and felt that they were grateful to him for providing a useful service on Mure as well and that that was all that mattered.

'You have to tell me what it is.'

'I'm afraid I can't.'

'Can I bring the boys?'

There was a long pause.

'Best not.'

Chapter Thirty-four

Thank goodness for Mrs Laird, who could always step in, and Jeannie, the only person he could talk to that morning, explaining that he had to get to Glasgow urgently. Jeannie understood this meant government business and simply nodded, concerned about the shy, dedicated doctor she'd come to be very fond of, and set about trying to find a locum in Christmas week who'd drop everything to come to a remote island for an unspecified amount of time, as hapless a task as she knew.

Fortunately, the surgery was quiet at Christmas. Jeannie had several private views on how much better people felt when they were busy and didn't have time to sit around bothering themselves about nothing and taking themselves off to the doctor's every five minutes. Of course, they'd all be back after Christmas, complaining about stomach aches when the answer was clearly that they'd been entirely unable to lay off the mince pies.

Jeannie also thought that people were unnecessarily harsh on the subject of medical receptionists.

Saif kissed the boys as they finished their breakfasts, telling them he just had a couple of things to do on the mainland.

'Are you going to see Father Santa?' said Ash, who had the whole thing completely confused.

'There's no such thing,' said Ib shortly. This didn't upset Ash quite as much as it might have done as he had only begun believing in Santa Claus five weeks before.

'Bring a tree,' he ordered peremptorily and Saif kissed him on the head once more, ordered them both to finish their porridge and headed off for the early morning ferry. He had two minutes to grab a coffee at Flora's and did so, finding himself unable to stop checking out her stomach.

'Stop that,' she hissed at him.

'I'm doing nothing,' he protested.

'You do! And it's a secret.'

'There's nobody else in here. And you need a scan. We have ultrasound.'

Flora blanched. She hadn't thought about that. Oh God, she would too.

'Can you do it here? In the kitchen?'

'No,' snorted Saif. 'I do not walk about village with a scanner. Come to the surgery.'

'Hmm,' said Flora. 'Where are you off to?'

Saif didn't want to think about it. He had been

terrifying himself with what it might be ever since Neda had phoned. Or delighting himself. But when they'd found the boys ... he'd got a letter.

But they were juniors. He should call the Home Office line.

He couldn't bear to. That tiny fragment of hope sparking in him ... he couldn't bear to extinguish it. Not yet.

He couldn't allow himself to think of Lorna at all.

Chapter Thirty-five

Neda met him at the featureless detention centre door. She offered him what he already knew would be a cup of the worst coffee in the history of the world, and he shook his head.

Neda was about five foot ten inches, her hair cut close to her head except for a small flat-top, large gold earrings swinging from her ears, wearing a bright pink trouser suit – normally she was the last person to look intimidated in the world. Her confidence, straight-talking and certainty Saif had never found anything other than comforting.

Today she looked concerned, and he began to feel nervous. He followed her through to her tiny office, over-flowing with bursting files that looked to Saif like great big compendiums of heaving misery, tied up in string but spilling out everywhere, each one of them families divided; war and misery and separation. He tried to look somewhere else.

A tall man entered the room and introduced himself as being from the Home Office. Saif was suddenly so nervous he couldn't remember the man's name and could barely shake his hand.

'Okay,' said Neda. 'As you know there's been a lot of cutbacks in the refugee service, and they're winding up the programme.'

Saif did know. He could not – would never – understand the government's reluctance, particularly in sparse, underpopulated areas like Scotland where they desperately needed people to work, to stop taking in desperate doctors, engineers, workers, families who only wanted to pay their way in exchange for a safe place to lay their heads, without bombs. But questioning politics was absolutely not something he was going to go anywhere near.

Neda glanced at the tall man apologetically.

'They thought this might be easier with someone you know. I'm sorry.'

She tailed off. Saif simply nodded. Please let her get on with it. Please.

'We have . . . we have some footage.'

She looked at him.

'I have to warn you. It's rather upsetting.'

Saif found himself blinking very rapidly.

'We can't . . . we can't identify the person in it.'

He remained silent.

'We think it might be your wife.'

** ❇

Saif was gripping the side of the chair. He wanted to be anywhere else right then. Back home with the boys draped on him watching *Hey Duggee*. In the surgery listening to Canna Morris who thought that he needed to hear his full theory of exactly how he'd come to get a haemorrhoid. In Lorna's . . . No.

He squeezed his eyes tight shut and opened them again, full of misery.

The man had moved forwards and Saif noticed that a television and an old-fashioned video recorder had been set up in the corner of the room. Neda started closing the blinds in her office. Saif started to shake uncontrollably.

'We have no DNA match,' said the man. 'But the pick-up was near Yarmouk, and we think the timings might match.'

There was a lot of fuzz and rattling at the beginning of the tape; the date stamp was for November. At first, he couldn't make out what he was looking at; then he realised it was a stone wall, which he was obviously seeing through a camera mounted to a man's helmet – a soldier, clearly. There were orders being barked in his own language and they seemed to be moving through some sort of tunnel. Dust was falling from the ceiling. Someone called a halt, then they moved into a small space; a cellar possibly.

In the corner of the cellar was a figure, crouched over. Saif felt his heart beating incredibly fast. Neda was next to him then, sitting down. He felt her hand on his arm, attempting to be reassuring.

A figure was bowed over, shaking in fear. It was filthy, dressed in a head covering and a shapeless dress. Saif leaned forwards. The darkness of the cellar meant that everything was lit by torchlight; people's eyes glowed strangely.

Someone asked the figure her name and who she was, but there was no answer. Eventually, someone else leaned out and gently touched her arm to try and get her to turn around, and she flinched and shook like a dog.

Saif found tears springing to his eyes. He couldn't tell – he couldn't see – she was the right height, more or less, but it was so difficult to tell. He could see a long strand of dark hair escaping from the head covering, but that told him absolutely nothing.

'Please turn around,' he muttered to himself, even as the soldiers, clearly nervous about being rough, asked her to come out with them.

One shone his light directly on her face and she veered backwards, her hands to her face as if she was being blinded. Saif immediately wondered how long she'd spent in the dark. Her clothes were filthy.

'Where is she now?'

The man looked awkward.

'We tried . . . we tried to bring her in. But she ran away.'

Saif moved closer and closer until his nose was nearly at the screen. He put his fingers out.

'Freeze it,' he ordered, and the man did so, as close onto her face as he could get. It was so dark. Then Saif noticed something up the side of the woman's face. He gradually made out a scar.

How could he not tell? It had only been three years. Surely he would know her anywhere? Surely? How could he ever forget that beautiful face, the long straight nose, the tinkling laugh? How could he be looking into another face and not even know if it was that of his wife?

'Move it on,' he said. The idea that Amena, so funny, so clever, had been reduced to this – an animal, living in a hole. His heart was breaking. Was that her?

The man pressed play.

'Stop it again.'

Now the woman had moved her head to the side and he traced her profile, frowning. Her mouth was open and he saw that several teeth were missing, and it felt like a punch in the stomach. He did not want to think of how she had lost them. Her beautiful smile. But was it her?

How much of how you recognised someone, after all, was in the turn of their head, or the way they stood and moved. And this person was contorted, feral ... but he was making excuses.

They had moved it on several times when he saw it.

'Stop.'

It paused.

'Move it back. Stop it again.'

There. It was right there. And he didn't know how he felt about it.

Chapter Thirty-six

'It's okay. We understand,' Neda was saying, her voice gentle. There was a plastic cup of the horrible coffee next to him. Unable to think of anything else to do, he picked it up and drank it. It was foul.

The man was packing up in the room. Nobody mentioned what Saif had done to the video player after he'd apologised profusely, offered to pay for the damage.

The fact that it was the woman's ears that gave her away was ridiculous to Saif. He would have known Amena's little curved ears anywhere; both the boys had exactly the same ones – little shells, flat to the skull. She thought they were too small and rarely wore earrings; he adored them. This woman – this poor bedraggled creature – had ears that stuck out more normally, and not in a way that violence could have caused.

The man had let the video run on: she had started to scream, and Saif had pulled the machine out of the wall to make it stop and hurled it at the ground.

'How dare you show it to me?' he had shouted.

'Because we wanted to help,' the man had said mildly, picking up the heavy machine as Neda settled Saif back down, made him take deep breaths until he was at least semi-calm. He ran his hands through his thick black hair.

'What happened to her?' he demanded.

'The soldiers got her out of there,' said the man. He did not add that she had been chained to the wall. 'Then she just ran ... But we've ... '

He turned to Saif.

'We've been trying to find her. We're worried. And she matched the description we had on file – which means, as your wife, she counts as under allied protection.'

Saif's head jerked up, surprised.

'Which means it's our job to find her.'

Saif shook his head.

'I am so sorry. That is not her.'

The man nodded.

'Well, I think they're still pretty determined to find her anyway.'

'I'm sorry you had to come all this way,' said Neda. 'I'm sorry you had this shock. We couldn't discuss it over the phone; you understand.'

Saif could barely speak.

'I hope you do find her.'

The man nodded and left the room. Neda opened the blinds.

'I'm so sorry,' she said again. 'About all of this.'

'It's fine,' said Saif. But it was nothing like fine. Everything was churning up in him; everything threatened to overwhelm him. What if Amena was in similar circumstances? What if she was living through this daily hell, this living agony? Suddenly he wanted to lay his head on the table and sleep for a hundred years.

'Don't think about it,' counselled Neda. 'There's every chance . . . '

There was not every chance. There was zero chance that his wife was alive in happy circumstances and hadn't come looking for him and her sons. In fact, the military man had made it even worse; confirmed that if she had come forward, the British government would treat him as a priority case, would help them search, would have offered her protection. And here was a woman, who must be someone else's mother, wife, daughter, sister, being kept underground like an animal. And this was going to be in his head for ever now. Saif thought he was going to be sick.

'Are you going to go back today?' said Neda. Saif nodded. Then he looked up. He had made a decision.

'Do you have time for lunch?' he said.

Neda nodded. Of course.

Saif couldn't eat when it came to it, so he bought a sandwich to play with while Neda drank more coffee and carefully ate a salad, waiting for him to say what he had to say.

'I want to ask. Is it possible to move?' said Saif directly.

'What do you mean?' said Neda carefully, putting down her fork.

'Move from the island. Move somewhere like here. Glasgow.'

Neda blinked.

'Why?'

'Is it possible or not?'

'Well, there's a huge shortage of GPs ... ' mused Neda. 'But I have to tell you. It would be in very difficult areas. Drug abuse, alcohol abuse, child abuse, stabbings ... Everywhere most staff don't want to be. I know you think Britain is a rich country, but there are some very, very poor areas, and a lot of them are around here.'

'Good,' said Saif. 'At least I could be useful.'

'You're useful in Mure. Very, if the reports I get back are anything to go by.'

Saif shrugged. 'It is blood pressure, vaccinations, stitching. Nothing difficult.'

'Isn't that good for you though?'

Saif shrugged. 'I am good doctor,' he said without false modesty.

'And the boys – they're settling in well, aren't they?'

'But here in Glasgow ... ' Saif was still feeling stung about the nativity play. And something new: that he needed to be around people who would understand. People who were suffering. Not the contented people of Mure who knew so little of what passed beyond their own tiny borders. People who had lost, people who had been through hard times. It was a sign, he was convinced, even though he was not a man who was remotely superstitious. He was being punished. To see that woman's feral face. Because he had dared to love another.

Saif pressed on.

'There would be more boys like them. There is a mosque. There are people who look like us.'

'Yes,' said Neda. That was undeniably true. 'But they've made friends ... '

'They don't need friends. They need their family. Which is me,' said Saif shortly.

Neda leaned back in her chair and looked at him.

'What's really going on, Saif?' she said. Saif was silent. These were not the kind of conversations he generally got involved in.

'You saw what happened in there?'

Neda shook her head. 'No. You've had this idea before. This isn't new.'

She leaned forwards.

'There'd need to be a very good reason to move you from somewhere that is working out so well. Of course it's not been easy, Saif. Nobody expected it to be easy, to move to somewhere so different from everything you know; to take the boys on yourself. But changing the landscape isn't going to change that.'

'I realise that,' said Saif.

'So is it anything else?'

Saif coughed and – amazingly to Neda – a blush stole over his face. And she realised immediately. Of course. It made sense. She supposed it was natural. He was a young man. A young, handsome man. Put him anywhere, you were going to get trouble. And now he was feeling the full weight of guilt on his shoulders.

'Oh, Saif,' she said, sighing. 'Is she nice?'

Saif's look of horror was almost comical. Neda leaned forward and patted his hand.

'I'm sorry,' she said, a smile playing on her lips. 'Come on, Saif. It's not the most surprising thing in the world, is it? You're the biology expert. Honestly. You shouldn't beat yourself up about it.'

Saif shook his head, his face flooding with colour.

'You don't understand. It's ... She's the boys' teacher.'

Neda screwed her face up.

'*Seriously?* Come on! There must be at least ... ' She thought for a moment. 'Well. A dozen girls on Mure, at least. Nine, maybe. Anyway. You picked the most inconvenient one!'

Saif couldn't speak.

'Really.' Neda was genuinely cross, but she could see how it happened.

'She's looking after your boys every day ... Is it that girl with the red hair?'

Saif simply nodded. He didn't trust himself to say her name.

Neda sighed.

'Oh Christ. Is it . . . serious?'

Saif stared at the floor.

'I suppose I have to take that as a yes. Oh goodness, for one person you do seem to attract an enormous amount of trouble.'

Saif didn't answer.

'And you don't think you could . . . just finish it and stay there?'

Saif shook his head.

'Right,' said Neda briskly. 'I can pass it on to the right person . . . but you'd have to be sure.'

Saif lifted his head finally. He felt like a man tossed on stormy seas. He couldn't live like this, that much was clear. He couldn't be torn between one woman whom he loved – and one whom he had adored since he was twenty years old, was married to, had a family with, and whose whereabouts he didn't even know. Life was not giving him a choice. So the best thing to do was going to be to start over once again.

'I'm not sure about anything ever,' he said. 'But it seems to me the best thing to do.'

Neda sighed and snapped her file shut. 'I'll have to take a view on the boys,' she said.

'But being in a more mixed environment . . . '

'Yes, you said that,' she said, uncharacteristically snippy with him. She had been so proud of Mure; so proud of a community that had accepted the family; for a placement that had felt like a genuine, measurable success. And so proud of Saif for making a success of the job and for the way he had introduced the little scarred boys to the Murians. They had been a success. In Neda's line of work she didn't always see a lot of those. She thought moving was absolutely a dreadful idea. She looked at Saif's face. It was clear he didn't agree with her analysis at all.

'Right . . . you should probably get moving. It's a long journey back.'

Saif nodded. It was.

Chapter Thirty-seven

Lorna was rehearsing the lower class and wishing she was doing a better job of it. It was only 'I Saw Three Ships' which everyone loved because it was easy to sing, sounded so merry and struck the very small island children as entirely sensible that Mary and Joseph would have sailed into Bethlehem, since in the world they lived in, you had to sail to get anywhere.

They were bellowing out the carol but all she could think of was where was Saif? Ash had told her that morning that he'd gone to 'GAZZLE' which she'd eventually realised must mean Glasgow. But why? What was happening? Why wouldn't he tell her where he was going?

She realised she thought she had some kind of claim over him and of course in fact she didn't, which was upsetting enough in itself. Mrs Laird, huffing her way up the hill to collect them even though Ibrahim had complained bitterly that he was eleven years old and didn't need a babysitter, something Lorna would have scoffed at if she hadn't known that of course they'd had to depend on each other more than any children she'd ever known and were probably entirely competent, and so he huffed in turn on their way down the hill.

Mrs Laird didn't know any more than the boys did, only that their father been called away suddenly. A curious feeling clutched Lorna and she felt it in her stomach. The last time he'd been called away to Glasgow, he'd come back with his sons.

She bit her lip and smiled at Mrs Laird and told Ash for the ninety-fifth time to practise the difference between his 'B's and his 'D's, and as usual he flashed that dazzling grin at her and said, 'YIS, MISS LORNA,' and skipped off and did absolutely nothing about it.

Maybe it was nothing. Paperwork. But to be called away so suddenly like that . . .

She couldn't let her imagination run away with her. And she ought to change the sheets, she knew. But she couldn't bear to. She felt every single hour as he got further and further away from being with her. She missed him like she'd miss a limb. Rather than spoiling the dream she had of him – the crush, like some teenager with a crazy, idealised view of another human being – this had done exactly the opposite. The way they had been together was way beyond her wildest dreams. Was like nothing she'd ever known in all her years. She blushed every time she thought about it. She thought about it all the time. She wanted to see him like she wanted to breathe air. And all she could do was wait.

Why couldn't he just text? Just to see if she was okay? Why wouldn't he do that? It nagged at the back of her mind. Why wouldn't he just drop her a line?

She didn't know that Saif had never dated. His parents had known Amena's parents and, while strictly speaking it wasn't an arranged marriage, they were certainly highly encouraged to spend lots of time together, which hadn't bothered Saif in the slightest as Amena was beautiful, clever, fun and liked him too, and what more, he truly believed, could anyone want out of life? And when the children had arrived he had realised, almost to his surprise, that he loved her very deeply indeed.

It had never even crossed his mind, before he got the call, to text Lorna. Rather, he'd tried to put the problem to the back of his mind – to deal with the two completely contradictory impulses in him of staying a loyal family man or loving Lorna – as far back in his mind as possible in the forlorn hope that somewhere, somehow, a solution would present itself.

And it had. It was not going to please Lorna.

☆ * ❄

The odd thing, Saif thought in retrospect, was how much he had thought she would understand. It had sounded so clear in his head. That he had thought the boys' mother might be alive – how could anyone argue with that? And it had proven not to be, but reminded him of his responsibilities.

And that he was needed elsewhere. That he was being moved to another community; that it was out of his hands. He lied. He would spare her that, at least.

So there he stood, by the schoolhouse door, the boys out throwing snowballs in utter delight (it had snowed in Damascus, Ash had informed Lorna solemnly, but he hadn't had any 'glubbs'), their cheeks pink, and he had stood back as if he was having a perfectly normal professional conversation, and while they were in full view of the playground, there was absolutely nothing Lorna could do, even if she wanted to kick him and kiss him all at once, her heart cracking, as he told her.

He sounded so clinical about it. And clearly she was expected to say she understood. And she did. But she didn't. Her entire body yearned to scream, 'NO!' at him, damn it all to hell. Life was short and loss was long and if anyone could find a bit of happiness – a tiny bit – they had to cling onto it like a lifebelt thrown to a drowning man, because she knew – she knew – she was never going to have anything like this ever again, and she had felt . . . she had felt so sure that Saif had felt the same.

If Saif had had any doubts about whether he was doing the right thing by leaving, they were assuaged by her face. Her sadness and disappointment in him were clearly etched there. And the agony of knowing that he could change that in a moment by doing the thing he most longed to do: taking her in his arms, kissing her, holding her, telling the rest of the world to go to hell.

He'd been to hell. It wasn't worth it.

But it took everything he could, staring at the ground, to end the conversation. All he wanted to do was talk to her for ever. And every second with her was torture. Oh God.

'I have to go,' he muttered, calling after the boys, who ignored him.

Lorna nodded stiffly, trying to calculate how long it would take her to get to a quiet space to have a cry. The stationery cupboard, maybe? Just lock the door for a little bit. There were other parents – there were always, always other parents – but she nodded and excused herself for a moment, then dashed inside and sobbed her eyes out into a pile of exercise books and HB pencils. Normally there were few things she liked better than the smell of exercise books and HB pencils, but from that day on, she always found it very difficult.

She actually sank to her knees – she'd thought people only did that in films. And she tried to swallow the horrible choking noises coming out of her. Then she slid into the bathroom and threw freezing water on her face to try and make it look like she hadn't been crying, nearly started again but managed to grab it back. She still had parents to see and little bits of admin to do. She glanced out of the window. Amazingly, all the parents were still there. Oh God. What was up? Had someone fallen over? Was there a fight?

Still scrubbing frantically at her face, she tried to plaster a smile on as she left the building. Everyone was shuffling in the cold but looked pleased to see her. Gwen – the mother of the feral Ferguson children who had arrived from England, their parents' intention to let them have a free and natural childhood and be home-schooled having fallen by the wayside by the end of the first winter, and her husband having scarpered back down the length of the country to his cosy centrally heated triple-glazed bungalow in Guildford, leaving Gwen to cope alone – stepped forward. She had never forgotten that it had taken a lot of help from Lorna to manage her life on the island.

'Um, we . . . ' She gestured the other parents. Saif had left. Of course he had, thought Lorna viciously. Of course.

'We just wanted to say thank you. For everything you do for us.'

Normally Lorna was used to a mixed bag of presents at Christmas time: lots of handmade pictures and bits and bobs from the children which was nice but not entirely useful; lots of bath salts (ditto) and the occasional gem of a parent who'd sneak a bottle of fizz in. But Gwen was holding out an envelope. She took it, frowning.

'We thought . . . we thought you work so hard, you might like . . . ' Gwen's voice trailed off, and Lorna opened the envelope. Inside was a voucher for two nights at a swanky hydro on the mainland, famous for its hot pools and a spa.

'Oh!' said Lorna, completely overwhelmed. 'I didn't . . . I didn't . . . I mean. This is a bit much!'

Gwen shook her head.

'We had a whip-round. You do a great job,' she said, and all the parents clapped at which Lorna nearly burst out crying again, particularly when Gwen leant over and whispered, 'Also, one of the parents – I won't say who – gave us an incredibly large donation. I think they might be sweet on you!' in a confiding way, and Lorna felt all cross and weird again. Fortunately her tears were interpreted as grateful surprise and she hugged them all and the children too, and everyone in the playground felt that happy sense of satisfaction you get when you give someone something they obviously really, really want, except for Lorna, who was fully conscious of the fact that she had just lost the only thing she had ever wanted and didn't want to speak of it or think of it ever again.

Chapter Thirty-eight

Joel kept thinking a solution was about to present itself; that it had to be nearly there – like in a complicated legal case, all he had to do was work a little harder, concentrate a little more and everything would become clear.

The problem was, it kept not doing that. Sometimes, he thought, he could just about imagine it being all right – them living somewhere nice, such as in Lorna's flat, a little ... screaming thing ... there all night and all day ... wailing, demanding something from him that he didn't know how to give ...

How could he love – become enslaved by – a tiny thing? And what if ... what if he gave it everything he had: the pain, the anxiety, the worry?

It will be like Flora, he thought. Warm and safe and

loving and kind. Then he thought, It will be like my parents: cold and addicted and frenzied and dead.

He stared at the sea, but he couldn't find any answers there. It felt for the first time that the island, instead of being a safe harbour, a haven from the harsh vicissitudes of life, was instead a prison.

He couldn't even speak to Mark and Marsha any more. He knew how kindly they meant, and what they thought would be best: it was in the tone of their voices. He was dreading their visit.

And indeed, he thought bitterly, who would understand? The lovely girlfriend, the beautiful island. What did he have to be unhappy about?

But the fear was so strong. So very strong.

It was his day for helping Charlie and Jan's charity, helping out with the boys who came from the mainland. As an ex-foster child himself, he didn't see that he had much choice, even if he was pretty limited to helping put up tents (not terribly well) and cooking sausages. But apparently it was very helpful.

Jan's large face was uncharacteristically beaming.

'She told you then?' she announced once he had hiked up the hill to where they made camp. The boys, from somewhere called Giffnock, were wearing basically all the winter gear available as far as Joel could see. They were just small pairs of eyes peering out of balaclavas. He smiled as cheerfully as he could manage. In fact, after the blustery cold of yesterday, today was fine: bright blue skies and a piercing breeze blew the light snow cover around until the flakes looked like they were dancing. Marching up the hill had woken him up, at least, after a characteristically poor night's sleep. The freezing air was so fresh, it felt like it cleansed your entire system, washed out your lungs. He still felt wretched, but at least he was awake. He stared at Jan in confusion.

'Yeah, hi?' he said, rubbing condensation off his glasses.

'Did she tell you?' said Jan gleefully, then clocked his face. 'Ooh, she didn't. I wonder if she's jealous. She's always very jealous of me, Flora.'

'Shall I start the kettle boiling?' said Joel, still totally mystified and hoping for a cup of coffee. 'Hi, lads.'

The boys clustered round him as they usually did, particularly when they found out he was American, something they seemed to find as exotic as he did them.

Jan whispered conspiratorially, 'About the baby!'

And Joel's mouth fell open.

After a pause he said, 'So, does *everyone* know?'

'Well, you know what the island is like,' said Jan, giggling, and Joel felt a momentary flash of anger at – once again – his supposed girlfriend's inability to keep things to herself. He didn't want to share her with the world, and as far as anyone was concerned around here, Mure *was* the world.

'Hmm,' he said.

'So are you pleased?' said Jan, startling him. It really wasn't her business. 'I mean, it's going to mean more work for you.'

He stared at her, then simply stomped off to check the kettle.

Charlie came out of a tent as Joel approached.

'Ach, aye, hey there,' he said. He was still a little shy around Joel.

Joel grunted rather rudely, but he was still utterly taken aback at how upfront Jan had been. Flora was only just pregnant, after all – you couldn't just discuss things like that.

'Did Jan tell you ... about the baby, aye?'

Joel blinked.

'About my baby?'

'*Your* baby?'

Charlie burst out laughing. 'No, Christ. No. Ours. Why? What baby?'

'No baby,' said Joel quickly, astounded at how he'd managed to get himself into this mess. 'I just didn't ... Sorry. It's early. I didn't sleep well.'

Charlie just stood there grinning.

'Oh ... and congrats. That's great.'

Charlie beamed even wider.

'I know. We're just ... I mean, I know you expect it after a wedding, I suppose ... '

I suppose you do, thought Joel sadly. Why did everyone else in the world find it so straightforward? The expectation that it would be nothing but joy; a new beginning for everyone. But he himself felt like he had barely begun.

Suddenly he felt something flung around his legs. He glanced down. It was a wide-eyed boy. He knew this cohort was at least ten years old but this chap looked very much younger. He had dark curly hair, a quiet countenance.

'Hey, Luke,' said Charlie equably. 'Hands off, please. You know the rules.'

'I'm just saying hello.'

'Not like that. Come on.'

Joel smiled at the boy as Charlie unpeeled him – they weren't really allowed to touch the lads at all – and said, 'Hey there. What's up?'

Luke stared at him.

'Don't worry,' said Charlie. 'He's just . . . Och, you don't want to know the story to this one.'

Joel knew all those stories.

'Just needs affection, that's all. Not exactly sure how to get it.'

'Mm,' said Joel. 'Hey, Luke, I need some help to make lunch, are you up for it?'

'Yes!' said Luke. 'Are you really American?'

'No,' said Joel. 'I just watch a lot of movies and pretend.'

'Oh,' said Luke, thinking about this for a second. Then he put on a terrible American accent. 'Can ah do thit?'

'Sure,' said Joel, and led the boy off to what Jan called the mess tent.

He managed to remember to apologise and offer his congratulations to Jan on his way.

'Sorry,' he said, pushing up his glasses, and she'd smiled smugly and said that kind of little fuss didn't bother you when you were pregnant because you knew something much more important was happening and as usual she'd completely bamboozled him so he'd gone back to the team.

The boys were starting relay races over the snowy meadow, and the shouting and breaths in the air sounded nice to him. Once he'd organised the lunches, he joined as a team leader, realising as he did so that running flat out oddly reminded him of horrible sterile gyms he'd wasted so much time in when he'd stayed in city hotels – they were all the same, with all the same drawn-looking people staring at themselves in mirrors, obsessed with themselves, everything about them and how they would look on Instagram and in their selfies; hard-eyed, self-obsessed, looking for abs and perfection. It had been him too, he supposed, once upon a time. Plenty of times he'd work out and catch some girl's eye and take her out for lunch where she'd talk about diets and being vegan and juicing and oats and he'd just be figuring out how to sleep with her, and both of them would be exhibitionists, still trying to look in mirrors the entire time.

He tried to imagine Flora in a gym and the thought made his lips twitch. He simply couldn't; the two things didn't go together at all. Flora with her soft curves, her skin so pale, elastic would mark it like a bruise . . .

But this was better than hotel gyms in every way: pushing his body hard, with the boys laughing, and Charlie falling behind, good-naturedly putting a hand up – there wasn't a doubtful, mean bone in that man's body, Joel had thought many times. Flora could have ended up with him, and would have been completely fine.

Maybe she should have. Maybe that should have been Charlie's baby – or Teàrlach as she called him, in that old tongue. It shouldn't be Jan grinning like a circus clown. It should be Flora happy.

It absolutely shouldn't, he knew, be Flora crying alone at home. He absolutely knew it. He did. But he couldn't. He just couldn't. And so he ran faster and faster in the frosty air, feeling it burn in his lungs – a good burn – even as the boys jeered at him for not giving them a chance and his team leaped for joy. He would have run beyond the campground, if he could, kept on running till he got to the top of the mountain, then leapt in one bound to the outer isles, or the mainland, run from hill to hill because something was chasing him, something was always chasing him, and he didn't know what it was or how to stop it.

And so the day went and the late winter sun was already setting. He glanced around. Luke, the dark-haired boy, was standing, stock-still, watching it sink down over the sea, his face at peace.

Chapter Thirty-nine

Lorna and Flora were starting to resemble two survivors of a war.

Flora, Lorna noticed, looked so tired. Really drawn actually – it wasn't hard for shadow to appear on her pale skin, but the colour under her eyes was dark and violet, and her stunning pale hair was dry and wispy-looking even as her waist continued to thicken underneath her apron.

'Flores!' she said, hugging her with real concern. 'Have the boys not noticed? Really?'

'You know what they're like,' said Flora wearily. They were propping each other up at the Harbour's Rest where Lorna had insisted Flora have a bowl of soup, even though they made good soup in the Seaside Kitchen, of course – a good hearty cock-a-leekie and vegetable.

But she knew Inge-Britt bought it in wholesale and it would be Heinz, and sometimes a bowl of Heinz tomato soup can absolutely restore the soul. And anyway, she wanted some.

'Fintan's head is elsewhere, and Innes is trying to work something . . . Well,' she said. 'I think Eilidh is coming for Christmas.'

'Oooh,' said Lorna, surprised. Innes's estranged wife had hated living on the island, which was why they had separated in the first place, and she had moved towards the bright lights of Inverness. 'Do you think . . . ?'

'I think Agot has her heart set on Mure,' said Flora. 'Can you even imagine what a pain in the arse she is at her mother's house?'

'I can't,' said Lorna. 'You know, every time I see her she says, "HELLO, MISS LORNA, I HAS DONE MY HOMEWORK FOR MY SCHOOL".'

Lorna's imitation was spot on and Flora laughed. 'What's she actually done?'

Lorna rolled her eyes. 'She brought me a dead bee once.'

'Grade A student,' said Flora automatically.

'Are things . . . ? How are things?' said Lorna, not wanting to dive in unless Flora was willing to talk about it.

'Let's talk about something else,' said Flora. 'Because I get more pregnant every single second of the day and we still aren't speaking and I absolutely can't bear it.'

'Ah,' said Lorna.

'But you!' said Flora. 'You're having gorgeous sex with

the second most gorgeous man on this island, and the first one is a *nobber* so you totally win!'

Lorna immediately did what she had promised not to do and burst into tears.

'Oh for fuck's sake,' said Flora. 'This is worse than last year when neither of us could get any for love or money. Now we've got some and it's making everything worse.'

Lorna shook her head.

'Flora . . . don't. You can't tell anyone. But . . . '

'What?'

Lorna swallowed hard. 'He's leaving.'

'What do you mean, he's leaving? He can't leave! He was sent here!'

'No, he was sent to Scotland,' said Lorna. 'There's loads of places they can use him on the mainland. They're short of doctors all over. They're sending him somewhere else.'

Flora shook her head.

'I don't understand. We still need a doctor here. If they take him away, we'll still be short.'

The two girls looked at one another. And Lorna realised, with a sinking sense of horror, that Saif had lied to her.

'Oh God,' she said. 'Oh shit. He told me . . . he told me he has to go.'

Flora held her friend's arm.

'Maybe he does.'

Lorna rubbed her head.

'Look,' said Flora. 'You saw the nativity play. Maybe it's not you. Maybe he doesn't think ... he doesn't think it's the best environment for the boys.'

'What? It's a perfect environment for the boys!'

'He wants to be somewhere ... There's a mosque. Maybe more Middle-Eastern kids.'

'Bute has a mosque,' said Lorna sadly. 'Well, a very wee one I think.'

Flora looked at Lorna.

'But I thought the kids were happy here! Ash is at the farmhouse all the time.'

'I don't think it's about the kids,' said Lorna miserably. 'Is it?'

Flora shook her head.

'That sucks. I am so, so sorry.'

Lorna let the tears flow.

'At least you got a baby,' she said, sobbing into her drink. 'The best, the most gorgeous man I have ever met in my entire life – he's going to leave. And I'll be stuck here. For ever. On my own. Getting older and greyer and more stuck in my ways. And I will always know that the perfect guy for me was close and ... and ... '

Big bits of snot were coming out now. Flora dug in Lorna's pockets for her tissues and handed them over.

'Here,' she said. Lorna blew into one.

'Oh God, look at the pair of us,' she said. 'What on earth is the matter with us?'

'I always wanted to fall in love,' agreed Flora. 'And now I have and it is absolutely *bloody rubbish.*'

They put their arms around each other.

'I don't know what to say,' said Flora.

'I know,' said Lorna. 'I don't think there's anything to say.'

Flora hugged her tightly.

'But you've always got me.'

'And you've always got me,' said Lorna.

'Oh good,' said Flora. 'Can you babysit?'

Chapter Forty

'So what are your plans for Christmas, Dr Hassan?'

Mrs Laird was talking but Saif wasn't listening, just staring out of the window. He'd had an email that morning asking him in for a chat with a large corporate GP group in Glasgow, which had mentioned that as well as having vacancies, there were plenty of Arabic speakers who would really do well from having an Arabic speaker in the practice.

Good. Maybe this was the answer. He couldn't deal with what was happening; the ups and downs of an emotional life. At night his dreams were dreadful so he was terrified of falling asleep. A writhing, glorious Lorna would transmogrify into the terrible, pathetic shape of the woman in the video, and then into Amena, and he would wake up in a sweat, pulling Ash to him, using the child for comfort even though the little one slept in his bed because he was still in desperate need of reassurance that a parent was still there.

It was no good, it was not going to last and it was hurting him. A fresh start was what he needed. He had not been on his guard here. It had never even occurred to him, after everything he had been through to try and help and safeguard his family, through all the miles, through the hardships, the terrors of the boats and the checkpoints and the Mediterranean and the guards and the dogs and the inspections.

He had thought and planned and worked, made his way, found a job. Everything he had planned for. And then there was the one thing he didn't and could not have planned: falling in love.

'The boys must be looking forward to it?'

Jeannie had said the same thing at the surgery and Saif hadn't really paid much attention then either. This had not gone unnoticed, nor had the fact that there wasn't a Christmas tree in the window or a wreath on the door. Opinions were divided between whether it was inappropriate to mention it, as not everyone wanted to celebrate Christmas, and the absolute sense that the boys were fully expecting to participate. But Saif didn't say anything now. Mrs Laird pursed her lips and got on with things. *She* was going to buy the boy's gifts, even if Saif didn't want to. She could pretend it was for something else.

'Mmm,' said Saif. 'Can you look after them on Thursday? I have to fly to Glasgow.'

'Again?'

'Busy time of year.'

'Well, make sure you go to a toyshop,' said Mrs Laird, but it fell on deaf ears.

Chapter Forty-one

Dr Mehta regarded the potential new practice member carefully. She'd read his file, and had been amazed at what he'd managed to achieve in the short time he'd been in the UK. Her own grandparents had fled partition, so she knew a little bit about the emotional costs. She leaned forward.

'You know, in this area we have a lot of issues,' she said. 'Separated and broken families. Social problems. Do you get much of that in Mure?'

Saif shook his head.

'No. Lots of sheep.'

Dr Mehta nodded.

'Do you feel – and apologies if this is delicate – do you feel emotionally equipped to deal with, for example, abused children?'

Saif blinked. 'As well as anyone. Perhaps better.'

Dr Mehta nodded.

'And why are you leaving Mure?'

For the first time, Saif hesitated. The truth ... it sounded so weak. So pathetic. He took a deep breath.

'I just felt there were places my skills could be more useful.'

'Hmm,' said Dr Mehta, marking something on a piece of paper.

'And I thought it might be a better place to integrate my sons.'

At this, she took off her glasses.

'Is that the word you meant? Are people excluding them?'

Saif blinked again.

'No. I mean, find more people like them.'

'I see.'

'And that's okay?'

'Of course.'

Saif left not knowing how it had gone. Dr Mehta spent the rest of the morning meddling with her conscience. She felt the island probably needed Saif more than he knew. And that it was probably the best place to raise a family – here they had gang problems and sectarian issues. If there was remaining PTSD – his notes didn't show it but on the other hand not many people fled a civil war unscathed and Christ knows what the boys had been through – then it might be a triggering situation.

On the other hand, you didn't pass up a good doctor, whatever his reasons. And he was clearly that. She sighed.

Chapter Forty-two

Even flying nice class, as they had, and changing at Reykjavik then hopping down, the journey to Mure was still quite tiring, so Mark and Marsha were both jet-lagged and trepidatious when they arrived on Mure. Mark was annoyed and concerned that Joel might be stumbling; Marsha was more sanguine that Mark could fix anything; both were desperate to see 'their' boy.

There was no sign of Flora at the tiny landing hut they used as an airport. It had been a bumpy trip and they deplaned in pitch darkness to a howling gale. 'Isn't it awesome!' Mark had announced loudly as they descended, and Marsha had done her best to agree even though they appeared to have arrived in Mordor.

Joel was looking thin again, Mark noticed worriedly. It was always a bad sign. He did his best to smile when he saw them though. Marsha noticed he was wearing a blue shirt and heavy Burberry twill overcoat, which was most unlike him, and smiled happily through her exhaustion.

'Darling,' she said, opening her arms, and Joel was ashamed to show how desperate he was for her to encircle him in a hug, despite the fact that he was nearly twice her size.

'Hey, Marsha,' he said. 'Merry Christmas!'

'Yadda yadda yadda,' she said. 'We're here to sort you out.'

'Marsha!' said Mark crossly, shaking Joel's hand, squeezing it tightly in both of his. 'Nobody can fix anything for other people. Basic rule of thumb. Sorry, Joel.'

'That's okay,' said Joel.

Mark looked around.

'She's not . . . ?'

Joel's face was bright red.

'I haven't . . . '

Marsha rolled her eyes.

'Well, can I just get to bed please?' she said. 'I'm exhausted.'

Joel drove them up to the Rock even though he was slightly anxious that at any moment Colton was going to kick him out as soon as he heard how he was treating Flora. However, the fires were lit and a small dinner had been prepared, and the beautiful tartan and deep reds of the small lounge were so cosy and delightful that even exhausted Marsha was charmed.

'Well,' she said after tea. 'What have you decided?'

Joel's face was a picture of misery.

'Marsha,' he said. 'I'm just not ready.'

'You're never ready,' said Mark. 'Well ... ' He put a steadying hand on Marsha's shoulder. 'We were ready. But we weren't lucky.'

Marsha took her husband's hand in her own tiny claw and squeezed it. The sadness had diminished but it had never vanished entirely.

'That makes it worse,' said Joel. 'I mean, of course I'll support it. Anything Flora wants ... She won't have to work if she doesn't have to.'

'She loves to work!' exclaimed Marsha.

'Well, whatever ... whatever she needs. But I think ... I think they'd be better off without me. She's got all her brothers and, well, an entire island. I can fly in and out. I think that'd be best, don't you?'

He looked up hopefully at Mark and Marsha, his face like the anxious twelve-year-old of so, so long ago.

Mark put his hand on Joel's shoulder.

'I think there's more in you than that,' he said gravely. 'I think you can be a man and face up to your responsibil- ities. I think it's in you. I think you might even enjoy it.'

'But what use is that,' said Joel, 'if I was resentful and bitter at everything I'd been made to do?'

Chapter Forty-three

Following the party, Flora was doing the Christmas planning with very, very bad grace.

Fintan would be up at the Manse of course, but they couldn't all go there: it would tire Colton out. The boys obviously thought she liked doing it, when hanging over a stove was what she did all day. Eilidh was coming over so Agot could be with her dad at Christmas, which was lovely but it did rather add a layer of complications to things, plus Innes had assumed she'd be at the Rock with Joel so had commandeered her bedroom for his ex-wife. Then obviously she was planning for Marsha and Mark, but that excluded Joel. Who had chosen to exclude himself, of course. He could go where the hell he wanted. Which, she knew, probably meant to Jan and Charlie's, which annoyed her even more.

So they would be: her, Lorna, Lorna's brother Iain, who only came back from the rigs occasionally and didn't really have anywhere else to go, Innes, Eilidh and Agot, Hamish, Hamish's girlfriend, who could be literally anyone on any given week, Eck, Fintan possibly but he didn't know what time, Mark and Marsha, who didn't eat bacon or sausages which was slightly problematic for stuffing and chipolatas, and Saif whom she'd invited but hadn't heard from (in fact, he'd been invited to nine separate Christmas lunches and hadn't known what to do with any of the invitations so had ignored them all) but was now concerned about that because she'd asked him before she'd found out about him and Lorna and now wanted to disinvite him but as he hadn't replied to the first invitation she didn't feel she could automatically retract it, but it was no guarantee he wouldn't just appear. (Lorna was no help on this issue as she was half desperate to see him – possibly believing a fair amount of bonhomie and Christmas spirit might actually change his mind about going – and half desperately teary at the prospect.)

And Flora had a horrible, horrible feeling she might have to cater for that horrible Tripp as well who had shown absolutely no sign of moving on, and might start talking about American politics and then they were really in trouble. So anywhere between eleven and sixteen people, depending. And a great big empty chair. A great big hole in the middle of everything. Well, two big empty chairs, because even though she sat in her mother's seat now, it never felt quite like hers. She had never looked forward to Christmas less.

Flora sighed again and looked up a recipe for vegetarian stuffing. She felt awful. So far she'd got away fairly easily with everything – no sickness – but today she felt absolutely awful. The Seaside Kitchen had been absolutely mobbed the entire time, up to and including a team of carol singers who had sung 'Paiste Am Bethlehem' so beautifully that she had been unable to stop sobbing and so drowned them in cake which was all very nice but not particularly helpful to her bottom line.

Chapter Forty-four

To be clear, Tripp had no idea it was going to be like this. Back in Texas, people were respectful but wary. They knew he was from an important family, and they were in awe of his (relative) money and known bad temper. People knew to mind their business.

Here, he couldn't get two steps without old ladies asking how Colton was, boxes of shortbread pressed into his hands, people giving him the benefit of the doubt because they all knew Colton and Fintan and all felt the awfulness of it. Flora wasn't keen on him, but everyone else was incredibly welcoming.

Day after day, as he wandered, he saw evidence everywhere of the esteem in which his brother was held. These people didn't give two craps, as he saw it, for whether his brother liked boys or girls – or for his money either. He was just one of them; he had come and joined in, and that was all that mattered.

And every day, when he thought about turning his back and going home, he didn't. And as time went on, he realised that it would help his mom – a lot, he felt – if she knew that Colton was not with strangers. That he was loved, even though that was not a word Tripp thought very often.

It helped that the village had become a fairyland. In the very depths of winter, when it was dark for so long you couldn't believe anyone could stand it, there were lights everywhere – great icicles of light along the length of the buildings, strung-up bulbs between every gable and huge Christmas trees glowing and shining in every window. Out of the darkness, the little island had made itself a haven of the brightest, purest joy he could imagine – a tiny spot of glorious fortitude in the midst of a dark black sea.

It never really got cold in Texas at Christmas time. The weather was the same all year round: hot in the winter, damn hot in the summer. The sun rose and set at more or less the same time every day. This astonishing world of freezing darkness – this was mighty strange to him.

He thought he rather liked it.

✳ ✳

Innes was doing his best to have a quiet pint which was frankly never easy on Mure, particularly the closer you got to Christmas. Farmers' days were shorter this time of year and he and his cohorts could often be found in the Harbour's Rest, craving a warm room, a friendly smile from Inge-Britt and a cheery word. They were less concerned about the cleanliness of the carpet than the warmth of the welcome.

Tonight, he was trying to get a few minutes' peace to think about his ex-wife, who'd been on the phone again. Of course, Flora and the lasses wanted them to get back together; as for Agot, she was loudly insisting on it as if it were simply a matter of obviousness. And now Eilidh . . . Well, he wasn't sure . . . He'd asked Hamish, who hadn't been much help. But it felt like she was almost hinting at them getting back together again.

However, he still remembered the complaints: how much she had hated the draughty farmhouse; how the lack of a cinema or decent shopping made her want to visit the mainland more and more until eventually she hadn't come back at all. It certainly wasn't an unusual trajectory for island girls.

If they had enough money, maybe to keep a wee flat in Inverness (which was to Innes's mind the most cosmopolitan place he could imagine) . . . He sighed. If they ever got that dang hotel open . . .

Lost in thought, he didn't notice Tripp until it was almost too late. He was knocking on the window just above his head, looking frozen to the bone.

Kindly, he popped his head around the door.

'Do you think,' said Tripp humbly, 'you might ask that

beautiful lady at the bar there to let me come in and take the weight off my feet for a moment?'

Inge-Britt was staring straight at them. Innes raised his shoulders and Inge-Britt rolled her eyes.

'Is he going to behave himself or be an arsehole?' she said shortly.

'I won't be an asshole, ma'am, to the best of my abilities,' came the plaintive, shivering voice from the other side of the door.

'Can you vouch for him?' said Inge-Britt.

'No,' said Innes. 'But I'll help you chuck him out if he gets mean again.'

There was quiet in the barroom as Tripp stood outside, hoping for the best. Eventually, the heavy black studded door was thrown open.

'One wrong move . . . ' warned Inge-Britt.

'Thank you, ma'am,' said Tripp. 'Uh, can I buy everyone a drink?'

This went down rather well as far as apologies went, and he paid carefully for his beers with this strange-coloured money they insisted on using, and Inge-Britt only overcharged him a tiny bit more than was strictly necessary and was then almost embarrassed when he gave her a tip although, being Inge-Britt, was only *almost* embarrassed, and everyone raised their glasses and shouted, 'Merry Christmas! Slàinte mhath!' and Tripp found himself doing the same, even the weird bit.

Tripp joined Innes in the corner, who tried his best not to sigh as he put aside his phone on which he'd been attempting to type the pros and cons of having Eilidh for Christmas, not really managing to get past the fact that Agot would be there, and Agot was the moon and the sun and the stars and everything else more or less came down to that.

Plus a Christmas without children in a home without a mother was a sad state of affairs, everyone knew that, especially with Colton as he was and Flora moping about for some reason like a mumpy fish.

'How's Colton?' said Innes. It was the first question everybody asked. Tripp harrumphed into his beer.

'Well, he's not real pleased to see me.' He sipped the beer. It was awful. He tried another experimental sip. Well. Maybe.

'Maybe that's a good thing.'

Tripp shrugged.

'Here's the thing ... I was wondering ... perhaps ... '

And Tripp told Innes his plan, and Innes sucked his teeth and attempted to be non-committal about it but failed miserably until they were interrupted by Mrs Laird, shaking a tin quite aggressively at them.

'What's this for?' said Innes. There was always something – school roof, church hall, community play. The way it traditionally worked was that everyone would give ten pence and then Colton would make up the difference with a gigantic cheque and they would all bask in the glow, as he reached into his pocket cheerfully enough.

'It's for the nice doctor,' said Mrs Laird. She sniffed. 'I don't think he's going to celebrate Christmas.'

'Well, that's all right isn't it?'

'Only, och, I felt for the wee lads. It's not their fault things are different. And they've been doing it all at school. And after what they've been through – I don't think we need to call them Christmas presents. I think we can just call them welcome presents and that will be all right, don't you think?'

Before he'd come here, Tripp realised, he'd have had some very choice words to say on people of other religions. Not that he'd met many. Now, he watched Innes carefully consider this situation.

'You could probably just say it was a passing gift,' he said. 'Just something we would do for every new child in the village?'

'Aye!' agreed Mrs Laird. 'That's an excellent idea. Call it a tradition! But not disrespecting anything they believe in – just for fun.'

'Just for fun,' agreed Innes. 'Okay, here we go. What are you getting them?'

'People are being really very generous,' said Mrs Laird. 'We might make it to a PlayStation.'

'I think that'll do it,' said Innes, smiling and handing over some money. 'Great. How nice of you to think of it.'

Mrs Laird smiled back and moved on to the next table.

'Eh, wait up there,' said Tripp suddenly. Mrs Laird stopped and blinked politely. She knew who Tripp was but she'd also heard he wasn't very nice.

Tripp fumbled in his pocket.

'Uh, I don't really unnerstand the money,' he said, proffering a huge red fifty-pound note. 'Is this all right?'

'Oh, don't—' started Innes

'I'd like to,' said Tripp, going an angry shade of pink. 'We got money. We're not here to take Colton's money, no matter what you heard.'

'Uh, of course,' said Innes, sitting back and raising his hands. 'Of course.'

Mrs Laird accepted it cheerfully.

'That'll be some games too!' she piped up.

'I didn't have you down as a gamer, Mrs L,' said Innes cheerfully.

'I play *Soldier of Fortune* while I'm waiting for my bread to rise,' she replied pertly. Innes gave her a look.

'So it's *you* who's stealing all the internet.'

She smiled cheerfully and headed off.

Chapter Forty-five

'Is that bastard coming today?'

You could see the pressure on Colton's face, the sweat on his brow. Fintan grimaced. Yesterday he'd said that no, Tripp wasn't available and Colton had relaxed, taken his medication and dozed off into a medicated sleep which was, Fintan knew, by far the best thing for him.

And Fintan had wandered the empty corridors and rooms of the great Manse, the people who worked there quietly scattering out of his way, the thick carpet utterly silent under his feet, and he thought to himself, This is what it will be like. This is what it will be like when he is dead.

So, selfishly, when Colton woke again and asked after Tripp, Fintan said yes, he probably would be coming today, knowing it would make Colton groan but heave himself up and take less of his medication so as to force himself to be alert and awake in the world even though now Fintan simply touching him caused him great pain.

But Fintan could sit next to him on the bed – feel him there, a hair's breadth away – even as Colton raged somewhat incoherently over his brother and he would nod and agree, even if deep down he knew this was futile – cruel even. So Fintan called Innes, telling him to send Tripp up.

Today, however, Tripp sidled in looking almost ashamed of himself.

'I got an idea,' he growled, staring at the floor.

'You've never had an idea in your life,' said Colton. 'Not one you didn't get off Fox News and is a bunch of crap.'

He coughed, and it felt like the fit would go on for a while. Fintan gave him a handkerchief.

'No, listen,' insisted Tripp. And Colton glanced at Fintan, who shrugged. Fintan's mind was made up on this issue. He thought Tripp was right.

* ❋

And so it was arranged. Joel went along because there was going to be some stuff he knew he was going to oversee. Fintan, obviously. Saif, just in case he was needed. And Tripp, so there was a lot of testosterone in the room.

Colton had every new computer ever made so it was a simple case of taking it out of its box and setting it up. In despair at the island's internet, he had also installed a large satellite dish so he had his own. Then he had so many people loitering on his property trying to download iPlayer programmes that he told Joel to get it sorted out in the village too. It was in hand. Frankly, though, Joel wasn't rushing with it. He felt rather strongly that the ability to get lots and lots of work done and to be contactable every minute of the day and freely available in a million corners of the world that weren't Mure was vastly overrated, so hadn't exactly been all over it.

Plus he'd had other things on his mind, such as the struggle between being 'a selfish a-hole' (Marsha's words after two whiskies) and 'a cold, distant, harmful father' (according to himself at 4 a.m., staring out of the window), and his constant, agonising missing of Flora that happened every second. But the Flora who loved him, not the one who was furious with him. How could he be such a coward?

Unable to sit still at the Rock, Joel arrived first and sat down on Colton's bed. Fintan was busying himself with wires; Tripp was pacing nervously up and down the hallway.

'Don't . . . don't tell Fintan about the baby,' he said straight off.

'Uh yeah, whatever, man,' said Colton crossly.

'Can I get you anything?' said Joel.

'All the morphine in the world and a vat of Drambuie,' growled Colton.

Joel moved closer.

'Getting tougher?'

'Every fucking second.'

A look passed between them.

'Oh, it makes him happy,' said Colton, meaning Fintan of course. 'Every frigging morning. If I can say hi, he's like a fricking spring lamb all day. That's why my brother is around. Gives me the energy to be awake and hating that SOB.'

Joel blinked.

'I thought your whole policy was not to fight this thing.'

Colton grimaced again.

'I know. I know.'

Joel tried to work out if he would endure so much pain for the love of Flora.

He would. He knew. He just needed to sort out the next bit. He needed to get there.

Joel sighed and didn't realise he'd done so out loud.

'Hey, what, you got problems?' said Colton, squinting at the thirty-point options page Joel had brought him.

'Sorry, man,' said Joel. 'Stupid of me.'

'No, I mean it. Distract me from it please. If I have to be conscious, I don't want to be thinking about it.'

It would, Joel realised, be a huge relief to talk about it. 'Flora's baby . . .'

Colton winced and indicated to Joel to pour a little whisky into the tumbler by the table and feed it to him. Joel did so.

'So, a baby. What's your problem?' he said when he'd gulped it down, winced, then — after a moment or two — looked slightly happier. 'I'm not paying you enough?'

Joel shrugged.

'No, it's fine. I just ... I mean ... it was just a bit of a shock, that's all. I don't think I'm dealing with it very well.'

He paused.

'No, I am definitely not dealing with it very well. It's just ... it's come as such a shock.'

'How old are you?'

'Thirty-six.'

'When were you thinking would be the right time exactly?'

'I never thought about it at all ... Are you giving me advice?'

Colton strained to lift his head up a bit and made a throat-clearing noise that might have been a laugh.

'No, man. No.'

'Well, could you?'

Colton stared down at his withered left hand. It was trembling; it couldn't be stopped.

'I would have loved a kid,' he said. 'One that looked just like Fintan. But was smart like me. Would have loved it.'

Joel sat quietly.

'I know people talk a lot of crap about seizing the day, Joel. I have never heard so much crap spouted at me as I have in these last few months. Man alive. If I ever see that homeopathy woman again I will shoot her. Also Captain "Bananas cured my Second Cousin". I have had every piece of crap advice under the sun and it all sucks ass at the end of the day, I can tell you that much.'

Joel smiled ruefully.

'But,' Colton went on. His voice sounded cracked and painful, like he was dragging it over gravel.

'If you can't enjoy having a motherfucking baby with the motherfucking woman you love, fuck you, son. And also. Fuck you.'

His energy gave out and he collapsed back on the pillow, wheezing, covered in sweat. Then he turned around.

'Oh. And you guys need to live here. Fintan hates it. He wants to go home to that cruddy farmhouse. I forgot that. Write it down.'

'What?' said Joel, but Colton had taken on a deep and prolonged coughing fit and didn't seem to be able to stop.

'What can I do?' said Joel, rushing over and looking around for the nurse.

'Nothing,' said Colton grimly, eventually managing to control himself. 'If I go back on the morphine, I nod out again and apparently we have shit to do today, and Fintan will be all sad puppy dog face . . . '

Joel put a hand on Joel's arm.

'I'm saying this as your lawyer,' he said. 'But also as your friend.' He paused. 'You can choose when you want to go.'

Colton squeezed his eyes shut. But he didn't say anything. Eventually:

'You think?'

'I think Fintan would hate to know what it's really costing you.'

'Huh,' said Colton.

'Just . . . don't lie to him about the pain. Tell him about the pain. Nothing good comes of shutting up pain,' he added, a little ruefully.

'Huh,' said Colton again. Then he tried to lift a wizened hand to pat Joel's, but he couldn't make it.

'I'll get the nurse,' Joel said. 'Want me to get Saif too?'

Colton waved a hand that could have meant anything. Joel took a few steps towards the door to tell the others to come in. Then he turned back.

'We're not calling it Colton,' he said.

There was a silence.

'Good,' came a hoarse growl. 'It's a crappy-assed name.'

And Joel called Tripp and Fintan up, and retreated to the corner.

* *

Joel sighed. And then he vowed. Yes. He would. He would go over there. Straight after what had to be done here, he would go over. He would. He would pick her up, grab her out of the café – hell, shut the damn café. He would fall on his knees, beg forgiveness for being such a terrible idiot. Hope against hope that it was clear why he had needed time; why it had been a shock. It occurred to him too that it had also been a shock to her, and he immediately felt guilty that he hadn't been there for her; couldn't have made her happy right from the start. And they would take over that tiny little flat and start living.

Well, if she'd still take him; if she still had a moment for him – which, hell knows, he didn't really deserve – then he would spend the rest of his life making it up to her. Making it good. He took out his phone to text her.

Just then, Tripp stood up in front of the bed, looking florid and solemn.

*�֍

The great house, as usual, was hushed. Fintan, who had lost weight too, was sitting on Colton's bed, holding his hand. Colton looked like he was in so much pain – great big crevasses of it carved into his paper-thin face – but every time Saif asked if he could help, he shook his head, just a little.

Fintan was trembling even though the room was toasty warm, the carpets thick, a great fire burning in the grate; the house was so insulated that you couldn't even hear the snowy wind outside. The vast Christmas tree in the hallway was more beautiful than ever. None of them had noticed it.

'Okay.' Tripp cleared his throat. He glanced at his phone. 'Okay, I think . . . I've been working with my sis on this, okay? She – Mom – she doesn't know. Okay?'

Colton waved a hand. His heart was fluttering; Fintan could feel it.

'If she doesn't . . . I mean . . . well. She should . . . ' said Tripp. 'Forget about Pa for a minute, okay? He wouldn't understand. We got his carer to take him to IHOP.'

Colton nodded.

And then Tripp pulled up Skype and they all listened to the plinking bongs with bated breath.

*✖

There was a crackle, then the screen opened up onto an old-fashioned room with brightly patterned wallpaper and ornaments everywhere. Outside was blinding sunshine.

A middle-aged woman was fussing with the computer. She looked mostly like Tripp, not Colton, but when the focus changed to show an old lady on the couch, Fintan could see the resemblance to his husband immediately. Tripp must look like their father; Colton, with his fine features and high forehead, resembled his mother. She must have been beautiful once, he mused. Beautiful, young, with a baby . . . where had it gone so terribly wrong?

The old woman blinked. 'Hello? Hello? Who is that?'

The other woman – Colton and Tripp's sister Janey – spoke.

'Put your glasses on, Mom.'

The old woman did so, from a tie around her neck, and leaned forward, peering offputtingly into the camera lens.

'Mom!' came a booming voice, loud in the quiet room. 'It's me, Tripp.'

'Tripp?' The voice was frail and querulous.

'That's right, Mom!'

'Where are you, son?'

'I'm in Scotland, Mom, remember? I called you yesterday?'

The old woman blinked.

'Oh. Did you? Did you? Yes. That's right. That's right, Tripp.'

Fintan's heart sank. This woman was half out of her mind. And Colton wasn't really up to talking to her. It might just be best to let bygones be bygones after all.

Tripp, he realised, was still talking. And suddenly he felt something oddly like respect for someone who, for whatever reasons, had come all this way to find his family.

'Mom, there's someone here . . . there's someone here who'd like to talk to you.'

'Eh? What?'

Her face, riddled with cracks, was very near the screen now.

Tripp then sat down next to Colton, the laptop balanced on his knees. He tilted the computer closer to Colton's face.

'Mom . . . it's Colt.'

The room held its breath as the old woman squinted into the lens.

Finally Colton, in a terrible attempt at his old, laid-back drawl, said, 'Hi, Mom.'

Her hand went to her mouth, and Janey immediately put her arm around her shoulders to support her.

'That's Colton?' She could be heard whispering, thousands of miles away. 'That's my Colton?'

And Janey, in tears, nodded and hugged their mother to her. Neither of them remarked on his terrible appearance or the prognosis that Janey, at least, was well aware of. Instead, Colton's mother leaned forward and said just three words.

'My baby boy.'

Chapter Forty-six

There wasn't much said after that. No long-drawn-out conversations. No explanations.

And everyone was thinking of their mothers. Joel felt extraneous and excused himself to the bathroom, where he threw water on his face. Saif was staring very, very hard out of the window for a completely different reason: he was wondering, God help him, how long it would take his boys to reunite with their mother. Even if was never ever too late. Fintan was thinking of just how much he missed his mum; how grateful he was for her unconditional love, all his life; how he wished he'd told her. He hoped she'd known. She'd known a lot of things.

Meanwhile, Colton's mother was actually touching the computer screen as if that could bring them there, as if she could touch her son. And Colton was saying, 'I'm going to look after you, Mom, I promise. Don't worry,' as if it were she who needed reassuring, not him, but Fintan could feel off him – sense the effort it took but the way it made him feel so much better about himself just by doing it.

Just by saying it, he felt like strong, powerful, world-beating Colton once more.

And then his mother was saying, 'I miss you, my boy.'

And Colton said, 'I know,' in a low tone of voice. And, Fintan, who knew him better than anyone in the world, realised that he felt seven years old.

'I'm so . . . You know, I didn't mean . . . '

It felt as if his mother was about to start on an apology. Colton shook his head sharply.

'It doesn't matter, Mom,' he said, his voice a rasp. 'Nothing matters now. Except that you're my mom.'

'I love you.' The voice was querulous.

'Yeah, yeah, yeah,' rasped Colton. And then, quietly, very quietly, 'You too, Mom.'

Chapter Forty-seven

Afterwards, there was a heavy silence in the room. Tripp looked as if he was in church. Fintan turned to him.

'Thank you,' he said quietly.

Colton had his eyes closed. Fintan went to him.

'Get Joel,' he said, sweat clear on his forehead. Joel returned immediately. Colton pointed at Tripp.

'Change the will,' he said. 'Make sure ... just make sure my family is taken care of.'

Tripp shook his head.

'Look, man, I don't ... I've thought about it. Don't. You don't need to give us your money. Forget it, man. We're all right.'

'Just for Mom and Pa – not for you, you old bastard.'

But amazingly he had conjured up a smile as he said it. His dry lips curled over his teeth.

'But. Make sure Mom is okay. And Pa is taken care of. All of it.'

Tripp nodded. Joel said quietly, 'I can sort all that out, don't worry.'

Then Saif stepped forward out from the shadows of the dark window and Fintan reflected that he looked like a sad angel, like a portent of the days to come, his silhouette long against the curtains.

'Fintan . . . '

And Fintan looked on the bed where Colton had fallen back on the pillows, the suffering clear on his face – and the atmosphere in the room changed, and something else had changed: they had reached the end game, and they all knew it.

Then two phones went off, and the noise was almost unbearable in the silent room. Saif's first, then Joel's.

Saif's was Charlie. He was brusque and serious.

'Can you come to the Seaside Kitchen please? It's Flora.'

Joel's caller was more blunt. It was Lorna.

'Get your arse down here if you give two shits about Flora.'

Without another word, she hung up.

Chapter Forty-eight

Christmas Eve had been absolutely mad-busy in the Seaside Kitchen: everyone was out doing last minute bits and bobs of shopping and wanted to pop in and chat about their purchases and what they were doing and could they just get a couple of extra slices of cake in a bag, just for tonight, or some mince pies for leaving out for Santa. They'd sold hundreds, it felt like. Flora was dead on her feet, and she knew she still had to go home, get the turkey out to defrost, pre-make the red cabbage, the bread sauce and the venison.

She was so weary just thinking about it. The girls were clearing up rapidly, both excited – Christmas Eve would be a big night in the Harbour's Rest, and they were ready – or rather, they would be – the faster they cleaned up. Then there was make-up to be put on and party dresses to be changed into and mistletoe to carry about and Russians to be surreptitiously met. Flora couldn't begrudge them any of it – they'd worked so hard – so she smiled and handed them the Christmas bonuses they hadn't managed to afford the previous year but had this, and the girls jumped up and down in excitement, and they all hugged each other as they said goodbye and wished each other a happy Christmas and Flora thought bitterly that if it wasn't for *that*, what a sweet moment this would have been.

She really didn't feel well though. Just exhaustion, she knew. Just the strain of all the work – which was good of course – and everything she had to do ever since she'd taken over being officially 'mother' to just about everyone which was also fine except she apparently also had to take on being a real mother and . . .

Suddenly, Flora felt an odd cramping sensation in her stomach and at the same time an odd light-headedness. It was very strange and very quick. Simultaneously, she felt the blood drain from her head and wanted to throw up.

She leaned forward to put her hand on the countertop. Unfortunately, she missed it and slipped forward and hit her head, and the next thing she knew was . . . nothing . . .

*   ❄

It had been Charlie who found her. Charlie often stopped by just after the Seaside Kitchen closed as that was the best time to pick up leftovers, but he didn't have any of his mites with him today; he just wanted to say 'Merry Christmas!' and was taking the opportunity of Jan not being there to do so. He had absolutely no idea what went on between the two women, but he sensed it didn't make Flora happy and it didn't seem to make Jan very happy either so normally he just stayed well out of it. But he did want to wish her a merry Christmas – and hope that everything was okay with her and Joel. He didn't feel he knew Joel very well despite spending time together with the Outward Adventures boys, and he had absolutely no idea what knowing Joel might be like; he was just aware that the man seemed even sadder and more distant than ever and he was worried about him.

Charlie was a simple man, and a decent one, and just wanted everyone to get along, so he was going to wish everyone a merry Christmas and . . .

The front lights were extinguished in the little café but the kitchen light was still on, and from it Charlie could just make out . . .

Fortunately, he remained calm. He tried the door and, finding it locked, rushed around to the back door, which almost never was. Flora was lying there, out cold, and Charlie's extensive first aid training kicked in without his needing to think about it. She looked so white, though, and there was . . . He noticed there was blood on the floor.

He pulled out his phone and called Saif immediately. Then, as soon as he'd hung up, he phoned Lorna, who called Joel. Charlie hadn't wanted to call Joel directly: he would have been very hard-pressed to explain why.

He took off his jacket and covered Flora up, and was considering calling the air ambulance when she started to come round, her eyes flickering, trying to get a grip on who she was.

'Ssssh,' said Charlie, and Joel, flying into the café before Saif, couldn't help but feel stabbed through the heart at the sight of another man cradling Flora so tenderly and carefully.

Saif pushed them both gently but firmly out of the way as Joel pulled his phone out.

'I'll get the ambulance out,' he said.

Saif shook his head and looked up.

'Let me check her – if I call the air ambulance out for someone fainting, they will laugh.'

Between them they made a fireman's carry as Lorna came tearing down, having run into Innes. Saif blinked. In a moment, half the village would be out there.

'Take her to mine,' ordered Lorna. 'It's warm and it's just across the road.'

This did make sense; Flora was trying to protest but still looked wan and very green, and outside a blizzard was growing higher and higher. Siberian winds had blown in from Russia, and the tempest wasn't yet near its peak. Joel looked into the battering storm and suddenly thought gravely that even if they did need the helicopter to the mainland, it wouldn't be able to land in this.

Then he glanced at Saif and, for the first time, said the words out loud.

'You know . . . you know she's pregnant,' he said quietly.

Saif nodded, his mouth a thin line.

'Of course.'

* *

Coming thundering up behind was Tripp, whose huge bulk was very helpful for carrying Flora, and together they staggered across the road to Lorna's, put Flora down on the bed, which Saif couldn't see without a very awkward flashback and reminiscences – even being in there made him suddenly highly conscious of the sense that Lorna was there, right behind him – and it took every ounce of his doctor's professional experience to put the mask back on and to keep his head cool.

'Okay, everyone out,' he announced, and moved to examine her.

Charlie's phone went off; it was obvious he was being summoned home and reluctantly he left, with Tripp saying he'd be right downstairs if anyone needed him. Everyone nodded as if Tripp had been a part of them all for ages and this was totally normal.

Joel and Lorna loitered awkwardly in the kitchen; Innes was waiting for news to then go and tell Eck. Not knowing what to do, Lorna put the kettle on. She was terrified, and dreading the worst – the idea that Flora might lose the baby – was so awful she worried she might spill the kettle on Joel accidentally on purpose.

For his part, Joel was utterly shell-shocked. It was ... it was poetic justice, he knew. Just as he'd been ready;

just as he'd decided to do – as he'd thought, with some reluctance – the right thing . . .

Suddenly a huge emotional tsunami burst over him. He wanted this baby. He was terrified, more terrified than he could imagine that something might be wrong with Flora. He might lose her – he might lose either or both of them.

Unable to speak, he sat down and took off his glasses. Lorna, whose shoulders were still rigid with frustration, eventually turned around to look at him. He was, she saw, crying, whether he knew it or not; great fat tears were rolling down his face.

Bit bloody late for feeling sorry for yourself, was her first, uncharitable response, but when she saw the way his hands shook, her kind nature overtook her and, calmly and quietly, she made a large pot of tea and set out five mugs. Innes grasped her shoulder. With her eyes she thanked him, but nodded at Joel. Innes rolled his eyes. Lorna nudged him. As she poured the tea, she watched Innes tentatively pat Joel on the shoulder.

* *

'I am so . . .'

Flora was trying to explain to Saif that she was embarrassed, but she wasn't really getting the words out. She felt as if she had a terrible hangover, a splitting headache and an utter sense of dislocation from the world.

'I am . . .'

'Ssh,' said Saif, working briskly. 'Do not worry. You're going to need one stitch in your head. Is fine. Looks worse than is.'

'Okay. Yeah,' said Flora, blinking. 'What happened?'

'And watching for concussion. Keep talking.'

'I can . . . I can do that. I can.'

Then something else.

'Saif. I can feel something. My tummy. My tummy hurts.'

Saif nodded. That was what was giving him the most concern.

'Saif, there's . . . Is there blood?'

Flora realised suddenly she was lying on a towel.

Saif looked at her, face full of concern.

'A little.'

Flora, her face still covered in blood, burst into tears.

'Sssh,' said Saif. 'Please. Do not upset yourself. It will not help.'

'Am I going to lose the baby?'

Saif straightened up and went into the bathroom to wash his hands. If either of them had been paying more attention, they'd have noticed how he automatically knew exactly where the bathroom and the towels were.

He returned and stood by the bed. This was not a part of his job any doctor ever enjoyed.

'Maybe,' he said. 'Sometimes there is bleeding with a pregnancy. Sometimes these things just happen, Flora. Often. You say you felt cramping?'

Flora nodded miserably.

'Just before I fell.'

'You feel now?'

Flora nodded quietly. Saif's face was full of pity.

'I think,' he said. 'I am sorry. You will just have to wait for it to pass. I have paracetamol for you. But . . . '

Flora burst into noisy sobs.

Joel, next door, could stand it no more and pushed the door open.

'What's happening?'

'Excuse me,' said Saif. 'I will have to ask you to—'

But Joel was already on the bed, his arms around Flora.

'I am so sorry,' he said, burying his head in her shoulder. 'I am so, so sorry.'

'Oh, it's all right,' said Flora, unable to keep the bitterness out of her voice. 'It's what you wanted, isn't it?'

'No!' said Joel. 'Oh God, Flora. No. You haven't . . . Tell me you haven't lost the baby?'

'I think I'm losing it now,' said Flora, her voice cracked and weak. 'Right now. That's what I'm going through.'

Joel put his arms right around her.

'I love you,' he said, for the first time in a very long time. 'And I love the baby. I love you, and I love the baby. Or another baby. Our baby. We will have a baby.'

'But I wanted this one,' said Flora, her tears bubbling over.

'I'm so, so sorry.'

'This is nobody's fault,' said Saif.

Joel looked up at him, eyes burning. He knew that wasn't true. If Flora had had a little more sleep. If she

287

hadn't been emotionally unsettled. If she'd had a home of her own to come back to at night. This was his fault.

He buried his face in her shoulder again.

'I will make it up to you,' he swore. 'I will. I promise.'

'I don't care,' said Flora.

＊ ＊ ❄

Saif had to put a quick stitch into Flora's head. At first, she was going to refuse the local to protect the baby; then she remembered. And so she accepted the drugs but snuffled throughout. The anaesthetic made her a little sleepy, but Saif told her in no uncertain terms she wasn't to go to sleep: she had to keep awake to make sure she wasn't concussed, and to make sure she didn't bleed more. There was a possibility of ectopic pregnancy and a possibility of haemorrhage, and if either of those two things happened she needed to be on a helicopter straightaway.

Joel insisted loudly they should get the helicopter now and Saif responded quietly that on a crazy stormy night like this there would be trees blown over and car accidents and exposure injuries, and nobody was going to allow a helicopter to take off in dreadful conditions for a suspected miscarriage, however serious it felt to them.

Innes came in, hugged his sister tight, tried to take in the information that she had been having a baby and now she probably wasn't and went to report back at the farmhouse.

Lorna busied herself in the kitchen, making soup for everyone. Saif's phone went off again.

'My life is not my own tonight.'

'Where are you going?' said Joel crossly. 'We need you here.'

Saif swallowed.

'It's ... it's the Manse,' said Saif. 'I need to go back.'

Flora bit her lip. Outside the wind was shrieking. It really was a dreadful night.

'Oh Christ. What a night.'

'I'll come back as soon as I can.'

Flora swallowed hard.

'Please,' she said. 'Please go. I'll ... I'll be fine.'

She half hiccupped, half laughed.

'I don't know *how*. But I will. I always have been before.'

'And I'm here,' said Joel, but Flora ignored him.

Saif picked up his bag reluctantly.

'I will call you,' he said to Flora. 'Keep your phone on please. And charged please, and answer it please. You –' He turned to Joel. ' – if she changes, if she gets feverish, you call immediately. If there is a lot of blood, you call 999. If she passes out again, you call 999. Do you understand?'

Joel nodded.

'Do not leave her side.'

'I won't.'

Lorna met Saif as he was leaving. She held up a flask of fresh vegetable soup.

Suddenly, as he always felt with Lorna, everything weighing on his mind and everything he had to do that evening melted away, and they stared at each other as he reached out to take the flask and inadvertently found the back of his hand running gently down her smooth cheeks, even though he knew it was not fair. His heart was heavy with a deep and profound sadness even though they both knew there was nothing more to be said, that prolonging the inevitable helped nobody.

'You're ... you're definitely leaving?' said Lorna, a tremor in her voice. 'After all this?'

'Yes,' said Saif. 'I am. I think it will be for the best. Don't you?'

Lorna didn't trust her voice.

'I don't ... '

She swallowed hard.

'Good luck,' she said. 'I hope you find her.'

'Thank you,' said Saif. 'Thank you for ... for everything you have done for the boys.'

'Of course.'

'Call me if you need me,' said Saif, and he meant Flora of course, but Lorna so, so wished he meant more.

'But maybe they need some time together, yes?' He tilted his head in the direction of the bedroom and Lorna nodded. They stood there a moment longer.

'Well. Take the damn soup,' said Lorna finally. And Saif did.

Chapter Forty-nine

Saif didn't rush to the Manse. It didn't feel appropriate. There was nothing to be gained by him making a lightning dash that would only get there in the nick of time to save the day.

He still hadn't heard from Glasgow, but with Christmas upon them now it was entirely possible this would be the last medical call he would make on Mure. That felt very strange.

There had been no light that day, not really. The storm had been building; the wind absolutely howled in his ears now. Snowflakes danced and circled the sky without settling; or if they did, then a huge gust would appear as if from nowhere and melt them away, and then the whole cycle would start again.

Now it was freezing. Clouds in various shades of

grey bounced through the skies, tumbling, chasing one another. Ash had been fascinated with them and had stared when he was meant to be putting his shoes on for school and so had had to be chivvied. Saif wondered how he would spin the move. A room of their own, perhaps. A chance to meet other Arabic-speaking children, definitely. Ib would love it. Ash would settle, for sure. Well. They all would. Eventually.

It saddened him greatly that this could be his last call out to the Manse. He hadn't known Colton particularly well, but he had respected him, and the way he had planned and faced up to his own death was utterly courageous in Saif's opinion. Refusing to go to hospital was absolutely right as far as Saif was concerned: if you could ever possibly stay out of hospital, you absolutely should.

Refusing any extra treatment had left him in two minds though. Part of him theoretically could see the sense of this. Part of him thought that if he were Fintan, he would fight and fight and make him try absolutely anything. But the outcome was always going to be the same, he knew. And he had never once lied to Colton about that.

To die in a beautiful house, at peace with your ancestors, with the person he loved, overlooking the ocean.

Yes. He could see it … he supposed. He checked his locked bag; he had everything he needed if the time had come.

* ❄

Fintan's face was grave. Colton's breathing was shallow; Saif barely need to take his pulse to know how thready it would be. He was sweating and was in so much pain he couldn't speak.

Any dose now, Saif knew. Any dose now.

That was what it boiled down to in the end: palliative care. The balance was to keep the patient alive and pain-free. But sometimes those ends conflicted. You couldn't do both. And you had a choice.

You could let the patient spend their last hours – possibly more than twenty-four – in the unconscionable agony of a disease as vicious as cancer, which ate you up from the inside out, crawling and thrashing on the floor.

Or you could give blessed relief even if you knew it would – no, it *might*, Saif told himself strictly – it *might* let them drift into a sleep in which there was no agony, no pain – and no return.

Saif had seen enough in the war; he had witnessed things which meant he knew there was no such thing as a glorious death. That there was no honour in agony; no dignity in a human abased to a tortured animal.

Nonetheless.

'Mr MacKenzie,' he said in his gentle voice, taking off his long coat, placing his black leather bag on the bed, as charming, Fintan thought later, as death paying his final visit could be.

'Mr Rogers. Good evening.'

* ❄

'Stop this.' Colton was hacking. 'For the love of God. Christ. Stop it.'

Spittle dropped onto his grey bristled chin.

'I'm done, I'm done, I'm done.'

The tone was begging. It was hard to hear, even to someone as relatively experienced as Saif.

Saif turned to look at Fintan, who was staring mutinously out of the window at the passing ships; he would not turn around. From downstairs, weirdly, Christmas music was playing.

He walked over to Fintan, who wouldn't meet his gaze.

'I am going to give him another sedative now,' said Saif quietly. 'It is the appropriate dose. But I need to have your consent – both of you – that in Colton's weakened state it may . . . it may make him sleep.'

Fintan blinked.

'Will it kill him?'

Saif shook his head.

'Absolutely not,' he said. 'The cancer is going to kill him. Very soon now. But it will ensure he is not in pain as it does. This is end, Fintan, whatever we do. And this will help him sleep.'

Fintan turned to him, his face a mask of misery.

'Will he wake up again?'

'It is out of our hands,' said Saif quietly.

Fintan nodded. He looked over to the bed where Colton was coiled up.

'Okay,' he said.

'Is there anyone else he needs to say goodbye to?' said

Saif in a low voice. Fintan half smiled. 'He's been doing nothing else since the summer. One long party.'

Saif nodded.

'I'll just fetch . . . '

He didn't need anything but he just felt the need to be out of the way for a little bit. Fintan nodded. Saif left the room, and the two of them were alone.

Chapter Fifty

Fintan sat next to Colton and put his arm around him.

'Please,' said Colton.

Fintan had a speech prepared. He had a lot of things he wanted to say. How Colton had been the first – the only – man he had ever been in love with. How he had believed it was never going to happen for him. And then it had. And the wonder and the glory of all of it. And every single moment they had spent together and everything they remembered ...

But he saw now how selfish it would be to make the person he loved most in the world endure another single moment.

'Yes,' he said, and two great tears rolled down Colton's cheeks. Fintan went and found Saif, hovering in the hallway, barely having reached the stairs.

Fintan held Colton's shaking body in his arms as Saif skilfully inserted the morphine into the syringe driver already set up over the bed.

Outside, the winter geese swirled around the house, caught up in the burling snow, almost indistinguishable from it.

Inside the room, everything was quiet, except for Fintan, Colton in his arms, whispering fiercely, 'I love you, I love you, I love you,' over and over again in his ears, their fingers tightly knotted together, and Colton briefly lifted his other hand, but he did not speak again, and gradually, his breathing slowed, and the pain left his face and his body started to relax.

'He's sleeping,' said Saif.

'What happens if he wakes up?'

'I'm not going anywhere,' said Saif, glancing at his phone. Nothing from Flora and Joel, which was good news, he supposed.

Fintan gently disentangled himself and kissed Colton on the forehead. Then he went to the door and beckoned the other person who was sitting waiting patiently outside: Tripp.

Chapter Fifty-one

Flora's headache had started to abate, but strangely, now that the drama of passing out and needing stitches had passed, she had more time to reflect, and she felt worse and worse with every passing moment.

Joel was sitting on the floor, holding her hand like a courtly knight at a grave. Finally, she turned to him. 'You're being ridiculous down there,' she said stiffly. 'Can you get me some more tea?'

Lorna had gone out after checking on Flora, giving her the biggest hug and whispering she'd see her tomorrow and not to worry about Christmas dinner, she'd bring some sausages and that's all anyone wanted.

Joel and Flora needed privacy; that much was clear. Except it was odd, seeing everyone in there. She thought she'd have been quite happy to rent the place to Joel and Flora; move out and on with her life.

Somehow though, even though she and Saif couldn't be together now, it felt like their place. Their special place, at least once upon a time. She didn't want to move. She wasn't sure how she'd break it to them.

She definitely needed a drink. A stiff one. She headed to the Harbour's Rest. She'd have to deal once more with the fact that very soon she'd be seeing Saif for the last time – watch him step onto the ferry and head for the mainland, never to return – and that was the kind of image only a whisky was going to put a stop to.

She had thought the Harbour's Rest would be jolly on Christmas Eve, and she was right, even through the sadness. Tripp was sitting, crying in a corner while people were being incredibly kind to him and buying him drinks and whispering things about it all being for the best and hadn't he done the right thing, and Tripp was saying they were all the best people on God's green earth, and he was going to move there, goddammit, and fulfil his brother's legacy, so that was something even if it wasn't entirely clear that he'd remember it in the morning, but she realised, then, that Colton was dead, and was sad for it: two deaths on the island in one day.

She ordered a large whisky and sat at the bar and Inge-Britt smiled sadly and said she could have whatever she liked – Colton had ordered all drinks on him – and Lorna reflected and decided to stick to the whisky on balance and Inge-Britt said suit yourself but she had two bottles of Bolly stashed away for later and Lorna gasped and said that was hardly in the spirit of the thing and Inge-Britt winked and said Colton wouldn't have minded in the slightest and Lorna reflected that no, he probably wouldn't have.

'How's Flora?'

Hamish and Innes were immediately at her elbow.

'Can we go over?'

'Seriously, I wouldn't,' said Lorna. 'I think they have some stuff to sort out.'

'Yes,' said Innes. 'How to kick his arse from here back to the States. I'll help with that.'

'It might not be that simple,' said Lorna.

'Very simple,' said Innes. 'Hamish's boot; Joel's arse. Simple.'

'Will Flora be okay?' said Hamish, looking worried.

'I'm sure she will,' said Lorna gently. 'Sad, but all right. You'll have to be very nice to her.'

'Nice to her *and* Fintan,' groaned Innes. 'For God's sake.'

And then all the lights went out.

Chapter Fifty-two

The red warning for snow and storms had been in place for so long that everyone had kind of ignored it. The ferries were off, but everyone was well stocked up with food and flour and the milk and eggs were local anyway, so as long as you weren't in absolutely desperate need of, for example, a sudden pineapple, you could cope all right.

Neighbours were checking in on neighbours; cows were warm and safe in their barns. Hamish was one of the local volunteer gritters and adored going out in Gritty Gritty Bang Bang and making sure the roads were safe, so mostly life continued as normal.

However, a freak gust of wind had overturned the Land Rover of the man charged with checking the convector coils, which led to a circuit break, and as the wind heightened and everything seemed to get more ferocious, the entire island – that tiny beacon of light and warmth in the North Atlantic – suddenly went black. The cold battering waves rendered the scene dense and dark for endless miles and miles across the sea; only the lighthouses, with their back-up generators, could send a signal to lonely, tempest-tossed boats that there was now danger here.

Everything went black in the room at the Manse.

Fintan didn't even notice.

He was sitting by the window, staring out to sea. The undertaker was on his way, even in this weather. There would be a sea burial, which was as close as they could get to the full Viking burial Colton had actually wanted. This would have to do instead. Saif had signed all sorts of papers to say he wouldn't require an autopsy, which meant, unusually, that the body wouldn't have to be transferred to the mainland at all. But it also meant that Hector, who ran four fishing boats and also acted as the town's undertaker when required, that the body wouldn't be kept in particularly fancy conditions.

Fintan didn't care about any of that. He just knew that Colton had died exactly as he had wanted to in the end: surrounded by people who loved him. Even if some of that love had taken a lifetime to show itself.

So it took him a while to hear the commotion and for

someone to come upstairs with a clutch of lit candles, and in fact in the room they made a rather soothing vigil – a place to sit and contemplate in utter silence, and Fintan was glad.

＊ ❄

In the Harbour's Rest, there were whoops and cheers and candles and torches immediately lit – they got cut off all the time, Inge-Britt was always forgetting to pay the bill – and more logs thrown on the fire and more whisky taken out and more toasts made to Colton, for as everyone knows there is nothing more enjoyable on a stormy night than to be somewhere cosy and comfortable which suddenly doesn't have to shut for legal closing hours (as if it ever did).

All except for Lorna, who snuck out of the door unnoticed to check that Joel and Flora were okay.

＊ ❄

At Lorna's little flat, Flora blinked in the darkness and half smiled.

'What is it?' said Joel.

'It must be the weather,' said Flora, stretching.

'Don't get up,' said Joel fiercely, pulling gently on her arm. 'Please.'

There was a pause.

'Are you still bleeding?'

'I can't tell,' said Flora. ' It's too dark. And . . . I don't want to check.'

'Does your stomach still hurt?'

'A bit.'

'Do you want more tea?'

'That's kind of what a "power cut" means. No more tea.'

In the darkness, Joel risked putting his head next to her stomach, and in the darkness she let him.

'Is this the flat you thought we could live in?'

'Uh-huh,' said Flora. 'Stupid thought, I know.'

'No,' said Joel. 'It wasn't. It's nice. It's lovely. It would have been perfect.'

He didn't mention Colton offering them the Manse. It didn't feel like the right time. Nothing was the right time.

'Well, it doesn't matter now,' said Flora.

'It's still for rent, isn't it? I can't stay at the Rock now anyway; it's Fintan's now. I'm just a lodger.'

'So you'll move in with me because you're homeless?'

'No,' said Joel. 'In fact, I could go literally anywhere in the world. But I don't want to. I've made such a mistake, Flora. Such a mistake. Do you think you can ever forgive me?'

'Joel . . . ' Flora's voice was trembling. 'I'm in the middle of losing a baby. I'm in the middle of everything I thought might happen in my life falling apart. It's pitch-fucking-dark. So would you mind terribly if it's not all about you, just this once?'

Joel didn't say anything after that, just stayed exactly where he was.

Up at the Rock, where Mark and Marsha were getting changed, there was a momentary flicker as the lights went out, then came back on again – the Rock, of course, had an emergency generator for exactly this type of situation. They looked at each other and peered out of the window; the snow swirled and visibility was incredibly poor, but the line of lights down the end of the Endless Beach had popped out, all at once.

'Oh goodness,' said Marsha. 'Seriously, what is this place you've brought me to?'

'Everything must be down,' said Mark. 'Do you think people know the Rock is still working?'

'Maybe they're used to power cuts,' mused Marsha. 'What do you think?'

She had rather been looking forward to some mussels and a nice glass of wine in the Rock's lovely restaurant, but Mark had a look on his face she knew meant that whatever it was he had in mind, he was almost certainly going to do it whether she agreed or not.

'I think we should go and help,' he said. 'Flora's vulnerable, for starters.'

'She'll be at home with those fifty-five brothers of hers you told me about,' said Marsha.

Mark frowned at his phone and texted Joel that there was power at the Rock and did they want picked up? A second later came the reply: an enthusiastic yes.

'I'll go,' said Mark, smiling. 'You stay here – stay cosy.'
Marsha gave him one of her looks.

'You think?'

Then she pulled on the bright yellow nor'easter jacket she had for Januarys in New York that was a shade too big for her and made her look, to Mark's eyes, like a teenager (and to everyone else's, a tiny fisherman) and went to fetch her boots.

It was a bumpy route down; Mark went incredibly slowly. There weren't even street lights to mark the route; everything had to be done by the high beam of the Land Rover Colton had left at their disposal. It wasn't until much later that Mark recalled he'd driven on the wrong side of the road the entire time.

'At least they're together,' he said comfortingly to Marsha.

'I think we should do it now ...' she said, and he nodded, knowing exactly what she meant.

The two of them never forgot that ride through the dark night, achingly slow, Marsha's hand over Mark's as he manoeuvred the unfamiliar gearstick, the crashing dark all around them, snow whirling violently. It felt like the end of the world, a million miles away from their cultured, metropolitan lives.

A deer bounded out into the road, eyes red in the head-lights, and was gone. The air was so thick with swirling snow it was almost impossible to see. It seemed endless: a constant spiral of white, a shock of wind, so that the snow drifted hither and thither across the landscape which in itself seemed to change and shimmer in front of their eyes.

'We're going to have to collect lots of people,' said Mark eventually. Marsha nodded. 'And people will see the lights up there.'

'They will,' Marsha said, and patted his hand. She could feel his tension.

'I'm sure they're fine,' she added.

Mark sniffed.

'And if they're not, Marsh? What is that going to do to our boy?'

Marsha shook her head and looked out of the window, even though there was absolutely nothing to look at. They both knew this was his absolutely best shot – the best way Joel could break the cruel carapace of his childhood. Flora was his only hope. But could he realise it in time? And if he did, could Flora accept it?

* ❄

It was still warm in the little flat, which was easy to find, but dark as pitch. Flora and Joel were there, Flora lying on the bed. She sat up awkwardly as Mark and Marsha cheerily knocked on the door and announced themselves, and shot Joel a look.

'There's power up at the Rock,' he said, illuminating the room with his phone. 'I thought . . . I thought maybe we should be there. That it would be safer.'

'I'm not supposed to move,' hissed Flora.

'Oh yes,' said Joel. 'I know. Sorry. But I thought. Maybe ... if we carried you ... if you kept lying down? Then you could be more comfortable? My phone is going to run out of battery soon, and we won't have anything ... and you can get tea.'

'But I'm in bed!' complained Flora.

'Lorna will have to go to bed at some point.'

Flora sighed at that. It was true: it wasn't fair to annex her friend's place, not on such a wild night as this. And she didn't feel quite as bad as she had earlier. Still sick and wobbly and upset, but not as if she was going to pass out again. She touched her stitch briefly.

'How is it?' she said.

'Dunno,' said Joel. 'I can't see it. So – gorgeous.'

Flora almost smiled but winced instead.

'Hang on, what's going on?' said Mark, shining the torch.

But when both of them turned to look at him with such anguished expressions on their faces, Marsha tugged at Mark's arm. It was a look she knew very well. The devastation. The sadness. They had known it; she would have given anything to spare them.

'Something happened,' said Flora. 'I had an accident. I think ... I think we might have—'

Marsha interjected.

'Let's just get them back to the hotel,' she whispered. 'Let's just go.'

'Here.' Joel leaned down to pick her up with such

tenderness Marsha and Mark swapped glances. 'Wrap the blanket around yourself. I'll take you out to the car.'

'You can't lift me!' said Flora.

'I can bench-press two-eighty,' said Joel mystifyingly. 'I don't think I'm going to find you a problem.'

And indeed he did lift Flora up into his arms like she weighed nothing, and she pressed her face into his neck and smelled his smell and cursed how weak with love he made her feel and how much better she felt when she was in his arms.

The Land Rover bumped painfully back up to the Rock, tracing the line of the Endless Beach, but Joel held onto Flora absolutely fiercely the entire way, absorbing every bump into his body in an effort to keep her safe.

Flora found at one point that they had their foreheads pressed together; she could feel Joel's tears run down her cheeks.

'I'm so sorry,' he kept whispering. 'I love you. I love you both.'

And Flora felt it was incredibly unfair of him to do this when she was feeling so weak and so awful, but on the other hand suddenly grateful for the strength of his arms around her, and for his simply being there.

'Shut up,' she tried to say, but she was tearful too, and found, in the end, as they drove through the storm, that it was all she could to simply hang on.

Chapter Fifty-three

In fact, as it turned out, half the population who weren't cheerfully locked into the Harbour's Rest had moved up to the Rock, attracted by the lights and wishing to toast Colton one last time. Joel took one look at the crowds and carted Flora straight off to his cottage. There was no one he wanted to speak to right now.

Mark and Marsha looked at one another.

'Do you think . . . ?' said Mark.

'I think,' said Marsha with a sigh. 'That there might be . . . a better moment.'

Mark grimaced, still unsure. But Joel turned back to them, the storm roaring outside.

'Thank you,' he said simply. 'Thank you for coming to get us. Thank you.'

And, figuring they might as well get it over with,

they decided to follow them to his cottage after they had divested themselves of their outdoor gear in their own room.

✳ ✳

As usual, inside it was scrupulously neat and tidy. Typical Joel. There was almost none of his personality in the lovely room at all, but it was so warm and comfortable.

Joel laid Flora down with infinite tenderness and Flora looked up at him. This – this was the man she had always wanted him to be, longed for him to be. Was it only guilt that was making him behave like this though? Was this the real Joel, or someone feeling punished and pushed around by life?

So she asked him.

He pushed up his glasses.

'I think,' he said slowly, in his serious way, 'that it took something awful for me to see. To see how I feel. To admit how I feel. Does that make sense?'

'So whenever I need to talk to you I just need to have something . . . something terrible . . . '

Flora started crying again.

'No,' said Joel. 'No, my love. Never again.'

She looked at him, swallowing hard, ridiculously aware that she must look absolutely terrible.

'What did you just call me?' she said.

Chapter Fifty-four

Saif had arrived home an hour before, utterly exhausted – mentally, spiritually, everything. He wanted to see his boys, physically have them crawl all over them. Thank God for Mrs Laird to whom he was planning to give a large chunk of money: she had done everything for them. He'd even got used to her lasagne.

Oh, he was so tired. And felt so old. And the idea of having to pick up everything and start all over again, in a new place . . . oh, it was so wearying.

He didn't bother locking his car – nobody did here, he'd learned, and he had a lockable drug safe in the house – and almost couldn't manage the walk, nearly getting blown over and then suddenly feeling a wave of tiredness so huge he leaned against it. That's when he saw the house.

Ash and Ib were at the front window, obviously having done nothing but wait for him since ... since whenever he'd been called out the first time, he couldn't even remember now. They were bouncing up and down in their jim-jams, so gorgeous, the both of them. Through his tiredness, he couldn't stop smiling.

But what was that behind them? He squinted. It must be a reflection from the car. It looked glistening.

His step lightened a little in anticipation of having Ash and Ib's arms around him, trying to wash away the sadness and stress of the day, and of everything. But as he got there, it was Mrs Laird who met him, with a worried look on her face.

Oh no, he thought to himself. Please. Please not more problems. Please let there be nothing wrong with her. Please let nothing have happened.

'Yes?' he said, and it came out more brusquely than he meant it to.

'Oh, Dr Hassan,' she said. She wouldn't ever call him anything else. 'I'm so sorry ... It was meant just to be a little whip-round. It got a bit out of hand ... '

At that point, the boys came charging through, even the normally reticent Ib a streak of pyjamas and scruffy hair.

'ABBA! ABBA!' and they pulled him into the sitting room.

The old manse was normally a cheerless place, but tonight it was transformed. A vast tree shimmered in the corner, hung with lights – and underneath were presents, uncountable numbers of presents, all wrapped gaily and tied up with shining ribbons. Saif stared at them in consternation.

'I'm so sorry,' said Mrs Laird, her voice wavering. 'I told them you might not like Christmas or it might not be right or lots of things like that. But people just kept bringing things . . . '

'Why? They feel sorry for me?'

Saif could have bitten his tongue as soon as he'd said it. Mrs Laird looked completely puzzled.

'No, Dr Hassan . . . They like you.'

* ❄

The boys were in such a high pitch of excitement, Saif let them open a present each – a Tonka truck for Ash, which made him bounce up and down, and a transformer for Ib, which he should probably have been too young for but, in his shy way, he half smiled as he examined it, which meant, Saif could tell, that he loved it.

Saif sighed and sat back in the chair. Mrs Laird had kindly brought him some tea and supper on a plate.

'Thank you,' he said again. 'I have not bought you a present, I am sorry.'

Mrs Laird was going to her daughter's tomorrow, once she'd covered Saif's on call, where she would be swarmed by her grandchildren, her nephews and nieces and many, many Lairds who'd descended en masse just before the storm had hit and closed the tiny airport.

She would have more bath salts and pyjamas than she could handle.

'Don't worry about that,' she said. 'I'm just glad . . . you don't mind.'

'It's amazing,' said Saif, staring at the tree again. 'I'm a bit overwhelmed.'

'I was worried you might be offended.'

'Well, I'm not,' said Saif, watching the boys rattle about with their new toys. A sudden burst of energy came from nowhere, and he grabbed the boys and held them tight to his chest and they giggled and squealed. 'I think it is all right, no? Merry Christmas?'

'Merry Christmas,' they shouted back as he growled like a bear and knelt down, and they squealed as he tickled them.

Mrs Laird shook her head.

'We'll miss you when you go,' she said. He had mentioned to her that he wouldn't require her services in the new year.

Instantly the boys froze.

'What?' demanded Ib in Arabic.

'We go home to Mama?' said Ash.

Mrs Laird jumped to her feet.

'Oh my God,' she said. 'I'm so sorry. I didn't . . . I'm so sorry.'

She was bright pink with consternation.

'It's all right,' said Saif, sighing. Oh God, he was tired. He put a hand up. 'Don't worry about it. We have to talk about it.'

The boys' eyes were huge. It was so late now. He still had to check on Flora and Colton once more. And now this.

'Well . . . ' he began.

And then the lights went out.

Chapter Fifty-five

Back at the Rock, there was a knock on the door. Joel answered it, confused. It was Mark and Marsha.

'We just wanted to know how things were going?' said Marsha.

'Oh well . . . ' said Joel, opening his hands.

'And?' said Mark, even as Marsha shot him a look.

They moved into the room.

'There's something I wanted to say,' Mark said. 'Marsha and I have been talking this over . . . We wanted . . . I know this should probably wait. But we can't . . . I know this will probably not feel like the time. But we thought, it might . . . it might actually be exactly the time. So that you both know . . . so that you both know . . . in case what happened makes either of you think of making rash decisions . . . '

Marsha stood next to him and took his arm as if to steady him.

Mark removed his glasses and took a deep breath to steady himself.

'Well,' said Mark. 'And I am meant to be the person who advises people to speak up about their feelings.'

His voice was wobbling.

'I'll do it,' said Marsha.

'Yes please,' said Mark, rubbing his eyes.

'What is it?' said Flora from the bed.

'Don't worry,' said Marsha. She turned to face Joel, who looked terrified.

'You need to know that we have been planning this for a long time. We read about it in a book, and we didn't realise you could do this but . . . but it feels like you two . . . are at a crunch point. And we are so sad to see that, and don't want to interfere. But if this could tip the scales, or . . . well . . . We figured it's worth a shot.'

She took a deep breath.

'A long time ago, we made a mistake. A terrible mistake. We got to know you a little – or Mark did. The boy you were. And we saw the potential you had and how special you were to us and how much you needed someone – a family. And we should have given you a family. We were wrong. So wrong. So it feels like we absolutely do not have the right to ask you what we're about to ask you.'

Flora was bamboozled. Joel looked frozen in place.

'We won't . . . '

Then it was Marsha's turn to be unable to speak. She turned to her husband, who was still clutching her hand, his knuckles white, but he nodded and took over, and for the thousandth time Flora loved how simpatico they were – how simply in tune with each other's ebbs and flows – and dreamed of the day they too would be like that. She looked at Joel. Was it possible? Was it?

Mark cleared his throat.

'We thought we had managed to get over never becoming parents.'

Marsha's mouth twisted a little.

'... but somehow the pain has come back with everything we'll be missing out on. And so we wondered when we heard about the baby ... if it was at all possible ...'

'And Flora, this is up to you too,' added Marsha.

'But if you would like ... we wondered if ... We heard ... that you can adopt grown-ups. I didn't know. And we thought we might be able to adopt you ... and then your children – and we are so, so sorry about the baby. We are so sorry. But one day. One baby. Your children ... would be our grandchildren and then ... we could be in their lives the way we always wished we had been in yours. And of course when we die there'll be certain benefits and so on ... We'd like to be able to pay for school and all of that ...'

But Flora wasn't listening – she was so shocked her mouth had fallen open. And she was staring at Joel to gauge his reaction.

Marsha's hand was at her mouth; the other one, that was grasping Mark's, was shaking.

Joel was still standing, rooted to the spot. From the bed, Flora gently touched his hand, and Marsha and Mark both saw it.

'Joel?' she said softly.

But he didn't answer; couldn't trust himself. Instead, he wobbled a little unsteadily. Then, without letting go of Flora's hand, he leaned over to them and put his arm around Mark and buried his head in his shoulder as Marsha's face lit up with a brilliant smile.

Within moments they were all hugging, and Marsha beckoned Flora in and whispered in her ear, are you sure you won't mind having a mother-in-law one day, and Flora cried and said she couldn't think of anything she'd like more, but it wasn't about her, she realised suddenly. With everything that had happened, it was about the future.

It was about the man she loved having more people to love him, not just her. That it wouldn't always be on her shoulders. That she wouldn't have to be watching her step all the time; a slave to his dreadful past.

Plus the pretence that Mark and Joel had a purely professional relationship had, frankly, continued a little too long.

She put her hand to her stomach once again, suddenly feeling how bereft, how sad she was. Marsha put her arm around her, and she leaned into the older woman.

'It'll be all right,' whispered Marsha, stroking her hair, and Flora knew that she wasn't her mother, and Marsha knew she wasn't trying to be her mother, but it was something they both desperately needed to do nonetheless.

'Oh and you don't have to look after us when we're old or anything,' said Mark when he'd recovered himself and Marsha had whisked some champagne from the fridge. 'We're all sorted – don't worry about that.'

'We're going together to the Home for Elderly Greeks Who Live For Ever,' said Marsha. 'It's all arranged. You have to drink quite a lot of olive oil.'

Flora smiled.

'Or you may have to shack up on an island with us . . . if we need the childcare one day.'

Mark's face was hungry. Marsha looked at the windows. 'Is it always like this?'

'Pretty much,' said Flora.

'Well, it will probably be fine,' said Marsha.

* ❄

Mark and Marsha left them to sleep, which of course was never going to happen in a million years. Instead, they clung to each other as if they'd just survived a shipwreck, with the bed as the raft.

'You don't . . . you don't feel bad about your real family?' she said. 'After all, there might be some remnants of it out there, somewhere.'

'I can't,' said Joel simply. 'I've never had anyone. Anyone on my side. Ever.'

And it was true: his real mother's family had disavowed

321

his drug addict mother long before his father had stabbed her in front of his eyes when he was four years old.

'Nobody ever loved me,' he said finally, quietly, his head under the blankets. 'And now three people do. And I will never, ever let that go. I promise.'

There was another knock at the door.

'What is this – Piccadilly Circus?' he grumbled.

'Santa?' wondered Flora.

'He knocks?'

Joel got out of bed. Saif was standing there, looking haggard and wiping snow off his jacket. He was carrying something that was banging off the walls and making a hell of a noise.

'I need do check,' he said apologetically

'Oh God, yes. Sorry,' said Flora. It was odd: she wasn't feeling as bad as she had earlier.

She clambered out of bed; Joel handed her a dressing gown and Saif took her temperature and blood pressure and asked if she'd had more bleeding and she said no, and he asked if she were still cramping and she said she wasn't sure and he reminded her that it could come on over the next couple of days, and she nodded.

Then he pulled in the machine he'd dragged all the way down from the surgery.

✳ * ❄

Iona had, frankly, been very, very busy snogging Anatoly and had barely noticed the power cut, as he was six foot four and pure blond with high cheekbones and frankly a total and utter ride by any standards, not just Mure standards.

Isla on the other hand was dancing with Vlad when the lights had gone out, and he – a serious-faced engineer from St Petersburg (and also, let it be noted, a total and utter ride) – had immediately glanced out on the pitch-black island and called his friends, who absolutely one hundred per cent were not hiding in a nuclear submarine out in the bay, and up they headed to join them.

Which is how, two hours later, the lights were back on in the Harbour's Rest and everyone was so jolly, they thought they were just seeing double – or possibly quadruple – as a vast number of pale young men poured into the bar and started attacking the vodka and teaching '*Tiha noc, divnaja noc*' to the assembled villagers.

* ❄

The lights came up as Saif was carefully inspecting the machine.

'Ah,' he said to himself. 'Easier.'

Flora was staring at it, her heart leaping.

'I thought you said . . . You *definitely* said you didn't walk about the village with the scanner,' she said.

Saif looked at her.

'People change,' he mumbled.

Joel jumped up, still not quite understanding what was going on, as Saif washed his hands and then took out a cold tube of blue gel and squeezed its contents onto Flora's stomach.

There was no sound at all as the snow danced past the windows until the machine started up with a steady hum, and the room held its breath.

'Don't move,' said Saif. He wouldn't look either of them in the face, just picked up the probe. He wanted to say something – something comforting about how these things just happened – but as he did so, the probe brushed the gel and even before the monitor was properly warmed up, he got an odd sense through his fingers. He pressed harder. He kept the monitor turned away from both of them, as was appropriate. He waited until he was sure.

Then he turned it around. And pressed the volume on the scanner, so they could hear the rustle-thump, rustle-thump, quick and strong and true.

'Someone,' he said, 'is hanging on.'

Which was true for the baby. But that night, everyone in that room felt it was true for each of them too. And, possibly, everybody in the world.

Chapter Fifty-six

Saif walked out into the blackness. There was nobody around on the freezing streets, although the storm had abated. He wanted to get a little fresh air before he went back – he'd left the boys curled up in front of the fire, having convinced them that the power cut was an adventure even though it was also a reminder of long ago. And they had finally fallen asleep, Ash clutching a huge fluffy tiger – he appeared to have completely lost control of the present-opening situation – and Ib still overwhelmed with amazement that someone would think enough of them to buy them a PlayStation, his lifelong dream. He genuinely couldn't believe it. There was, Saif thought, a hint in the boy's eyes of an understanding that people could care for him even if he was angry or disagreeable.

Saif went and stood on the sea wall. It was exactly

midnight: Christmas Day. Suddenly the wind fell still and everything was silent and the stars prickled into view overhead and Saif stared at them. The phone in his pocket dinged. It had been completely out of charge; he'd plugged it in for a moment in the car. He stared at the email he hadn't picked up before in some surprise.

He didn't know Neda had been a busy bee, working behind the scenes. Of course she knew Dr Mehta. She knew everyone.

And she knew a good thing when she saw it.

'Dear Dr Hassan,' read the email.

'We regret to inform you that on this occasion your application has been unsuccessful ... '

He didn't read on. Just blinked and carried on staring out to sea.

* ❋

Lorna wobbled back rather unsteadily from the Harbour's Rest through the dark streets. She had received a garbled text from Flora, something about all not being lost but also bring all the chipolatas. She smiled and shook her head as she walked carefully on her way, her heels clopping just a little beneath her.

When she first saw the dark shape ahead, she was a little afraid: it was so still, just standing there by the harbour's edge, staring out over the dark sea.

And then she realised who it was.

Epilogue

Bramble was perturbed, by dog standards. For a start, it was first thing in the morning but someone was jumping up and down and yelling at everyone to 'GET UP GET UP SANTY IS HEAH GET UP EVONE!'

Secondly, there was a huge tree in the corner of the room that he'd already tried to cock his leg on and been severely told off for, so he and the tree were enemies as far as he was concerned.

And there was also the delicious smell of things cooking which made him think it must be suppertime, except there was nobody offering him anything to eat.

So Bramble was confused, even by his standards.

He went out on his usual walk down to the village. There were lights on in some windows, and, oddly, people staggering out of the Harbour's Rest, also looking very confused and smelling not remotely nice. The paper shop, on the other hand, was not open. He stood outside politely for a while, but nobody was going to give him a paper today.

Neither were the fishermen tending their nets. Nor was Milou dancing up and down the beach.

Bramble waited, and sniffed, and mooched, and waited some more until the weak winter sun was almost over the horizon, bouncing pinkly off the snowy hills. Finally, Mrs Johanssen passed, walking Henzil, a growly midget Bramble didn't like, and told him to get on home, there would be no papers today, and Henzil snapped at his heels, but he still sat there until a heavy-set man emerged from the Harbour's Rest, and came over and buried his hands in his fur, as if he'd really been in need of a dog, and Bramble finally shook himself all over and headed for home.

And what a different scene awaited him.

There was a huge breakfast spread on the table, put on by Hamish, Innes – and a 'stranded-by-the-storm', pink-faced and extremely happy-looking Eilidh, who was snuggling up to Innes and being leant upon by a contented-looking Agot who was dressed up as a unicorn and a bear at the same time, having decided to wear all her Christmas presents at once.

There was French toast and bacon and maple syrup and porridge with thick cream fresh from the dairy as well as scones and new warm soft bread from the Seaside Kitchen, just waiting to be cracked into and the new honey poured on so it spilled everywhere. Bramble positioned himself carefully to catch any leftovers.

There was tea poured from the ancient pot into huge chipped earthenware mugs; Flora's fancy coffee machine was working overtime too.

Joel was there, looking exhausted but unbelievably happy, his arms around Flora's waist, never taking his eyes off his gorgeous girlfriend. He stood behind her, leaning against the sink and holding her tight – but not too tight – as if they had a huge goblet of molten gold, and he could not spill a precious drop. Eck sat by the fire, being waited on by everyone. Hamish was still hopping around the room as Colton had told Fintan to get him what he most wanted in the world, and what Hamish had always most wanted in the world was a Scalextric, and he could barely contain himself with glee. And Marsha and Mark had arrived with breathtakingly expensive and carefully chosen gifts for everyone, which was awkward as they'd got shortbread and tartan gloves in return, everyone having been a bit preoccupied to do much in the way of specialised and thoughtful shopping that year, but everyone pretended that shortbread was just as good as real jewellery and cashmere jumpers really and that was fine too.

And as they chatted and ate and opened gifts and got ready to wander down to the church to see everyone, the door opened quietly. Bramble looked around first, but then the others did too, as the pale, wan figure of Fintan sidled in.

And in an instant they engulfed him and sat him down; he had tea in his hands and a dog on his feet and a four-year-old climbing up his arm and, for some reason, a tinsel crown on, and before he even got the chance to explain to Joel and Flora that he couldn't – not ever – go back to the Manse, that (to him) hideously oppressive house and please please please could they rent it, he had a full plate, and the arms of people he loved around him and he felt like the lost snow child come home, and then Flora turned around again and saw another figure lurking outside looking awkward and a bit hopeless, and she left Joel's protective embrace, went to the doorway and, with a look to Fintan, beckoned Tripp inside too, even as Agot was announcing yet again, 'I DO NAVTY, UNCA FINTAN!' and Fintan smiled tiredly and said, 'Go on then, la,' and she stood up straight in her best angel pose, and hollered at the top of her voice:

'I GOOD NEWS! PEAS ON EARTH! PEAS ON EARTH! GOOD NEWS!'

Acknowledgements

Thanks: Maddie West, Jo Unwin, Milly Reilly, Joanna Kramer, Charlie King, David Shelley, Stephie Melrose, Emma Williams and all at Little, Brown; Deborah Schneider, Dan Mallory, Rachel Kahan, Alexander Cochran and his frankly astounding team at C+W; the Faceboard and my Beatons, big, small and those getting ridiculously big and taller than me even though in my head they are *in fact* quite small.

Laraine, of course, without whom I couldn't function; Sandy Tjolle and Major Kat for suggesting I told the entire book through the medium of dogs. (I did not, obviously, but I did borrow a chapter.) And apologies to cat-lovers who always write to me after books with dogs or puffins in and say, 'Cats are very nice too.' I agree. Cats *are* very nice too.

Some sad things, because life always has both types of things, and both should always be acknowledged. I have written about cancer in this book. As I was writing about it, two people I was profoundly fond of died of that horrible disease. All love to my beloved Tantan, Anne Kilkie (1942–2018), and Kate Breame (1979–2018), and to the NHS who cared for them so well.

Also, this year, my dear, dear friend Susan's nephew, Luke Hoyer, was killed, aged fifteen, in the Parkland shooting in Florida. Thanks and respect to his parents, Tom and Gena, for letting him tread, very briefly, through the pages of this book.

Recipes

LANARK BLUE SCONES
Remember with scones: HOT OVEN COLD BUTTER!

✳

200g self-raising flour
75g butter, cubed
75g blue cheese, Scottish *obviously*, cubed
1 teaspoon mustard
1 teaspoon baking powder
liberal sprinkling of salt
splash of tonic water
milk, to consistency (approximately 100ml)

Set the oven to 220 Celsius, 200 if fan.

Mix the flour, salt and baking powder, then rub in the butter and cheese to make crumbs. Add the mustard, plenty of salt, a splash of tonic for luck (my friend Sez swears by it) and then add the milk slowly until it's a proper, quite soggy consistency. Roll the dough out nice and thickly, then cut out with pastry shapers or, if like me you can never find them at the right moment, any jam jar or glass you have to hand.

You can paint a little beaten egg for shininess onto the tops if you like but I think that's for sweet scones really; savoury don't need it.

If you're feeling particularly adventurous, good things to add include cooked chorizo and if you have any leftover roasted peppers, they are delicious in them. Otherwise a few chopped fresh chives are lovely too.

Stick baking paper on a big tray and space them nice and far apart so they can expand, then 10–15 minutes in the oven: you'll be able to tell by the colour and by the amazing number of passing friends who suddenly just pop up, attracted by the smell.

BLACK BUN

* ❄

Black Bun is eaten on Hogmanay – New Year's Eve – so as to keep you nice and stodgified and warm enough to go out first footing, which is when you visit all your neighbours after the bells at midnight, and hopefully have a little dram here, there and everywhere. Hence you need something to soak up the whisky. It is heavy, but you only have a little bit. If you're modern, you can have it with cream ☺. It's a two-hour bake and can do with being thrown together the day before but it's not remotely difficult. You don't have to buy the pastry, obviously. But I buy the pastry.

250g plain flour
450g currants
250g raisins
125g brown sugar
125g mixed peel (that's what recipes traditionally
say for balance. If it's me, I like *all the mixed peel*!)
1 teaspoon bicarbonate of soda
50g maraschino cherries
1 glass whisky to taste
1 tsp each: cinnamon, mixed spice, ginger
1 clove
1 egg
Milk, to moisten

Mix all of these ingredients together – NB this will be even better if you leave them overnight (except the egg and milk!).

Butter a loaf tin and roll out the pastry so it fits (you are aiming for a large square sausage roll-looking thing). Tightly pack the mix together. Then stick down the pastry with a little egg and bake at 180 degrees Celsius for two hours. Let it cool thoroughly, then cut into small but utterly delicious slices – and may the first person through your door after the bells be the coalman.

SHORTBREAD

You can't make Scottish recipes without making short-bread, and this one is nice for kids to join in with as it's so simple. If you can't get your hands on Fintan's unsalted butter, buy the highest quality you can afford.

150g *very good* butter
60g caster sugar
200g plain flour

Pre-heat the oven to 180 degrees Celsius and line a baking tray.

Cream the sugar and butter well, then add the flour until you get a paste. Roll it out to about one centimetre in thickness, then cut it however you like – be creative (or lazy, like me, and just use the top of a glass ☺!

Sprinkle some extra sugar on top, then chill the dough in the fridge for at least half an hour otherwise they won't bake nicely.

Put it in the oven for twenty minutes, or until golden brown and delicious.

Loyalty Card

About the Author

Jenny Colgan is the author of numerous bestselling novels, including *The Little Shop of Happy Ever After* and *Summer at the Little Beach Street Bakery*, which are also published by Sphere. *Meet Me at the Cupcake Café* won the 2012 Melissa Nathan Award for Comedy Romance and was a *Sunday Times* top ten bestseller, as was *Welcome to Rosie Hopkins' Sweetshop of Dreams*, which won the RNA Romantic Novel of the Year Award 2013. Jenny was born in Scotland and has lived in London, the Netherlands, the US and France. She eventually settled on the wettest of all of these places, and currently lives just north of Edinburgh with her husband Andrew, her dog and her three children: Wallace, who is twelve and likes pretending to be nineteen and not knowing what this embarrassing 'family' thing is that keeps following him about; Michael-Francis, who is ten and likes making new friends on aeroplanes; and Delphine, who is eight and is mostly raccoon as far as we can tell so far.

Things Jenny likes include: cakes; far too much *Doctor Who*; wearing Converse trainers every day so her feet are now just gigantic big flat pans; baths only slightly cooler than the surface of the sun; and very, very long books, the longer the better. For more about Jenny, visit her website and her Facebook page, or follow her on Twitter @jennycolgan.

ALSO BY JENNY COLGAN

CHRISTMAS ON THE ISLAND

THE ENDLESS BEACH

CHRISTMAS AT LITTLE BEACH
STREET BAKERY

THE CAFÉ BY THE SEA

THE BOOKSHOP ON THE CORNER

SUMMER AT LITTLE BEACH
STREET BAKERY

LITTLE BEACH STREET BAKERY

THE CHRISTMAS SURPRISE

CHRISTMAS AT ROSIE HOPKINS'
SWEETSHOP

CHRISTMAS AT THE CUPCAKE CAFÉ